Julie

Enjoy!

Marilyn Kennamer

WIFE SELLER!

Cover Design & Photography: Marilyn Kleiber

Library and Archives Canada Cataloguing in Publication

ISBN: 978-0-9877607-6-0

Printed in United States of America

Published by Sun Dragon Press Inc., Canada
www.sundragonpress.com
First Edition, 2012

WIFE SELLER!

By

Marilyn Temmer

SUN
DRAGON
PRESS INC.

Dedication

To Catherine Anne O'Connor

Acknowledgments

To COC, without whose help it would never have been started.

To my writing group members, AU, MP and WR, without whose help it would never have been finished.

To my family for listening and reading.

CHAPTER ONE

Susannah trudged resolutely toward the church that served her small, Yorkshire village. Random stops to admire a budding plant, to shield her eyes against the wind, to gaze at a bird in flight or to admire the contents of a shop window all served to reassure her that Albert was not following her. She hunched her shoulders and crossed her arms under her breasts in a vain attempt to ward off the damp cold that easily penetrated her dress and thin shawl. In spite of the brave show offered by daffodils and crocuses, the spring weather was reluctant to let go of winter's bite.

"It'll do. It's big enough. Not the first time I've done this."

The echo of Albert's harsh voice resounded as visions of a small, dark rectangle filled her mind. He was right—it wasn't the first time, but the second. The memories shredded her heart. Time did not assuage her pain. Or despair. Or rage. The voice continued its relentless monologue.

Susannah's stomach threatened to erupt. She knew why Albert had dug those tiny graves. Even his self-indulgent drinking cronies would turn on him if he did not adhere to the social more that dictated a father must make a final resting place for children buried outside the church.

"No need for a headstone. The ground's not consecrated. Just mark it in your mind. It's a bloody waste of time to trudge up there. You can't fix it, anyway, you useless bitch!"

Her breath caught. She knew what was coming next.

"And whose brat is this? Mine? With all the rumours circulating about you being a round heels or a light skirt, who could tell?"

Only the fact that she was so numb with the pain of her loss kept her on her feet. They both knew he was the one who started those rumours. Clever enough to know that the village would not accept such behavior on his behalf, he had his mistress confide the information, in strictest confidence, of course, to one or two of the town's worst gossips. Their wagging tongues did the rest. Some of the sympathy and support of the village women had dwindled when the rumours became common knowledge.

Today's pilgrimage was much more than a wrenching goodbye to two small inhabitants occupying a minute parcel of ground in the area designated for those who died unblessed by the church. Walking along the village's only street, she remembered giggling with school chums as some of the patrons of the local pub lurched and leaned against walls when they left its cosy interior. The strong bonds with her classmates, Michael and Miranda, developed during this time.

Years of beatings had driven her to this last, desperate step. At first she believed Albert when he told her she deserved a slap, a punch, or a kick. Over the last two years, the beatings had increased in severity and duration. Shaming his wife by openly consorting with his mistress was not so effective a subjugation technique as he had thought. The humiliation was considerably less than Albert hoped and that others assumed; when Albert was with his "lady friend", he wasn't torturing his wife—verbally, emotionally or physically. Nevertheless, the latest beating would be the last. Exhortations from the only friends she could keep, combined with a body racked with pain beyond that which she could bear, despite long practice, forced the decision. That same desperate decision blossomed into a complete plan when Miranda told her the strange news from the market: it was legal for a man to sell his wife.

"Legally sell a wife? How could that be, Miranda?"

"Apparently if a husband wants to sell his wife, he can. Sometimes the wife's lover, the wife and the husband all agree to this. Sometimes the husband just wants to get rid of the wife. But he does have the right to sell her."

Susannah was stunned. She and Miranda both spoke at the same time.

"How could we...?"

"Do you think we could...?"

They laughed and then stopped abruptly while various scenarios developed in their minds.

"Well, Susannah, Michael and I had an idea."

"That's fantastic, Miranda. What is it?

"You know that we've been trying out the market in Upper Worthing. And you know that we've been spreading the word that the prices are considerably better there."

"Yes, of course I know."

"Well, your husband is nothing if not greedy," she sneered. "It's one of his finer qualities. We've been stressing that all the prices for goods are higher—*especially* for dairy products. Michael is going to suggest to Albert that you come with us.

"Knowing what we do about wife selling, Michael is prepared to make a special trip to put up a sign in the local pub that there will be a wife for sale."

"Michael is going to sell you? I don't believe that for one minute!" Susannah was shocked.

"No, no, Susannah. Michael won't sell me; he'll sell you!"

"But I'm not his wife, Miranda. How can he do that?" Susannah gasped.

"Michael's cousin, Daniel, who lives in Sussex, has a neighbor who needs a good dairywoman. Michael will tell him of your ability with cheeses and butter. Daniel will get the train to the first stop before Upper Worthing and hire a wagon. He'll buy you and whisk you away.

"Daniel's neighbor, we're sure, will jump at the chance to get someone with your skills. Of course, you won't really be his wife, because you're still married to Albert. You can't be, because Michael isn't your husband, so he can't really sell you. But, since you've never been to that village, let alone its market, no one will know who you are."

"That's all very well, Miranda, but they do know Michael."

"And my clever darling has thought of that, too. He'll bring a change of clothes and dirty his face before he sells you. Of course, he'll also have a different name. Your first name will stay the same, but you'll take his new last name."

Susannah continued to stare, fascinated. At this point, she was willing to do anything to escape Albert's clutches. The beatings had increased in frequency and severity. She wasn't sure just how much longer it would be before he really did kill her.

"What if Daniel doesn't agree? What if Albert doesn't agree to let me go?"

"Daniel is very anxious to be helpful to this neighbor. She has a bull that throws outstanding milk producers. Daniel has plans for that bull, but the woman is difficult to please. If she doesn't like you, she won't let her bull service your cows, no matter how much money you offer. Unfortunately, she is quite well off and can indulge her whims.

"Michael will manage to return any monies Daniel spends to buy you. The neighbor will have an amazing dairywoman; Daniel will have milk cows beyond imagining; you will have a life of peace; and Albert will look a fool. It's perfect!"

Miranda beamed. Susannah's mouth continued to open and close as she tried to absorb what her friends contrived to ensure that her life would no longer be in danger.

"But my family—what about them?"

"What about your family, Susannah? They are as aware as everyone that Albert is a brute and that your dresses with high collars and long sleeves, no matter how hot the day, cover the marks of his beatings. Those dresses don't cover the black eyes you sport on occasion. They know he flaunts his mistress, spends his money on her and his drinking cronies, and does as little as possible on the farm. You owe them nothing, Susannah. Certainly not your life, and that really is in danger."

Susannah contemplated a life free from Albert; a life where she would reap the rewards of her skills; a life that offered freedom from pain and terror. Miranda was right about her family. They were well aware of her husband's brutality.

They knew why those two little graves were in a rough field beside the church, and they did nothing. Not once had her father remonstrated with her husband. Her brothers had not stepped forward to support her. Even her sisters refused to acknowledge her losses.

"If Daniel agrees, Miranda, I'll do it! Oh, yes, it also depends on whether or not we can get Albert to agree to let me sell my cheeses and butter in Upper Worthing."

One week later Daniel's letter enthusiastically endorsing the "buy a wife" scheme was in place. Albert, responding to the lure of more money to spend, agreed to let Susannah try the new market—once, only. If the proceeds of her trip did not meet his expectations, he promised a good beating and withdrawal of his permission to go to market. Any market, he insisted, except the one in their own village.

Meanwhile, Susannah endeavored to avoid provoking Albert, but to no avail. The day before the market he arrived home, roaring drunk, and started to punch and kick her. Susannah was sure this time he would finally kill her. He picked up the poker hanging beside the fireplace and prepared to bring it down on her head. A knock on the door and a shouted greeting interrupted his pleasure. Panting, he lowered the weapon, kicked her for good measure, and wrenched open the door.

Michael stood on the doorstep, the vicar at his elbow.

"What the hell do you want?" snarled Albert. He then became aware of the vicar's presence. "Oh, hello, vicar." He was still panting with rage. He had yet to finish giving his wife a much-deserved lesson and to savor the pleasure gained by doing so.

Michael shouldered his way past the door, barely containing his anger and contempt. Only the knowledge that Susannah would suffer for his efforts held him back from beating Albert to within an inch of his life.

"I've come to load the butter and cheeses," he gritted. "We agreed that it would save time in the morning."

"And I've come to get the horse and wagon you promised to help haul supplies for church repairs. You insisted on driving, since you wanted to be sure no harm would come to either animals or wagon."

Faced with the reminder of his promise, Albert escorted the two men to the barn. He indicated the goods Michael should load and accompanied the vicar to the horses he had promised.

Tomorrow she would smuggle her pitifully small bundle of belongings amongst the cheeses and butter destined for the market, leaving her home, her husband, and her family forever. The hardest goodbye, however, was just ahead. Two small graves and an ache in her soul were all that remained of her daughters. She clutched her farewell gift more tightly and refused to let the tears fall.

The metal gate screeched in protest as she pushed it open. Closing it with meticulous precision, she winced at the noise.

This time she turned toward the street and checked for Albert's presence again. Still safe. She lifted her face to the wind, its coldness and fierceness matching her determination. Clambering over the stile to the rough field, she went slowly to the single board marking the final resting place of her daughters. No tidy walkways here; no monuments or even markers surrounded by flowers. These graves received only the attention bestowed by family members. Few showed signs of care. Rank foliage, sodden from the recent shower, threatened to trip the unwary. For the last time Susannah pulled the weeds and cut the grass with the scissors brought for just this purpose. Her kitchen garden provided two small bouquets of rosemary. As she prepared to put her gifts at the base of the marker, Albert's voice echoed in her head.

"If I catch you wasting time visiting those brats when you should be working in either the dairy or house, you'll be sorry. They're dead, you stupid bitch. Dead." Albert waited, gloating, for the wince of pain she could never quite disguise. Susannah learned long ago to ignore the repeated threats even as she increased her diligence. She had to avoid his cronies who sat outside the pub on fine days. Cronies and busybodies alike may have wondered at her always choosing inclement weather to pick up the pitifully few things Albert permitted her to purchase in the local store. She ignored their snide comments and knowing glances.

"Here you are, my darlings," she murmured. "Rosemary for remembrance. I'll never forget you." Her composure fled. It was all she could do to refrain from flinging herself on the ground that covered both her precious babies. "Mummy's going away, but you'll be in my heart forever." She rose and turned, the agony sharp in her breast. It was time to tend to the nightly milking.

Unable to withstand the cold and pain any longer, she retraced her steps. With her goodbyes completed, a new life beckoned in a few short hours. Prayers for her babies were augmented with thanks for Miranda's precious discovery that it was legal to sell a wife. That fact and the plan they had devised would soon be put to the test.

The tempo of her footsteps increased as she hurried to the dairy before Albert returned. He was especially cruel if he caught her away from the farm, but memory took her back to the first time she was pregnant. Albert's mother died three months before this occurred, and Susannah hoped he would welcome the new life. Her own family remained indifferent to her joyful news. As long as they could bask in the reflected glory of her marriage to the son of a prominent family, they ignored her.

"Albert, we're going to have a baby. It will come about the end of June." Susannah had waited expectantly for him to share her joy. Until then, he confined his rage to the odd slap, and ever-increasing verbal abuse.

"A brat—just what we need. Don't expect to slack your work in the dairy. You probably did this on purpose, thinking that you could spend time playing with it instead of working," he snarled.

As the pregnancy advanced and her body rounded, he taunted her growing ugliness. The slaps became blows and kicks. He took particular delight in holding her by the hair and punching and kicking her stomach. Mary was stillborn in the sixth month of pregnancy.

Albert continued his pattern of abuse followed by abject apologies and promises to never strike her again. Susannah began praying for him to spend the evening, and frequently the night, with his mistress. Two years later Sarah Elizabeth was born in the seventh month of the pregnancy, her puny cries soon silenced by her lack of ability to draw sufficient breath.

Albert no longer made any effort to keep up appearances and began to flaunt his mistress at public gatherings. Tales of his debauchery spread across the countryside. Susannah miscarried three more times. She tried to hide her bruises with long sleeves and high necklines. The deepest scars rested in her heart.

CHAPTER TWO

Ethan, oblivious to both the pleasant scenery and the shambling gait of his team, recalled the shock contained in yesterday's post. Settled in his chair, a snug fire in the grate, he prepared to enjoy a lengthy letter from his cousin. Recently Jackson had left for Canada to live on a friend's farm, while he decided whether to form a partnership or set up for himself. Ethan had refused repeated invitations to join this venture. Change meant things would not remain the same. Change was fraught with stress. Change invariably meant a great deal of effort spent on what often represented very little gain. Delivering a special order to a good customer living some distance from his store was quite enough variety for him. A mug of ale at his elbow, feet propped on a stool, he had smiled in anticipation as he broke the seal, and unfolded the sheets of paper.

The first intimation of danger came with the paper blazoned *Proxy to Wed,* followed by the name *Jackson Percival Stansfield, Age 28*, executed in a flowing script. Close perusal failed to indicate the name of the bride. Grasping the potential bomb between thumb and forefinger, Ethan placed it on the table beside him, fortified his mind for the ordeal with a libation, and began to read.

Dear Cousin:

By now you will have seen my Proxy to Wed. My friend, Edmund, is dead. Apparently he fell victim to a high fever, losing strength and weight rapidly. His Will stated that I was to inherit his entire estate that, as you know, included his farm. In a separate letter dictated from his sickbed, he commended to my care two young children for whom he felt a particular fondness. They are the son and daughter of his farmhand and wife, who also succumbed to this same fever some weeks earlier. There is a boy, Caleb, aged four, and a girl, Emily, aged six. You can well imagine my consternation. To lose my friend, be gifted with his farm, and then to be responsible for two mites has been overwhelming.

I know nothing of children, and very little more of housework. The new dairy, completed three days before he caught the fever, needs only a good dairywoman. Edmund spared no expense, and planned for the expansion of his herd of milch cows. My only solution is to hire a woman to take care of the children. More easily said than done in this community. Women are at a premium, and, as a single man, propriety does not permit their working on my premises without suitable chaperonage, of that none is to be found. Therefore, dear Cousin, you can see that my only recourse is to wed–thus the proxy.

The children are well-behaved, but it would break your heart to see how subdued they are. No one is interested in keeping them because of their extreme youth. They represent a great deal of effort expended, and no return in terms of labor.

The house, or cabin, boasts a kitchen, small parlor, and four bedrooms. It is desperately in need of care. Presently I am paying a neighbor to keep the children for me, but as she has four of her own and is expecting a further addition in August, this is a very temporary arrangement. The children will be returned to me on the first of May.

I can milk the cows, but that is all. My stock is dispersed amongst my neighbors, and tomorrow I shall begin to fetch them home. At the same time, I will enquire at each place if they know of someone who would be willing to make butter for me if I deliver the milk to their door. Field work remains undone now and for the foreseeable future.

I have enclosed a draught for ten pounds to pay for the passage of the wonderful wife I know you will find, with a little left over for her personal needs. I would suggest using the Allan Line. Their ships are superior, and the passage time quite fast. I devoutly pray to see a wife within a month. Please be sure that she has warm clothing and stout boots. You can book her passage from Liverpool through to Toronto, Ontario. The train comes right to the dock, and directions are available from any of the port personnel.

Ethan, please find me a strong woman. She must be in good health and under 30 years of age. A widow would be fine —in good health. I will arrange for her lodging at the Sign of the Ox. This establishment is quite respectable. Please assure her that she will be both safe and comfortable there.

She is to take the train to Marcher Mills, the funds for that rest with the innkeeper. If you will send a cable, giving only the date to save money, I will know when to meet her at the local station.

Cousin, I realize the size and weight of the load I just placed on your shoulders, especially in view of your blind panic when dealing with females, but I beg that you will be your usual efficient and understanding self. My need is very great and extremely urgent.

Your hopeful cousin,

Jackson

Ethan, shy and retiring, avoided women unless absolutely necessary. While this could be awkward in his role as a storekeeper, hiring a competent young woman to deal with female customers solved his dilemma. Jackson knew that he found females incomprehensible and frightening. How, then, could he request such an impossible feat?

# # #

When the beatings resulted in black eyes and a body too painful to move, Miranda and Michael Knowles, her dearest friends, took her dairy produce to market for her. They were the only outside contacts, aside from her infrequent visits to her family, that Albert permitted. The Knowles served a twofold purpose. They ensured the income from the market was maintained, regardless of Susannah's condition. They also provided an appearance of normalcy. Her friends' frequent urgings to leave Albert before he killed her had finally fallen on fertile ground.

Miranda's information about wife selling had involved a convoluted series of manoeuvres to ascertain its legality. The fact that it was deprecated by persons whose needs did not reflect those of the participants was of no concern to Susannah.

"All very well to turn up your nose at the common folk, but few indeed can afford the process of divorce." Miranda and

Michael's opinion of the irrelevance of opinions of persons other than themselves marched hand in hand.

Arrangements to have herself "sold" to Michael's cousin, Daniel were in place. She would then be spirited away to Daniel's neighbor's farm in Sussex and would disappear forever, safe at last.

"Daniel's neighbor has a reputation as a producer of outstanding dairy products, and she can hardly wait for your arrival and assistance," Michael reported.

"That's all fine and good, Michael," responded Susannah, "but whatever will I do without my dearest and only friends?"

She remembered Albert's comment last week when he agreed to let her try the new market.

"Listen, bitch, if you don't make a real profit with this new market, you'll feel my boot!"

That evening, she smiled coldly as she watched Albert mount the cob and canter out of the yard. The anticipation of meeting his mistress at the Blue Boar came before beating his wife. Punishing Susannah was a pleasure that could wait. Meanwhile, the combination of mistress and plenty of beer took precedence.

She recalled a conversation with Miranda when she had dropped in, after ascertaining that Susannah was alone, to review the plan once more.

"Michael heard Albert boasting to his favorite friend in the pub. He was anticipating teaching you another lesson, then remembered that the last time he had got carried away he passed out in the barn. The next time, he promised to watch how many pints he had. That way he could enjoy the power and pleasure of lessoning you while making sure that you could still work in the dairy."

Susannah hissed. "That bastard."

"And that's not all. You won't be the least bit surprised to know that he's waiting until you return from the new market. That way he'll have 'both the money and the pleasure'."

"I'm not surprised. Nor are you, I imagine. He congratulates himself that the village as a whole shares the view of his cronies—for whom he buys pints—that he's a fine fellow. The fact that he permits me to see you and Michael, attend church and visit my family shows him to be just such a fine fellow; stern, but fair. He also cannot fathom why anyone would chastise him for having a good time and a mistress. He's oblivious to the growing contempt of his flagrant exhibitions of cruelty and infidelity. As you said, high collars and long sleeves can only cover so much."

Even as horse and rider disappeared around the turn in the lane, Susannah hid herself from view. Sometimes he chose to enjoy the pleasures available at home before those of his mistress. She prayed that this would be a night like so many others, when he stayed away until morning. Her back, legs, and arms still throbbed from the last beating. Dizziness frequently overwhelmed her if she moved her head in the wrong way. *Never again*, she vowed, *never again*.

Careful surveillance of the farmyard determined that he had not sneaked back to catch her in some contrived crime. She slipped into the dairy. Carefully placing the rennet, that would accompany her on the bench just outside the door, she prepared to exact her revenge.

Albert had little interest and less knowledge about making cheese. There would be no opportunity to obtain a calf's stomach for some time, and even then it would have to age before it could act as an agent to produce curds. She knew he had no idea that rennet was not essential to cheese making and that there were other methods of obtaining the same results. She re-entered the dairy and began to put her plan in place. The goods for tomorrow's fateful trip had already been loaded onto Michael's cart. The remainder of the ripening cheeses she flung onto the dung heap, making sure to stab each one several times.

Milk and cream coated the floor of the dairy in a most satisfactory manner, promising a multitude of flies and a matching stench. The milk pans were hidden in the grain bins. She only rued the fact that her condition precluded flinging them into the pond, but the tiny holes she had managed to create would make their retrieval useless in any case. Best of all, because the holes were so small, he was unlikely to find them until a great deal of their contents had dribbled onto the floor.

Susannah had agreed to wed Albert was primarily for the benefits it would bring to her parents in their unending struggle to wrest enough from the land to support their family. As the eldest of five, she realized that they depended on her making a good match. She knew nothing specific against Albert, other than he sometimes drank too much at the pub. He seemed to be a dedicated farmer, and maintained the property left by his parents in good order. Unlike many young men, he was quite regular in attending Sunday services. The benefits would be considerable. Susannah was very aware that her marriage would raise her family's social status. Her own prestige as the wife of a prosperous farmer would also increase. Visions of renown for having the best dairy products in the district had helped to persuade her, for she knew she was an accomplished producer of both butter and cheese.

Mocking her fruitless thoughts, she hurried toward the house, mentally reviewing the things she would take for her journey. The final dimensions of her bundle could not exceed the size of a large cheese. The barest necessities would have to suffice. She snorted as she contemplated those few articles that qualified as worthy, and then only by the process of elimination. The dress with the least repairs, two aprons, her cap and shawl, a hairbrush, toothbrush, comb, a shift, and two pairs of much-darned stockings would fit. Her monthly rags would disguise the outline of her clogs and provide any necessary padding required to achieve the desired shape. Her money, three shillings stealthily kept back from market proceeds, represented her savings. Each coin had cost her a beating.

Straining and sweating, Susannah moved the heavy bed a few inches and raised the loose floorboard that protected her treasures. The final objects for her journey were the most precious. Tenderly she unfolded the rough cloth. Here was the christening gown she had stitched for those dear, dead children. Her mother made the tiny cap; her sister the sheer, cutwork chemise. Susannah was never really sure how she felt about these items, imbued as they were with hope, love, anticipation and heart-wrenching sorrow. They would be the only keepsakes to remind her of the past.

The light from the small fire pierced the dark as she returned to the kitchen and settled by the hearth. Apprehension dulled her appetite and prevented any chance of sleep. Nervously checking and re-checking her bundle, she watched the fire die to embers. Their angry red color suited her mood.

Twice before Albert had returned unexpectedly early to try to catch her in some misdeed. Just a few more hours and she would be free. Glancing through the window, she noted that false dawn that presaged morning's arrival. Discovery would mean certain death. She was ready.

Hearing the clip-clop of hooves and the jingle of harness, she left her seat beside the cooling hearth and latched the door behind her. Michael and Miranda called soft greetings. Such dear, dear friends—this escape would not be possible without them or the co-operation of Michael's cousin, Daniel. She stowed her bundle, noting with satisfaction as it disappeared in the pile of cheeses and crocks of butter, and took her place beside Miranda.

Susannah stared ahead, refusing to look at the graveyard or the rough field beyond. She stubbornly kept her gaze on the road as the horses slowly pulled the wagon around the first corner on the journey that would take her away from Albert, the beatings and Yorkshire forever. *How sad to leave my family with so few pangs*. Their refusal to acknowledge Albert's behavior had hardened her heart. Miranda's hand patted hers gently. She, too, had a babe in the cemetery. Michael chirruped to the team, and they increased their shambling pace.

"How long ago did Albert leave for The Blue Boar, Susannah? Do you think he knew of our plans?" Miranda snorted. "I'm sorry, that's a silly thing to say. If he thought for one minute that you were planning on escaping, you wouldn't be here."

"He didn't come home at all. I suppose he found better company. He said he was going to see a real woman, and not a sack of bones."

"Were you able to sleep?" Michael queried.

"Not really. I was terrified that he would discover our plot. I even imagined him unwrapping every cheese in the wagon and finding the few things in my bundle. She signed. "See this dress? It's my best dress. Before I was married, I wouldn't have considered it suitable for anything other than scrubbing floors. Now it's the only one I have with fewer than five repairs!"

"Are you sure you still want to go through with this scheme? Daniel is very trustworthy, but...." Miranda had long felt a great sadness for her friend's plight.

"Nothing could be worse than what I've endured the last seven years. I would do a great deal more than offer myself for sale in to escape. Albert will kill me if I stay. Besides, Daniel's not really buying a wife, just getting me away to a safe place where I can live in peace." She reassured herself that as no marriage would take place, she could not possibly be guilty of bigamy.

Michael cleared his throat. "Daniel is very dependable, Susannah; you're safe with him. He's made arrangements for you to work in the Farley's dairy, not his."

Miranda knew that Susannah had been apprised of every aspect of the plan and spoke only to distract her.

"The Farley's don't know who you are, other than a friend of the family. They only know that you are looking for and are experienced in dairy work. That way, even should, God forbid, Albert discover that you were the wife sold at the market, he'll never be able to trace you through a connection to me or my family. You'll be safe in Sussex."

Susannah nodded, her voice wholly suspended by tears she refused to shed. Except for her babies, she left nothing of value but these two good friends. Her parents, ignoring Albert's reputation for whoring and abuse, held firmly to their belief that a wife was absolutely the chattel of her husband. What can't be cured must be endured was their favorite maxim.

Miranda glanced at Susannah out of the corner of her eye.

"Are you all right, Susannah? Having second thoughts?" Her voice was filled with compassion.

"It's the right thing, and the only thing to do, Miranda." In spite of her brave words, Susannah's chin trembled and an errant tear traced a path down her cheek. Ignoring these small outward signs of the maelstrom of emotions within, she summoned a smile for her friend. "You know that if I stay, Albert will kill me. He came very close to doing so just a few days ago. I'm just giving thanks that he stayed away all night. When I think that he'll never have any control over me, that I'll never again feel his fist or hear his abuse, I can face anything."

Miranda placed an arm around Susannah's shoulders and cradled her gently. She never knew just where Albert struck or if the bruises had healed. "How strong you are, Susannah. I couldn't imagine having any good thoughts at a time like this. You must have been so scared." She withdrew her arm and softly patted Susannah's leg.

"Yes, I was terrified." Susannah allowed a faint smile crossing her face "But it was worth anything, anything at all to escape. I can't believe that we've got this far, and that he has no idea I'm never returning. Are you sure that you and Michael will be all right? Do you have your stories straight?" While desperate to escape, she was very concerned for her friends' safety and reputations.

"Now don't you worry, my dear friend. We know exactly what to say. Michael has brought a separate set of clothes, including another hat, to put on when he becomes your so-called husband. He'll put dirt on his face to make the disguise even better." Miranda's justifiable pride in their scheming shone through the overlying concern for her friend and sorrow at their parting. "At least we'll be able to write to each other. Daniel will forward the letters to you directly, even though they'll be addressed to him to avoid suspicion. You give your letters to Daniel and he'll write the address."

Suddenly Susannah was assailed by doubts again. So great was her concern about the prices her products would bring that she had forgotten completely about her ordeal to come. Her vision of standing on a table in the middle of a crowd of jeering, raucous men, even when the outcome had been prearranged, caused her to shrink with terror and embarrassment.

Try as she might, the word bigamy crept back into her mind. It seemed irrelevant that she was not marrying anyone, just escaping certain death. For some reason that dread word refused to give her peace. As the time for fleeing approached, she frequently found herself frozen half-way through a task, her whole being consumed flooded with shame. Logic could not budge her fear.

But such thoughts did not replace a very real concern about her immediate income. The only money she would have, except for those dearly-bought shillings, would come from the proceeds obtained at this market. *What a fool I was to think I would be able to afford even the poorest and cheapest of garments. I must save every penny against future need. What if it doesn't work out with Daniel? What if he's secretly like Albert? I absolutely must have enough to escape and support myself until I can find other work.*

Then a greater horror engulfed her: *what if Daniel was secretly in league with Albert? What if he told her husband where she was? What if there was no position in the dairy in Dorset?*

Wife Seller!

CHAPTER THREE

The horses plodded onward, accustomed to receiving little guidance, and inured to frequent stops and reverses as their inattentive driver surfaced from his rumination and corrected their direction of travel. He had chosen a less direct route as a way to avoid dealing with Jackson's terrifying request for just a little longer. He knew that only the most appalling circumstances would generate such a charge. God knew that he sympathized with having to deal with children—better a kitchen stove any day! He knew just as little about that as how to deal with the ladies, but there existed, however small, a chance that he might learn. Jackson would have to give him a day—or two—or four—to come to grips with such an overwhelming task.

Ethan tightened his grip on the reins and pulled into the Green Sheaf. On the infrequent occasions when he was in this area, he had enjoyed breaking his journey and partaking of the substantial lunch provided. Giving directions for the team to be fed and watered sparingly, he leapt lightly to the ground. He brushed dust from his clothing, adjusted the angle of his hat, checked to be sure the arrangement of his stock met his exacting standards, then headed for the taproom and his lunch.

After placing his order with the innkeeper, he looked around and saw that the majority of the men in the room clustered around a notice tacked to the wall. While he waited for his food, he ambled over to see the cause of such animation. A gentleman to his fingertips, he secured access by the merest touch on a shoulder, a nod or a smile. As he neared his goal, he became aware of comments, whether addressed to the group as a whole, or as an exclamation to a friend.

"Selling a wife! Can't be legal, that can't!" exclaimed an individual in a tattered smock. "Imagine getting rid of the old bag and having money in your pocket!"

"Might not be legal, but it sure is tempting," replied his companion, redolent of the stables. "That's the most exciting thing that's happened here for nigh on to twenty years.

Selling a wife? Ethan couldn't believe his ears. The notice, however, unequivocally advertised that a wife was for sale this very afternoon. He was filled with pity at the plight of a woman so shamed. No matter how bad a scold or slattern, no human deserved to be sold like livestock. The more he dwelled on the undeserved fate of the poor, unfortunate soul, the more incensed he became. Surely this couldn't be. It must be someone's idea of a joke. Consulting his pocket watch, he noted it wanted but ten minutes to the fateful hour. He joined the exodus to the site of the pending sale, lunch forgotten.

Susannah and Miranda stood in sight of the table used to auction items of particular value or small size. Their position allowed them to see, but not be seen. In a vain attempt to raise her spirits, Susannah wore the dress she had just purchased. Her old dress, plus her few, precious purchases, rested securely in her bundle. Not even the prospect of the coming ordeal could entirely wring the joy from the hanks of navy yarn, knitting needles and a stout crochet hook that caused the parcel to bulge in a peculiar manner. Michael and Miranda had scolded her when she gave them the wooden toys purchased that afternoon for their children. The ladies' anxiety, already high because of the imminent ordeal and subsequent parting, rose steadily.

"Where's Daniel?" Susannah hissed. "He was supposed to be here two hours ago! We have to go through with this. The auctioneer threatened us with the constable if we don't! It's grossly unfair, especially since," her voice deepened and developed a whine, "he refuses to have anything to do with the sale of one human being to another." She reverted to her normal tones, "I'm surprised he's even letting Michael use the table, given his disgust." She couldn't stop wringing her hands. "However, I noticed that the shilling Michael thrust into his hand disappeared quickly enough, and seemed to soothe his delicate principles! Oh, where is Daniel?"

"I don't know!" whimpered Miranda. "Daniel always keeps his word, and he's never late. I know he'll be here. Just have faith and patience." Miranda was devastated. How would she and Michael ever find Susannah if sold to someone other than Daniel? She had few illusions that the purchaser would permit Susannah to retain any ties with her old life.

"Faith? Patience! Miranda, I'm about to be sold to the highest bidder in five minutes! You know that I can't go through with this if Daniel doesn't turn up. And I can be taken in charge by the constable if I don't! Miranda, do something." Susannah's voice became louder and more frantic.

"Hush! People are staring at us. If Daniel doesn't turn up, Michael will think of something." Ignoring the death grip on her hand, Miranda stretched on tiptoe to scan the crowd in vain. No matter how hard she hoped or how carefully she looked, Daniel driving his hired rig at a smart trot to make up for lost time, failed to appear. Just then she saw Michael striding purposefully towards them, wearing the clothes and hat he had brought as a disguise, his features blurred by the dust and dirt he smeared on his face.

"Here comes Michael. He'll know what to do." Miranda, with wifely dexterity, deftly shifted the burden to his broad shoulders.

"Susannah, I checked with the auctioneer again." He kept his voice low, gesturing to the two women to form a tight circle for privacy. "The wife sale has been the talk of the town, and the mood of the crowd would turn very ugly if it were cancelled. We're in for it! I have no idea what has happened to Daniel. He's always as dependable as the sunrise." Michael raised his arm, preparatory to giving Susannah a quick hug. They had all agreed that he would act the part of her spouse to better build the illusion that he had every right to sell her.

Susannah realized that she was wringing her hands again. She wrapped her arms around her middle and clutched her shawl. The new bonnet afforded a modicum of privacy, but she kept her head down, tilting it as little as possible towards Michael and Miranda.

"Michael, you wouldn't be hugging the wife you were selling, so stop it," Miranda muttered. Abashed, he cast a quick glance around to see if they had been observed. Susannah fought to keep a smile off her face.

"Push me, Michael. Pretend you're angry and push me," she hissed. "If you're selling me, then we're hardly on good terms." Michael grimaced, placed his hands on her shoulders, and pushed. As she staggered backward, he snarled,

"Stupid bitch. I can hardly wait to get rid of you and acquire some good, hard cash. You're useless." Susannah lowered her chin to her chest. She clapped her hand over her mouth, and forced a couple of tears for effect.

"I'm sorry, I'm sorry," she cringed. Then she straightened and began to retreat. "And I can hardly wait to be rid of you, you pig. Anything or anyone would be better than living with you." Even as she spouted these brave words she flung up one arm as if to ward off a blow. The crowd, scenting ever more fodder for gossip, began to press closer.

"Get back, you louts. You'll have plenty of time to see the goods in just a few minutes." Michael yanked her closer and pretended to swat her behind.

He used the advantage of his height to scan the crowd again. Daniel was nowhere to be seen. Miranda, entering into the spirit of the action, ostentatiously looked down her nose at Susannah and turned her back, surreptitiously wiping her eyes. Susannah pushed against Michael to escape his grip.

She braced herself for the horrors to come. Somehow the perfect solution to her troubles when contemplating her escape from the terror of living with Albert, albeit embarrassing and shabby, was a means to an end. While she knew that being displayed on a table, stool or in the back of a wagon for all to see would be humiliating, she had dismissed it as a small interlude in a day that heralded her freedom. Now, as the crowd of men jostled for position, their crude remarks becoming increasingly pointed and audible, it was a very different pot of porridge. Her safety net had failed to appear.

Time telescoped alarmingly. The comments became coarser and coarser. Whore, hussy and bitch were the least of the epithets thrown at her. Suggestions as to her sexual preferences and the services she would be willing to perform increased in volume and invective. Frantically she searched the riffraff gathered around the auctioneer's table, hoping against hope that the elusive Daniel would magically appear. Her heart beat like a trip hammer. She had trouble drawing her breath. Hot tears blurred her vision and panic made her unable to focus. Hopeful that she overlooked him in the seething mass, she caught Miranda's eye. Miranda, valiantly controlling her sobs at her friend's plight, shook her head. Michael, with a tiny jerk of his head, echoed his wife's actions.

Bigamist! Bringer of shame! Susannah braced herself as the combination of fear and horror threatened to drop her to the ground. No Daniel! Panic at the possible consequences of her actions overwhelmed her. With Daniel performing his part of the escape plan, she acknowledged that her fears had been self-induced. Now those possible ramifications to her actions had become very real indeed. The safety net provided by her friends existed no longer. Unable to clutch Michael because of his duties as disgusted husband and auctioneer, she swayed. Michael, alerted by Miranda's frantic hand signals, pretended to shove Susannah, even as he held her arm to support her. "Stiffen your knees," he hissed. "I can't hold you and pretend to sell you at the same time." From an unknown well of strength and resolve, Susannah pretended to push Michael away even as she stiffened her back. She refused to catch the eye of anyone in the crowd by cantering on a distant point, an expression of extreme disinterest was fixed on her face.

Ethan, from his position near the back of the crowd, watched the public abuse of the wife with rising outrage. Normally a very private and withdrawn individual, his temper firmed his desire to do something, anything, about this dreadful situation. As his outrage grew, his usual reticence and bashfulness dwindled. He began to work his way closer to the front.

Michael swung Susannah onto the auctioneer's table, neatly avoiding being struck by the bundle she clasped in her hand, and leapt up after her. "Courage, Susannah, it's almost over. I'm sorry, but we must go ahead." Susannah shrank from him in a panic for what was to occur, inadvertently reinforcing the assumption that he was a harsh disciplinarian ridding himself of an encumbrance.

He grabbed her arm, ostensibly to prevent escape. In reality, it was the only thing that kept her upright. Fear overwhelmed her. She could neither see nor hear. Her knees felt as weak as water. Waves of nausea washed over her. Faintly, through her terror and shame, she was aware of rough male voices in counterpoint to the patter of Michael's attempt to imitate an auctioneer. Bursts of laughter impinged vaguely on her consciousness, but her concentration focused on two things: remaining upright and not vomiting.

Ethan, now past the mid-point of the crowd, determined to do something. He continued to edge forward.

"Attention. Order, here. Order. Wife for sale! Wife for sale!" Michael bellowed, his free hand motioning for silence. As the noise slowly diminished, he continued. "As you know, I've decided to sell this woman." he paused to spit at her feet, "my wife." Michael's voice took on volume and resonance as he continued.

"She's a skilled dairy worker. However, money now is better than money later, and I'm on my way to America. I know you'll agree that cash is better than a wife!" Hoots, guffaws and cheers greeted his spiel.

Ethan, fired with missionary zeal, suddenly connected the word "wife" to his cousin's letter. So great was his disgust at the proceedings and relief at a solution to his predicament that he jigged impatiently from foot to foot as he waited for the bidding to begin. He was almost at the front of the group. With a last thrust he wormed his way between two stalwarts, finally in a position to prevent this abomination.

"So, what am I bid? Do I hear two pounds?" Susannah swayed. Michael's supporting grip was all that prevented her collapse. The jeers and catcalls faded into the background as she focused on enduring the humiliation. She was unconscious of the fact that the bidding had become quite spirited. Acceptance of the fact that she would be sold slowly penetrated her consciousness. Then, as her knees began to buckle in spite of her best efforts, she heard the dreaded words, "Sold for three pounds to the man in the green coat!"

As the world came back into focus, Susannah looked at her new owner and husband. He was red of face and short of stature. He apparently did not think she was worthy of attention, as he stared fixedly over her head and seemed incapable of movement. While his appearance had nothing disgusting about it, a pleasant demeanour was no guarantee of kindness. Albert, a very handsome man, had displayed good manners until they were married. As she slowly absorbed the fact that her old life was over and a totally new one was about to begin, she groped for her bundle.

Ethan kept his eyes on the brute and his wife as he prepared to complete this most unorthodox of transactions. A wife. He had a wife! Purchased a wife, actually! Not even the knowledge that she would be married to his cousin by tonight, or tomorrow at the latest, offered him any comfort.

Suddenly he became aware of a burgeoning silence. *What? What was wrong?* Then he realized that this very wife stood on the table, waiting for assistance to descend. Belatedly he stepped forward to help her. The numbness that held him in thrall began to dissipate.

He reached up and clasped her waist. She bent forward to accept his support. Concentrating on completing the transfer with dispatch, he noticed that her hands trembled on his shoulders and she winced as he tightened his grasp. Torn between jerking his hands away, thus permitting her to sprawl on the ground, and maintaining his grip to assure control and causing her pain, he found himself on the horns of a dilemma.

Whatever his decision, they were both past the point of no return. He changed his action from supporting to pulling, the faster to get her on her own two feet. She gasped with fear or pain. Fortunately, just as his grasp began to loosen, the woman's feet touched the ground and he let his hands fall.

While his gaze apparently met hers, his eyes refused to focus. A wife. A woman for whom he must be reluctantly and, he prayed, only briefly responsible, was a terrifying prospect. A wife. In vain he reminded himself, Jackson's wife, she's Jackson's wife. She was still a woman, and he still had to get her to his home, arrange the marriage with the vicar, and see about her passage to Canada. And placate the doyenne of his abode, Mrs. Rumble.

Mrs. Rumble. Oh, my God, Mrs. Rumble! How would he explain this to Mrs. Rumble? Explain this extremely bizarre situation to the martinet who ruled his life. A redoubtable woman, her lack of patience and rigid moral standards were a byword in the parish. Could he present the case so that annihilation did not precede the completion of his explanation?

Her position was that of housekeeper, but Ethan always thought that the title keeper more closely described her actions.

Doggedly pursuing his goal, he stepped in front of the erstwhile husband and another woman, probably his new doxy, both of whom resembled statues. The shock on their faces echoed that of the purchased wife, and, did he but know it, of his own.

Why would they be shocked? Especially the man? He's the one who put her up for sale. These thoughts tumbled through his mind, and right back out. The immediacy of coping with the woman took precedence.

A telltale yellow of a fading bruise around her right eye had been impossible to conceal, large bonnet and lowered head notwithstanding. *Serves them right, doing such a damn fool, degrading, disgusting thing. I'm glad she won't sport bruises in the future. Jackson's a kind, firm man who wouldn't think of striking a woman.*

"Imagine actually paying for a wife. What a fool!" snorted one yokel.

"He'll soon learn." This from a man whose body and clothes reeked of a combination of odors gleaned from spilled ale, dried food and a particularly noisome stable.

"Remember to beat her if she doesn't mind!" The unsought advice assaulted his ears.

"Or even if she does!" This last sally brought loud guffaws from the crowd and earned the speaker many a hearty slap on the back.

Snide comments and sidelong glances from the crowd failed to pierce the miasma of terror that engulfed him.

"Three pounds, sir, as agreed." The dumb ox held out his hand for the money, a look of despair on his face. Dimly

Ethan realized that the man's reaction should mirror joy or satisfaction, but the dreaded repercussions that awaited him did not permit intrusions of logic. Even as he quailed at the thought of being responsible for getting the woman married to Jackson and safely ensconced on a ship heading for the Americas, he vowed to accomplish it in the most expeditious manner possible. He searched for his handkerchief to wipe perspiring brow and sweaty hands prior to retrieving his purse. It took three tries before he could control his shaking hands sufficiently to open it. He kept his head bent and took his time fetching the coins to regain some equilibrium. Until he saw her ship disappear over the horizon he would not draw an easy breath. Inhaling as deeply as possible, he proffered the coins.

"Here you are, sir. Three pounds, as agreed."

Dumbly, Michael took the coins, his expression epitomizing stupefaction, not delight. He was stunned. *What could they do? They had had to complete the sale or face insurrection from the mob.* His thoughts scurried like mice fleeing a cat. The first and foremost was how to track Susannah's whereabouts, closely followed by a roiling mixture of rage at, and concern about, Daniel. He clutched the coins in one hand, and reached for Miranda with the other.

"Come on," he whispered, "we'll follow her to the wagon and try to find out the man's name and address.

Ethan, turning to address the woman, suddenly realized that he didn't know her name. Well, that could wait. It was more important to get her out of this village before anything else untoward happened.

"My carriage is just over there. Come along, madam." He spun on his heel and charged toward his vehicle, face on fire. As soon as he realized his was the final bid, he had ordered a small boy to the publican with a message to have his horses put to and the wagon brought round. When he turned to help his most recent purchase into the vehicle, he thought he saw the former husband slide his hand into the bundle balanced on her hip. Ethan could have sworn he heard the chink of coins. Now he was both seeing and hearing things. There was no sense whatsoever in such an action. Sell a wife and then give her the proceeds? Ridiculous!

Jettisoning his first reaction, to loudly and forcefully tell the man to go away, he thought about acquiring proof of the transaction.

"One moment, sir. This should be recorded. Please come with me." He wheeled abruptly and charged off to the Green Sheaf. Numbly, the three followed in his wake. The innkeeper provided a scrap of far-from-white paper, a somewhat tattered quill and a viscous fluid purporting to be ink. Ethan dated the page and began to write, relieved that his shaking appeared to be under control: one wife, age—how old was she?

"How old are you, madam?" No sooner had he voiced his question than he cringed. One never asked personal questions, and asking a woman her age was the greatest faux pas of all.

"I'm three and twenty, sir," she murmured.

"Ahem, one wife, age three and twenty, price three pounds," he read aloud, and thrust the paper at the former husband with instructions that he was to make his mark. *I'll probably have to ask the publican to witness the mark*, he grumbled mentally, but was surprised to see a signature, albeit virtually illegible, gracing the page. The innkeeper, who claimed that the shilling he charged for the writing materials included his offices as a witness, signed with a flourish. Ensuring that this precious document resided safely in his pocket, Ethan shepherded his small flock outside. Addressing Susannah's head covering, he blurted, "I'll fetch the rig to the door, madam. Please wait here." *My God, I still don't know her name. Wait, that other woman called her Susy or some such, I think.* Even as he cursed himself for stupidity in not bringing the wagon with him, he prayed it would be where he had left it in his mad dash to the inn.

Frantic at the events of the last hour, Susannah whispered, "Michael, what will I do? What happened to Daniel?" She was barely able to choke the words past the lump of fear in her throat. Her friends were at a loss. "Do you realize that I'm a bigamist? Do you know the disgrace that will bring to my family? I know you have little use for them because they refused to support me against Albert, but they don't deserve this!" She drew a shuddering breath and fought for control. Michael nodded his head.

"Did he tell you his name or where you're going? We need to know how to contact you." Michael queried frantically. The deal had been completed and witnessed, in writing. They were stuck with the untenable results of their actions.

"I have no idea. I didn't even watch him sign his name." She braced herself for her new owner's return.

"I think his last name is something like Partridge or Parrot, but the way he held the paper blocked most of his signature and I didn't dare be too obvious. You had best go with this man for now, or he'll have the constable on us, right enough. I put the money in your bundle. But you be sure to get it into your pocket as soon as may be. Write to us when you get to your destination, and we'll see what we can do."

"Oh, Susannah, I never thought to ask, are you going to tell him your real name?" Miranda quavered. Susannah gulped.

"I'll have to, won't I? I don't see that I've much choice in the matter." She clutched Miranda's hand.

"Why don't you give him your maiden name, and not your married name? It might not help a lot, but it will buy you a little more time." Susannah nodded in desperate agreement.

The three fell silent as the man and wagon approached. Terror and despair filled their hearts.

CHAPTER FOUR

Two hours later, tired, dusty, and scared, Susannah knew no more than the name of her new owner: Ethan Parridge. She was reluctant to ask where they were going, caught equally between wanting to get the journey over with and dreading what was to come. Overwhelming any concerns about her personal safety, she tried in vain to stop her thoughts: *Bigamist, you're a bigamist, a criminal. Bigamist!* While her body swayed in rhythm with the motion of the wagon and her hands gripped the seat for added stability, all her attention turned inward.

She remembered with horror the treatment meted out to a family in a village not far from her own. The husband's family in another village caused vigilantes to stone and beat the man, leaving a drooling, useless wretch in their wake. The family was ostracized socially. The vicar refused to let the woman and her family attend services. When she took her goods to market, no one would buy them.

The entire community banded together, their actions supported and encouraged by religious and secular establishments. The children were refused entrance to the village school. People spat in their wake. Susannah swayed as she considered her family's disgrace if her infamy were discovered. Even parents who had refused to see or acknowledge the brutality of her husband deserved better than this. Her brothers, newly married with wives both increasing, might be banished entirely from their homes. Such an action ensured the demise of their parents, since the family resources were pooled.

The smallholding consumed the combined efforts of the adults. They toiled to wrest a living for too many people from ground that produced little, no matter how hard they worked. Every inch of land was utilized. Yet, because she chose to escape a situation that had become untenable, that had put her very life in danger, her entire family would suffer if anyone discovered what she had done. Releasing her grip on the wagon seat, she hid her face in her hands and moaned softly. Realizing that her new husband could hear her, she glanced at him.

Mr. Parridge seemed determined to concentrate on his driving and waste no time in idle chitchat. Just then he cleared his throat and mumbled, his gaze locked on the horses. He knew, from sad experience, that once a woman realized you were nervous around her, she had the upper hand. He was determined to avoid this distressingly familiar situation at all costs.

"Well, we'll be in Upper Melton soon, ma'am. You'll be taken care of."

Silence was the only response he received. He cleared his throat again. Staring at his left knee, he confided, "My house is close to the town, about two hours from here." The silence became palpable. Still no answer was forthcoming. He tried again, this time admonishing the whiffletrees.

"Ma'am, no one will hurt you. You'll be married right enough by tomorrow noon time at the latest."

Susannah became aware that the man was speaking. She had was so consumed with fear that her body felt frozen. Her mind, too. She swallowed hard, trying to get the lump in her throat to shrink enough so that she could talk. She realized that her silence was now embarrassing both of them. Desperately she swallowed.

"Yes, sir," she croaked. She was oblivious to his nervous gestures as the silence lengthened.

She contemplated telling the truth, but immediately rejected that idea. Except for Michael, most men assumed control of their wives, and with few exceptions felt impelled to exert that control at every opportunity.

Escape? How? If she jumped from the wagon, where would she go? Without a reference no one would hire her, or, if they were willing to overlook such a glaring omission, her wages would be so minuscule that her life would be little better than being Albert's whipping post.

Pleading? Mr. Ethan Parridge, as he had introduced himself, seemed to lack the brutish characteristics of many men, but appearances, as she well knew, could be misleading.

Why married? I can't get married. What if he discovers that not only am I married, but a runaway, as well. Even a thief, as I've taken all the money I got from the market today. Michael managed to slip the coins paid for me into my bundle. That's a good bit extra to use for escape. Oh, God, what will I do? If anyone finds out that I'm a bigamist, my new husband and children will be ruined!

Ethan, in blissful ignorance of the panic he had unwittingly created, resettled his hat, brushed his coat sleeve, and chirruped at the horses. They responded with enthusiasm and broke into a dust-making trot. Blushing, he hauled back on the reins, settling them to a steady, albeit faster, rate once more. Susannah opened her new reticule. Peered inside. Closed it. Resettled its position on her arm. Straightened her back. Inhaled to respond to Ethan.

Just as she opened her mouth, Ethan pulled up beside a small stream. He wound the reins around the brake handle and hurried to the other side of the wagon, vowing to do the job properly this time when he assisted her to alight. The concentration and cooperation of both parties effected an uneventful descent.

"I'm going to water the horses," he informed her left shoulder. Clearing his throat he continued, "Please feel free to walk about a bit if you like. This equipage is a far cry from a properly-sprung carriage." Apparently he was giving her a chance for some privacy behind several nearby bushes.

"Thank you," she murmured. Was the man blushing? Thanking the heavens that the rain had held off, Susannah hurried towards a clump of bushes that would screen her activities. Entering the clearing once more, her money now safely in the pocket she wore under her skirt, she washed her face and hands in the stream, patting them dry with her petticoat. Mr. Parridge had disappeared. She headed towards the horses. She was settled on the seat when Ethan ambled back into view.

He clambered into the wagon, picked up the reins, and mentally counted the minutes until his home came into view. Mrs. Rumble could take over with Jackson's new wife, thus permitting him a degree of comfort sadly missing from this afternoon's activities. He congratulated himself on his clever solution to a heretofore overwhelming problem. She…the woman…Susannah…had only supplied her first name, and he was too embarrassed to ask for her surname. While she got settled, he would call on the vicar to arrange for the marriage.

A visit to the Broken Barrel, the local stage stop, would give him the requisite information about times and costs of the Liverpool stage. Once at the port, he would see that Susannah acquired the warm clothes and stout boots recommended by Jackson, place her in the hands of the captain of the next passenger vessel to Upper Canada, entrust the letter to his cousin to the fastest packet at the docks, and then escape. In spite of his determination to hand over all responsibility to Mrs. Rumble at the earliest possible opportunity, he resisted the temptation to spring the horses, dust and distance combining to preclude the longed-for action.

The sound of the front door opening drew a young maid to the front hall.

"Hello, Maisie." He ignored her gasp of astonishment when she spied his companion. "Please bring some tea and ask Mrs. Rumble to attend me." Ethan heaved a sigh of relief. He led Susannah to a small parlor. The vicar would be here shortly, courtesy of the blacksmith's young lad. Light began to cast its lambent glow in Ethan's world.

The sitting room, furnished to a nicety befitting a gentleman whose interests tended toward the sedentary, confirmed Susannah's estimate of the social position occupied by her purchaser. The furniture fitted together in a way achieved only by years of sharing the same space. While nothing was shabby and each piece glowed with beeswax polish, neither did it obtrude with brash newness. The pictures were fashionable and sported several examples of the school of landscapes, lovingly rendered by an enthusiastic, if not gifted, amateur. No doilies peeked from beneath the pieces of bric-a-brac and there was that lack of ornamentation that proclaimed its owner a bachelor. Faced with these signs of undeniable respectability, her fears of nefarious plans on the part of Ethan evaporated. The room was cozy, welcoming, and extended its peace to Susannah's battered soul.

Settling back in the chair proffered by Ethan, she took a deep breath. His blush when they had stopped to water the horses, combined with her current location, reinforced her belief that Mr. Parridge suffered from acute shyness around females. Although her future remained clouded in mist, concerns for her personal safety abated.

Mrs. Rumble ruled the household, and Ethan, with an iron hand. He, oblivious, knew only that he was comfortable, that Mrs. Rumble's respectability was beyond reproach, and that he never had to cope with domestic difficulties. His plan to confide in Susannah about these matters went awry when the sitting room door opened with dispatch, and the object of his proposed discourse stood framed in the doorway.

Susannah saw a woman of certain years and comfortable size. Her black bombazine dress showed not a wrinkle, her cap framed her face becomingly, her gimlet gaze rested on Susannah, but her demeanour when she addressed her employer was painfully correct.

"Yes, sir? Maisie said you wished to see me." Her folded hands rested at her waist, and her posture indicated she expected to hear of a task well within her purview.

"Mrs. Rumble, this is, uh, that is, she's going to, well." Ethan stopped, drew a deep breath and threw his heart over the fence. "This is Susannah Ashton, the wife I bought today."

Ethan had taken advantage of Susannah's curiosity about her surroundings to consult the bill of sale and get her last name.

Susannah winced. She had forgotten her ploy of using her maiden name. Ethan's "the wife I bought" caused her heart to beat with fear as *bigamist, bigamist* pounded in her brain. She wrenched her thoughts back to the present.

Mopping his brow and finally daring to relax, Ethan was astounded to see Mrs. Rumble's complexion turn as white as wax. He hastened to help her to a chair, but she appeared to be stuck in the doorway.

"A wife, sir? You *bought* a wife? Here? You? A wife? Sir! I'm a respectable woman...." One hand flew to grasp the doorjamb, the other covered her heart.

Ethan, correctly reading signs of a peal about to be rung over his head, hastened to muffle the clapper.

"No, no, Mrs. Rumble, you misunderstand. This isn't my wife. She's Jackson's wife! Well, she will be Jackson's wife as soon as may be." Satisfied that the situation was clear, he heaved a sigh of relief.

Mrs. Rumble remained unyielding, clearly far from mollified. Her bosom swelled with indignation and inhalation, her eyes became slits, and her mouth opened in preparation of declaring her roiling emotions. The hand grasping the doorjamb now rested on her hip. The other hand remained over her heart. Ethan, shrinking in dread at observing these signs of a woman determined to empty her budget to some purpose, shuddered anew when he saw the stiffening of Susannah's posture. He had acquired a degree of comfort with Mrs. Rumble, partly because the years in her dish were approximately double his, and partly from their long association as master and servant. Susannah still scared him silly.

"This person, Mr. Ethan, is not a wife, for Jackson or anyone else. You can't just buy a wife like a peck of peaches. I suspect, sir, that she is no better than she should be!" Mrs. Rumble was affronted. So was Susannah.

"Here, here, Mr. Ethan," Mrs. Rumble continued, "that won't do. Mr. Jackson left for Canada some weeks ago. What do you mean this is his wife? When did the marriage take place? How...."

Susannah felt the room darken around her. She was already terrified that someone would discover her bigamous actions if she married this man, but to find that he would not be her husband took her breath away. Visions of white slavery clamored for attention. She clutched the back of a chair and prayed that she would not lose consciousness. Her voice rose in counterpoint to Mrs. Rumble's.

"Not your wife? What do you mean not your wife? Who is this Jackson person? Canada? You mean the Canada that's across the big ocean? You bought me fair and square, even insisted on a Bill of sale. You can't take me back...." Visions of her imminent demise filled Susannah's mind. She had no doubt that Albert's rage would lead him to kill her. How would she get home? Ethan, familiar with the byways on their journey, meandered down country lanes, seemingly at random. She had no idea of where she was or even the name of the village. Neither did she know how far nor in what direction she would have to walk.

Bombarded from both sides, Ethan tried gamely, and vainly, to smooth the waters of this tempest.

"No, no, Mrs. Rumble, I assure you, ma'am, Mrs. Susannah, er, Ashton. Surely I told you about…Mrs. Rumble, you don't know about Jackson's letter…ma'am…." The three-part disharmony was interrupted by the crisp sounds of the knocker on the front door. Grasping at this diversion, Ethan neatly sidestepped Mrs. Rumble, beating out Maisie by a hair and jerked open the door, only to come face to face with the vicar.

"Sir, come in." Ethan clutched the vicar's extended hand with the fervor of one going down for the third time and literally pulled him into the hall. He made sure of the vicar's continued presence by the simple expedient of placing himself in front of the door.

The Greek chorus turned as one.

"He has to marry me—he bought me. I may have been sold, but I'm no doxy. It's all quite legal. You…."

"Get that woman out of this house. The very idea! Bought a wife, just like a buying a sack of flour. What kind of a creature would let herself be sold! I never!"

"Sir, sir, you must marry this woman to my cousin Jackson. Look, I have the proxy right here. It's all legal. Please, sir, marry her quickly. I…."

As each of the combatants pleaded their case, they accompanied their arguments by jostling the other two for position, the better to focus the vicar's attention on the merits of their particular case.

"Stop!" The command, augmented by a raised hand and honed by years in the pulpit, brought instant obedience. Silence reigned. *Blessed silence*, thought the vicar.

"Now, one at a time, please. Ethan, I received a message from Jim Bolt's boy that you required my services to perform a marriage. He said you told him to fetch me as you passed the smithy. I didn't believe him, even though he's usually reliable. I haven't heard that you have been courting, Ethan, or negotiating for a marriage settlement. Now I find you with a strange woman, a wife whom you have apparently purchased, and Mrs. Rumble is very upset. Please explain." Privately, the vicar considered that Mrs. Rumble showed signs of apoplexy.

Delighted with an opportunity to present his case, Ethan launched his explanation.

"I met the young Bolt lad on the way into the village. Sir, you know that my cousin, Jackson, Jackson Stansfield, that is, recently emigrated to a place in Canada called Marcher Mills in order to farm. I received his letter yesterday. It stated that his friend, with whom he had planned to stay, had died. Jackson inherited not only the farm and all of his friend's assets, but also custody of two small children. The couple on the farm died and Jackson's friend took responsibility for them." Ethan paused for a much-needed breath.

"Yes, yes, but what has that to do with buying a wife?" The vicar understood Ethan's description and felt he had a firm grip on the salient points.

"Yes, sir, well, sir, I'm getting to that." Ethan prepared to rush his fences. "Well, the thing is, sir, that Jackson asked me to find him a wife."

"Find a wife? Surely, Ethan, you didn't expect to find one under a gooseberry bush. Whatever did Jackson mean?"

Ethan was wilting rapidly under the gimlet stare of the clergy. He realized that if he didn't complete his story quickly what little wits he had left would desert him entirely.

"Jackson sent me a proxy, duly signed, and I bought him a wife. Here it is. The proxy, I mean. And a perfectly good, wife, too, sir. She certainly meets all his requirements for someone to care for the children. There aren't any women in Canada, and he needs help." *But not as much as I do.* Ethan could feel the beads of moisture form on his upper lip. Perspiration trickled down his cheeks.

Susannah, riveted by Ethan's explanation, rapidly assimilated these amazing new facts. Surely Canada was sufficiently far away that Albert would never find her. Her bigamous marriage would be a secret. In addition, there were children. Susannah's arms ached anew to hold a small child, to make gingerbread men with currant eyes, to hear prayers lisped at her knee. Lost in her daydream, she almost missed Mrs. Rumble's pungent comments.

"That's all very well, Mr. Ethan, but I'm a respectable woman, and I won't have no doxies in my house. If she's to be married to Mr. Jackson, I want to see it done, and done now." The stridency of her tone was matched by the thrust of her chin and her pugnacious stance. Both hands now rested on her hips and one foot tapped ominously.

The vicar intervened. "Certainly, Mrs. Rumble. One concedes that you have very valid concerns here. But let's not jump from the pot to the fire." He twitched the paper from Ethan's hand. "I need to see that proxy, young Ethan, and I must know exactly what you mean by 'bought a wife'. It's a disgusting custom, just this side of legal, and only if all the requirements are met." The Vicar was caught on the horns of a dilemma. His own ethics were in direct conflict with the outdated common law, fortunately infrequently invoked, that permitted a man to sell his wife, providing she consented to the transaction. He could not conceive of circumstances so dire that they would drive a couple to hold themselves up to the ridicule of their community.

Wordlessly, Ethan handed over the bill of sale, duly witnessed. He thanked his lucky stars he demanded such proof. The vicar's reluctance to handle either document was obvious, but his position as moral arbiter of those within his community fortified him sufficiently to overcome his abhorrence. The document, duly witnessed, was signed by the husband (signature illegible), the wife's (shaky and unclear), the innkeeper-cum-witness, whose pen appeared to have been dragging a hair, and Ethan's. The probity of the proxy was unquestionable and complied with all legal requirements.

"Well, Ethan, it's true that the papers seem to be in order. However, I find myself unable to marry this woman," looking down his nose at Susannah "to your cousin until I have prayed on the matter. I will return at nine o'clock this evening with my final decision." The vicar took courteous leave of Mrs. Rumble, bid Ethan a perfunctory goodbye, and ignored Susannah entirely.

Susannah's spirits began to revive. Considering all the facts, it looked as if her escape from Albert would be effected in such a way as to give her the first sense of peace she had had in many a year. Even the horror of her soon-to-be bigamous state faded somewhat. The safety provided by distance and the acquisition of a new surname provided a cocoon of comfort.

Mrs. Rumble was mortified that the vicar had refused refreshment. She departed, huffily, to see to the matter of tea and the preparation of a room for their reluctant guest who was, obviously, no better than she should be. Ethan barely waited for Susannah to seat herself before he thumped into the opposite chair and heaved a premature sign of relief. As he restored his handkerchief to his pocket, he caught Susannah's eye.

"Jackson, sir? Your cousin? In Canada? Please tell me about this arrangement of marriage by proxy. What's a proxy? Why can't he find a wife over there? I heard you state that there weren't any women, but, sir, if he has two children to take care of there must have been at least one woman."

Susannah decided she would take pity on Ethan. Eventually. Her terror was slowly ebbing, and her limbs were once again under her control. It was difficult to contain her excitement. Canada. Canada! She felt like shouting. It didn't matter where in that vast country Marcher Mills was located. Canada—she couldn't believe her luck. Across Yorkshire to a port, then weeks on the sea until they reached her promised land. While it was impossible for her to remember more than Canada being a land of vast wildernesses and savages, with criminals abounding, it really didn't matter. It was blissfully far away. She would have a different name.

She would disappear into a community as wife to a husband whose credentials had been vouched for by a man who was already part of the community. Albert would never, ever find her. If, by some horrid happenstance, he should learn that her friends helped her and "sold" her at a local market, she had disappeared from the ken of those friends as soon as the wagon she was riding in had vanished over the horizon.

It was a measure of Ethan's agitation that he actually addressed her; not her bonnet or shoulder or the arm of her chair.

"Well, ma'am. That is to say...I mean...you see ma'am, it's like this." Ethan disinterred his handkerchief once more, observed its damp state with a grimace of distaste and returned it to its home. "My cousin Jackson, Jackson Stansfield, that is, has been saving for years to move to Canada to join his friend in a farming venture. He left early this year. They are, that is, they were, planning to have a large dairy herd and sell milk, cheeses, butter and garden produce. Now that the railway is through from Toronto to Marcher Mills, there is a large, ready-made market practically on their doorstep. He withdrew the handkerchief once more, grimaced, returned it unused to the designated pocket, and motioned to Susannah to take a seat.

"He arrived, however, to find his friend and the hired couple who worked on the farm dead of a fever. The couple's two young children, who looked upon my cousin's friend as a surrogate uncle, are now in Jackson's care. So you see, he needs a wife, and asked me to help him find one. Jackson is careful of the proprieties He included a Proxy to Wed with his letter, so that all could be right and tight before the wife, I mean to say his wife, left for Canada." Running out of words and breath simultaneously, Ethan leaned back in his chair with the air of one who has addressed all the components of an extremely complicated situation.

"But what...?" began Susannah, when Mrs. Rumble bustled in with the tea tray. While her manner indicated some softening, the hand of friendship was not forthcoming. Susannah, ignoring that over which she had no control, gave herself to the enjoyment of a substantial meal and refused to think of her predicament until she had rest and quiet. She got her wish, for immediately after tea, Ethan suggested that she might welcome a chance to retire to her room.

Mrs. Rumble, very much on her dignity, showed Susannah to a chamber that fitted to a nicety that category that fell between family and retainer. While it was painfully clean and neat, she noticed only the beckoning bed. Mrs. Rumble's voice droning on about calling her in time for dinner was barely audible. She did not hear the click of the door's closing. Draping her shawl on the end of the bed and putting her shoes neatly on the floor, she succumbed to her exhaustion.

# # #

"I now pronounce you man and wife." Ethan and Susannah stood in front of the Vicar, both numb with shock. Susannah's resulted from her bigamous state and the enormity of the step she had just taken. Ethan's arose from an extremely uncomfortable proximity to marriage, even at several steps removed. Mrs. Rumble and the vicar's wife had stood witnesses, mostly on the basis that the fewer who knew of these irregular proceedings, the better.

The group moved stiffly to the waiting chairs, and Mrs. Rumble prepared to serve sherry. Ethan insisted that she have a seat and a glass as well. He was aware of her discomfort at sitting in the presence of her employer, but refused to let her go. She was his anchor and a much-needed assurance that normalcy would return. The vicar and Mrs. Parsley made stilted conversation and left as soon as they decently could. The atmosphere lightened significantly with their departure.

Ethan informed Susannah of his plan to whisk them to Liverpool tomorrow on the stage. A caveat by Mrs. Rumble resulted in an adjustment. Ethan would take his own vehicle, sans post boys, and hire fresh horses at stages. They would arrive in time to assure Susannah of a place on the next available passenger ship to Canada. Ethan assured her that he would send a letter by fast packet to apprise Jackson of her arrival. He then suggested that they should retire forthwith to ensure an early start. Susannah gasped her agreement, curtsied quickly, and fled to her room.

CHAPTER FIVE

The bustle of leaving the inn, traveling to the docks and boarding the ship provided a welcome distraction. Ensuring that her bundles were safely stowed, Susannah gazed with satisfaction at the ship's slow manoeuvring from the dock. As the shore receded, then disappeared, she felt safe, at last, from Albert's rage and revenge. *Perhaps it was fortunate that Daniel didn't purchase me. A new country where no one knows me provides the best protection.*

Immune to the seasickness that reduced the majority of passengers to a retching, moaning humanity, she found the ocean air invigorating. Her sea legs let her endure any amount of pitching. The operation of the vessel, with its constant activity, was engrossing. She welcomed the opportunity to work from breakfast to tea time each day as a nursemaid/companion for one of the emigrating families.

The transfer from ship to train went smoothly, aided by the fact that the train came directly to the dock. She settled into a seat and assured herself that her reticule was on her wrist. The majority of her coins rested securely in the pocket concealed under her dress. Adjusting her bonnet, she placed the small basket loaded with provisions on the seat beside her.

There it would remain; a small, silent, and hopefully potent protector, until all the other seats were taken.

Canada offered a bewildering array of intriguing sights and sounds. Clothing styles varied from the familiar to the bizarre. She was sure she even saw a Red Indian. She wished she could write to Michael and Miranda and share her adventure. No matter how great her longing to connect with her dear friends, she knew better than to let her handwriting be seen on any correspondence passing through the hands of the curious in her village. Too many of her erstwhile classmates exhibited an unholy interest in the actions of their neighbors. Melda Starbecker, the worst gossip, was in charge of sorting the mail—and of reading postcards and informing all and sundry of their messages. She was also rumored to steam open interesting missives, but no proof of this latter activity existed. Yet.

The rocking and rumbling of the train seemed strange after her weeks at sea. She was more accustomed to bracing herself for an up and down motion, rather than one that jerked and swayed. As the train pulled out of the station, she remained unimpressed with the slums through which they travelled. Soon, however, they were in the wilderness. No buildings marred the landscape; or curtain of smoke defiled the deep-blue sky.

Lunch forgotten, Susannah's gaze focused exclusively on the unbroken vista. She could easily imagine wild animals in such a habitat. Would she see a bear? What if she saw a moose? She still wasn't convinced that such an animal existed. The panorama of trees, trees and more trees entranced her, whether viewed as a great rolling carpet or when their branches gently brushed her window.

Accustomed to a small village and farms with tidy fields edged with hedgerows, she found her soul expanding to embrace the lush growth. A bird, she thought, would see a trail winding through the wilderness, but no other signs of humans. Was Marcher Mills set amongst such an untamed forest? No, no, it had to have fields and farms and people. But surely there would be woods nearby.

Several hours later the sea of green, no matter how grand, began to pall. The odor of unwashed humanity, cigar, pipe and cigarette smoke pervaded. She was in dire need of the privy, but held back because everyone would know where she was going, and why. Eventually, acute discomfort overcame her reluctance. She left her basket and shawl to reserve her seat, checked her bonnet strings, and rose. She stepped into the aisle just as the train swayed. Her frantic grab for the back of the seat barely saved her from sitting in the lap of the man across the aisle. He smirked.

"That's OK, sister, you c'n sit here any time," he slurred, leering and then belching mightily. The whiskey fumes from his breath and the bottle he tenderly nursed, threatened to suffocate her. She glared and swept toward her goal. The embarrassment of using the facilities in front of strangers sank momentarily beneath the wave of rage that suffused her. She knew from long observation that it was empty, and her progress suffered no impediment as she turned the knob, entered, and then made sure the door was locked.

It was at this point that she began to shake. She washed her face and hands after using the toilet, let her bonnet dangle from her wrist by its strings, and resolved to take down and put up her hair. She struggled to get the comb through the snarls, but finally the long, smooth passes of the comb began to soothe her shattered nerves. Under no illusion that the drunk would ignore her progress, she braced herself for the return trip. Her real fear centered on his possible actions. What if he tried to sit beside her? Susannah had paid little attention to her fellow travelers, except to mark where other women sat, comforted that there were several of them should she need help.

Miranda had told her that some women carried a hat pin if they were nervous, but bonnets didn't need hat pins. Then she remembered the small sewing kit residing in her reticule. Her fingers brushed against the penny that had accompanied the gift. Miranda took no chances that sharp objects would cut their friendship. Swiftly she removed the small, pointed scissors and hid them in her hand. Armed with both weapon and resolve, she stepped from her haven and prepared to confront her tormentor.

Unaware that her shoulders had straightened, and a martial light had entered her eye, she prepared to defeat her enemy. She reached her seat without incident, smiling, smoothing her skirts, and surreptitiously replacing the scissors. The big, bad, bold, smelly man snored loudly.

"Toronto, next stop. Toronto in fifteen minutes. Have your baggage tickets handy. Toronto, Toronto next stop." The sonorous call of the conductor filled the air as he proceeded at a stately pace through the car. Hats were adjusted. Bodies bobbed up and down as objects stored in the overhead bunkers came to nestle in their owners' laps; coats and skirts received vigorous brushing, and attention turned to pocketbooks and reticules in a search for those all-important baggage tickets.

Toronto—finally. Now, I have only to find the Sign of the Ox and identify myself. Then tomorrow it's off to Marcher

Mills. Determinedly she thrust aside all thought of the morrow and its fateful events. Children were all very well, but a husband was another matter entirely. Her hand brushed her skirt to make sure the pocket swayed against her leg. The weight of the coins reassured her.

Before I leave the station I must discover how to escape if Mr. Jackson Stansfield turns out to be another Albert Ashton. Never again. Never, ever again, she repeated her vow, *will I permit myself to be treated so.*

Ethan's directions said that the inn was just up the street from the station. She covered the short distance quickly, enjoying the opportunity to stretch her legs. Susannah entered the Sign of the Ox and identified herself to the landlord.

"Oh yes, Mrs. Stansfield, we've been expecting you. My name is Baskins. Your husband reserved a separate parlor should you wish it, or you may have your meal delivered to your room. I'll just get my daughter, Sally, to help you. Some other small arrangements have also been made."

He beamed. Exactly the type of guest he enjoyed entertaining, Mr. Stansfield proved himself generous, easygoing and polite. His letter contained explicit instructions about the amenities to be provided for his spouse. The opportunity to proffer every consideration to the wife of such a good customer delighted him. Sally, quickly smoothing her apron and checking to ensure that her cap was straight, hastened to respond to her father's summons with a smile and a quick curtsey.

"Good day, ma'am. I'll show you to your room. What time would you like your bath delivered?" Susannah gaped. *A bath! Her new husband had ordered a bath?* She had heard of baths in a special tub, but had always made do with a basin or the creek.

She blinked twice and squeaked, "Bath in half an hour and could you serve supper in my room?"

Susannah nodded, suddenly bereft of speech. When her voice returned, it seemed to be coming from a long way away. "Thank you," she murmured.

"Well, then, Mrs. Stansfield, your luggage has already been delivered to your room, and Sally, here, will take care of you." The innkeeper returned from dealing with other patrons and motioned imperiously for Sally to lead their guest to her room.

"Oh, Mrs. Stansfield, I almost forgot to give you this." The landlord retrieved an envelope from behind the counter. "Mr. Stansfield left a letter for you." Moving like one of the mechanical figures she had heard about, Susannah retraced her steps to accept the missive.

"Thank you," she murmured. Sally headed for the stairs. Numbly, Susannah followed.

Seated in the bath, luxuriating in the warmth of the water and the scented soap provided by the establishment, Susannah eyed the pail of rinse water. Tempting as it was to linger in the bath, the water designated for rinsing, delivered at a temperature close to the boiling point, was barely warm. The faint odor of vinegar ensured that her hair would be entirely soap free. Soft towels rested on a stool, waiting to enfold her in their gentle embrace. As she reluctantly left her cocoon and prepared to give her hair and a final rinse, she mused. *Is this— the bath, scented soap, meal in my room and a private parlor— part of a scheme, or does this man respect, even value, women? His note welcomed me to Canada and assured me that he will meet the train tomorrow. I hope he brings the children.*

Three sharp raps on the door interrupted her thoughts. "It's Sally, ma'am, with your dinner. Seth is with me to remove the bath."

"Just a moment, Sally, and I'll unlock the door." *And move the chair from under the handle, but I'll not mention that.* Sally thumped the tray on the dresser, slopping some of the tea from the pot. Seth, studiously avoiding looking at Susannah, used the rinse pail and a large funnel he had been carrying to empty the water down a waste pipe discreetly located in the corner of the room. Then, placing the funnel in the pail, and the pail in the bath, he carried them out of the room.

"Just put the tray outside the door when you're finished, Mrs. Stansfield. Someone will collect it later."

Susannah nodded. "Will you ask someone to waken me at six?"

"Certainly, ma'am. I'll be sure you're up in good time." She whisked out the door, her skirts fluttering goodbye.

Wife Seller!

CHAPTER SIX

Clouds and an oppressive humidity foretold a downpour, probably within three or four hours. After playing a game of hide and seek for the past two days, the sun seemed firm in its determination to be hidden. Jackson hoped he wouldn't need the tarps he'd included "just in case". He had misjudged, yet again, the amount of time it took to organize the children. How two small people could take up so much time puzzled him.

They weren't disobedient and mostly did what they were told, but they always had to have a drink of water or visit the necessary just as the horses started on the journey. Visits to the privy were very different for boys and girls, he'd discovered. It was easy enough to take Caleb behind a bush or tree, but Emily, while insisting that she was a big girl, became panic stricken when she couldn't see her Uncle Jackson. Combined with an obsession for privacy, the logistics were formidable.

This morning was particularly trying. Caleb and Emily protested loudly when dragged from the fascinating kittens discovered only minutes before it was time to get ready. No reassurance on Jackson's part that they would meet their Aunt

Susannah and then spend the night with the Turner children soothed them. Only the fact that he loaded the wagon and hitched the team before he began to prepare the children for their unwanted journey would permit him to reach town in time, he hoped, to complete several errands before meeting his bride.

Experience had also taught Jackson that it behooved him to organize Emily first. She, at least, maintained some semblance of tidiness. Today, however, she remained obdurate about not having her hair combed. Jackson solved this dilemma by agreeing that wearing her bonnet would suffice.

"Do I look all right, Uncle Jackson? My dress and pinny seem sort of scrunched, don't they?" Emily regarded her guardian earnestly.

"Well, Emily, they probably look sort of scrunched because I found them scrunched on the floor of your room. Maybe next time you can remember to hang them up." Jackson held his breath. Priding herself on being a young lady, Emily could dig her heels in about any number of things, invariably when time was of the essence. "Your bonnet looks lovely, though, Missy, and you've tied a particularly dashing bow." He touched her nose and smiled, braced for what might come.

"Very well, then, Uncle Jackson. I'll wait in the kitchen. You know what a chore it is to get Caleb ready." Jackson smiled as she swept out the door and toward the kitchen, a world-weary sigh trailing behind her. Another potential catastrophe averted.

Caleb hated water unless it was in a creek or a puddle. He saw no merit in being clean. He didn't want to look nice to greet his new Aunt Susannah. There was no reason to change one's clothes just to go to town. He had many excellent reasons why this should be so.

"Uncle Jackson, if I wear my good clothes then you won't let me pet the horses or play with the kittens, and you make me stay away from the pump. If I had a shovel, Uncle Jackson, I could dig a real big hole for the water to splash into real easy. " Jackson gritted his teeth.

"That's right, Caleb, good clothes mean different rules. You can't get near the pump, pet horses or kittens or anything else, and you have to use your very best manners. We want to make your Aunt Susannah feel welcome." From the time he started to get Caleb ready until he had Caleb at the final destination, his eyes left the boy at his own peril.

"Well, at least I can show Aunt Susannah how far I can spit!" Caleb practiced diligently to perfect this new and manly art.

"No, Caleb, that's rude and Aunt Susannah won't want to see anything so stupid," Emily remonstrated in a voice of disgust. Her body might be seated in ladylike splendor in the kitchen, but her ears mentored the conversation between her uncle and brother with no difficulty whatsoever. She gave a wriggle of satisfaction at annoying Caleb.

"It's not stupid, Stupid. Charles Moffatt thinks he's the best spitter, but you just wait, I'm going to show him!" Caleb's red face and pugnacious attitude indicated the imminence of a first-class brawl.

"That's enough, both of you. Now settle down. You will mind your manners and greet your new aunt in a polite and respectful manner." "*Or so I hope*" thought Jackson. His hopes for a pleasant and mannerly beginning to a relationship between the children and Susannah began to fade.

Finally he had the children and the wagon on the road to town. The horses plodded, the children played counting games, and Jackson thought again of Ethan's letter.

# # #

Dear Jackson

You can imagine my state of mind when I received your letter. A wife! As well ask me to dance a hornpipe. You know that women are a complete mystery to me, and I find it comfortable to leave it thus. Just between the two of us, they scare me. (Probably not news, I know.)

However, I appreciated your desperation and very great need, and have purchased you a fine spouse, Susannah. She follows this letter on the steamship Astoria, due to dock in Montreal the last week in May. I have consigned her to the care of the captain.

She tells me she is familiar with dairy work. Her interest in the children was sincere. Susannah assures me that she can cipher and read.

She appears to be quiet and self-effacing. I fear her life was not a happy one, as her face sported the remnants of a black eye and several fading bruises when I purchased her at a local fair. She married you that same evening. Congratulations on your marriage, by the way!

My plan was to have the marriage on the following day, but what with Susannah, the Vicar and Mrs. Rumble carrying on like mad people; it was clearly a case of the sooner the better—especially for me. In spite of constant reflection, the precise sequence of events leading to this most bizarre of purchases eludes me. Vague memories of a notice posted in the inn where I stopped for luncheon and to feed the horses seem to end with having the innkeeper witness the bill of sale, included for your perusal.

Impressing upon her that the winters were very severe and that the weather on the voyage could be equally sharp, I insisted that some of the funds you sent be used to provide stout boots and a warm cloak and shawl. Susannah selected other, more intimate items. When I noticed that the pitifully small bundle she carried had grown to an unwieldy size, I purchased a corded box that I assured her was in the way of a wedding gift. Because she had so few articles of clothing, I was forced to tell her that the shawl was in the way of a wedding gift, as well.

I made sure that she had some lemons and potatoes for the voyage, and impressed upon her the importance of consuming them daily to avoid scurvy. While the time from Liverpool to Montreal is now about three weeks, I wished to take no chances with the health of your bride.

Please let me know if she has arrived safely. I can only be thankful that you will never again make such a request of me. My housekeeper is not at all convinced I merely accompanied Susannah to Liverpool and set her up in a boarding house until her ship sailed. I fear Mrs. Rumble has imbued me with many of the qualities of a rake. The scene that occurred when I brought Susannah home, and that subsequently provided grist for the village gossip mill for many years to come, I prefer to forget.

Since I cannot guarantee the exact date of her arrival, I gave her some coins and a message to the innkeeper requesting him to send a telegram to you.

Your obedient servant,
Ethan

Jackson spent a great deal of time pondering Ethan's repeated use of the word "purchased", unsure of what his cousin really meant. The selling of humans had long been outlawed. *Did Ethan mean* purchase *because he used the money Jackson had sent?* A letter asking clarification of this strange situation was already on its way to England. *No, he uses* purchase *several times, and refers to a bill of sale. Perhaps Susannah can explain when she arrives.*

He noticed that the phrase "my wife" did not come easily. Mrs. Stansfield was even worse, as it conjured images of his mother. He thought of her as Susannah.

He began to consider his desperate need for the warmth and heat of a woman's body—his absolute requirement that he could embrace someone soft and sink his body into hers. Most men would declare it was his right. They would find him wholly justified to claim his marital rights whenever he wished. He was her husband. Her body was his to use as he wished. In every way that counted, he was her owner. But Jackson refused to consider such treatment. He wanted a relationship that matched that of his parents. There were many loud and vigorous discussions between them, but no abuse of any kind. Always, always their respect for each other was evident.

The rising volume of noise from his two passengers interrupted his fruitless train of thought.

"I can so too, so there!" stated Caleb, a militant look on his face.

"No, you can't. Uncle Jackson won't like it. He might even take you out to the woodshed." Emily really did have goading Caleb down to a science. Jackson had yet to realize that he, too, was being whipped into shape by a small, but mighty, martinet.

"Stop, both of you! Now, what is the matter? I thought you were counting trees, or cows, or weeds or whatever." Jackson turned so that he could see both children clearly.

"Caleb said...," Emily began, nose in the air.

"Enough, Emily. Now, Caleb, just what is it that you can, too, do? Come on, out with it."

Caleb struggled with his feelings. Incensed with what he perceived as his big sister trying to boss him, he wasn't really all that sure that Uncle Jackson would approve of his spitting proficiency or permit him to carry out his plan. Nor was he sure of unqualified support for his side of the current argument with his sister.

"I just told Emily that I could, too, drive the horses, Uncle Jackson. You know you said that I had to learn to be a big boy and have chores. Well, driving the horses is a chore." Caleb's demeanour became more conciliatory and less confrontational as the presentation of his rationale unfolded.

Jackson struggled to hide a smile while simultaneously praying for the wisdom to handle yet another looming crisis.

"Right, Caleb. You do have to learn to be a big boy and accept responsibility and contribute to the family. However, it's also important to be sure you are able to do those things you want to do without harming yourself or anyone else." Jackson waited for a response. Two pairs of eyes regarded him solemnly.

"But Uncle Jackson, I can drive the horses. You let me help you take them from the wagon into the stable last week," stated Jackson's nemesis.

"Yes, that's true. However, if you recall, I was also holding the reins. Do you remember telling me how hard the team pulled and how glad you were that I was there to help? Those horses could get the bits between their teeth and run away from you. They could even choose to ignore your signals because they are so much stronger than you are."

"But Uncle Jackson," But Uncle Jackson was a recurring phrase with Caleb, "you said that they were stronger than you, too, because you couldn't pull the wagon all by yourself, especially up a hill." Caleb's smile was cherubic. Jackson sighed. Surely there must be a way to avoid these conversations. He fervently hoped that his new wife would be able to provide some valuable insights.

"Even so, Caleb, I'm much, much stronger than you are. Therefore, this discussion has ended. You will not drive the team right now, but when you are a man, you will." Caleb accepted the inevitable with as much grace as he could muster. At least Uncle Jackson hadn't forbidden him to drive the team, and he was sure that if he were patient he would have an opportunity to show his uncle just how strong and wonderful a driver he could be. He just wouldn't bother his uncle with comments about spitting right now. Jackson grappled with guilt, sure that he mishandled the situation.

As he returned to his rumination, he realized that the distraction provided by the children had given both an opportunity for reflection and an easing of the compulsion to throw his new bride on the nearest approximately level surface and obtain some much-needed relief. *I am not an animal. I won't force her. But I hope I don't have to wait too much longer.* Just then Emily piped up.

"Uncle Jackson, do you think that Aunt Susannah knows how to knit and bake? I really want to learn how to make cookies."

"I'm sure she does, Emily. Uncle Ethan says that she's extremely good with dairy work, and no doubt your aunt will know how to make delicious meals, including desserts such as cookies and cakes." Jackson mouthed the platitudes, not caring as much about the kitchen as he did the dairy and fields. Although, upon sober reflection, having good meals at regular intervals, especially without his participation in the preparation, did sound like heaven. He had discovered, to his dismay, that cooking and housework ranked right up there with taking care of children on his list of things he couldn't do and didn't want to learn.

His mind returned to his new wife. He wondered, as he had so often since reading Ethan's letter, about her appearance. Her skills in the dairy relieved a great part of his concerns about operating a farm capable of supporting a family. What did she look like? Was she fat or thin? Tall or short? Pretty, plain or even downright ugly? All that, however, paled in comparison to his need for a bed mate. He also discovered that thoughts of wife and bed required vigorous monitoring. His body reacted with embarrassing alacrity to the thought of marital relations.

At the children's behest, he let the team canter the last quarter of a mile into town. He checked his watch, appalled to see that the generous amount of time he allowed for a variety of errands had shrunk alarmingly.

"Emily and Caleb, you may go into Mr. Marshall's store and decide on a penny's worth of candy each." Hunching his shoulders in acknowledgement of the bribe, he reflected that desperate situations called for desperate measures. "I'm going to the livery stable to pick up the chickens that Mr. Jenkins has left for me and then stop at the blacksmith's for work he's done. I'll be back as soon as I can. Do not touch anything in the store. Do not move from the candy counter. Is that understood?"

Nods and smiles greeted him as he lifted them down from the wagon bed and sent them into the store. He put his foot on the wheel, anxious to complete his errands, sighed, then lowered it and trotted back to enter the store.

"Zeke, they're not to move from the candy counter, and they each have a penny to spend." Zeke grinned and nodded at Jackson, who was already charging out the door.

Marvin Sanderson's garrulousness was legendary. It didn't matter if his customers wanted to talk, he had enough conversation for both. In spite of his best efforts, fifteen agonizing minutes passed before Jackson was able to load the crate of poultry and make his escape. While fifteen minutes was far less than the two-hour round trip to the Jenkins' place, today was not the one to catch up on gossip, no matter how fascinating.

Leaving the livery stable, he rushed to the smithy. Blessing Nat Bodkins for his businesslike attitude, he carefully placed the hinges and nails under the seat and bolted for the general store.

The two children hovered by the candy display with anticipation. A penny's worth of candy each was a rare treat, and due care must be taken to get as much as possible for that precious coin. Zeke, one eye on the children, measured fabric for one customer as his wife extolled the excellence of last year's apples to another. Considering that the wrinkles on the apples rivalled those on the face of the community's oldest inhabitant, her eloquence was remarkable.

"Hurry up, children. Haven't you chosen your treats yet? Aunt Susannah will be arriving in five minutes, and we've still to get to the depot." Jackson all but danced with impatience and nerves, his plan to run into the store, pay Zeke, and leave, in tatters.

"But Uncle Jackson, this is really important," stated Emily, eyeing her uncle with determination.

"Yes, Uncle Jackson, it's really important, and it's hard to choose with so many different kinds." Caleb supported his sister. The giddy delights of anticipation were not to be rushed.

"Well, there'll be no need to choose in about one second, that is all the time you have to make up your minds, because in one second we'll be on our way to the station." Jackson, perspiration beading on his brow, was frantic. Bad enough to resort to marrying a woman by proxy to get a wife; he had shared the fact of her purchase with no one. The least he could do to show her respect was to meet the train on time.

"Very well, Uncle Jackson. We'll be quick. Mr. Marshall, I shall spend my penny on a bag of peppermints, and Caleb wants liquorices. That way we can trade." Emily placed the order with aplomb and a slight air of humoring one bound to be difficult.

"I can place my own order, Emily. I don't need you to help!" Caleb's outrage radiated from his rigid body.

"Well, then, what are you going to order," Emily queried.

"I'll have a penny's worth of liquorice, please Mr. Marshall." Caleb's glare dared Emily to comment.

The shrill whistle of the train and the screeching and squealing of brakes captured Jackson's attention. Panic, resident in his mind since the morning and burgeoning apace, increased its grip as the imminence of his bride's arrival and the impossibility of making it to the station in time fought for supremacy. Later, later he promised his recalcitrant body. *Concentrate on the children. The luggage. Dropping off the children at the Turner's so my bride and I can have privacy. No, forget that last thought—concentrate on the luggage.* His attention was caught by the sound of Emily goading Caleb.

"That's just what I said you'd have, Caleb, so why are you being so difficult?" Emily smirked. She knew well her brother's favorite candy and was not above raising his hackles to see his reaction.

"Enough, both of you! Wait for me on the porch, and I'll bring the candy. One more word, and there won't be any candy at all."

Recognizing tone and stance, the two combatants quickly and quietly left the store. Jackson started to swing the children up onto the seat as a special treat. Then he thought about the urgency of reaching the station as quickly as possible and deposited them in their usual place: in the back and as close to the seat as was feasible.

So much for plans, he thought. *I've three blocks to go, and the train is already here.*

He encouraged his team to a reckless pace, checking to be sure that his hat would not blow off in the resulting breeze. He ordered the children to stop their squeals of excitement and reminded them to remain seated. He learned not to say stay down, as Caleb interpreted that as an invitation to crouch to see if he could keep his balance as the wagon moved.

"There's a lady standing there, Uncle Jackson. She's all alone. Do you think that's Aunt Susannah?" Emily enquired.

"Probably," muttered Jackson. He eyed the slender figure obviously waiting for someone. "Now mind your manners, children. We want to make your Aunt Susannah feel welcome."

Wife Seller!

CHAPTER SEVEN

Susannah stepped down from the train, one hand clutching the ticket for her box and the other anchoring her shawl against the breeze. The sharp spring wind in no way reflected the fresh green of leaves and early flowers she had admired through the train window. She had waited to be the last to disembark to look for her husband as unobtrusively as possible.

No matter how many times she repeated Mrs. Jackson Stansfield in her mind, it still wasn't real. Susannah Stansfield had the same false ring. Scenes from her life in England rushed to replace any ideas she might have about this Susannah Stansfield. While she thanked God that so many miles separated her from her past and that she was safe from Albert, she could not quell all her fears that someday the truth about her bigamous situation might be revealed. Prepared to do her duty as a wife, she vowed not to tolerate any violent actions on the part of her new, albeit illegal, spouse. Over and over she told herself that marital duties didn't take long. And she would have the children. A great deal could be endured or overlooked for the sake of those precious children.

As she peered in vain for a glimpse of her bridegroom, she noticed that the sun lost its battle for supremacy over the clouds. If she were any judge, they were in for a downpour in less than an hour. The brisk breeze reinforced her forecast.

While the other passengers disappeared into the small restaurant cum hotel or were met by friends, Susannah's alarm increased. Where was her husband? A farm wagon driven with determination and almost reckless speed claimed her attention.

Strident cackles, led by the raucous crow of a lusty rooster whose head jutted between the slats of a crate heralded its arrival and claimed her attention. A collection of sacks and boxes provided bracing for the crates. The wagon's sturdiness was painfully utilitarian. The driver, who had very broad shoulders, sported a frown, and stained, wrinkled but clean clothes. Farmer's boots, albeit free from mud and muck, seemed out of place in town. Worn braces supported his canvas pants, and the hat pulled low on his brow obscured his features and provided some control for a wildly-curling mane that brushed his shoulders. He climbed down from the wagon and turned to assist the two children hidden by the seat.

They appeared to be about four and six years of age. The boy had a gleam in his eye that promised mischief should the grip on his arm weaken. The little girl surveyed Susannah with big eyes, her hair a tangled mess that straggled down her back. Their clothes, too, were also clean and wrinkled. Susannah's arms ached to hold them.

She straightened her spine and looked directly into the dark blue eyes of her new husband. She cleared her throat and swallowed twice, refusing to acknowledge that his strength could easily overpower hers, and spoke.

"Mr. Stansfield? I am Susannah." Each word was measured and uttered with the control necessary to maintain her composure. *Big. So big. Bigger than Albert. And strong.* She braced her body as if to receive a blow.

Silence.

"Mr. Stansfield? You are Mr. Jackson Stansfield, are you not? I am your wife, Susannah."

Silence. *Is he deaf? Is he disappointed? Maybe he's not Mr. Stansfield, but then why doesn't he say so?* Susannah looked down to hide the swell of emotions threatening to weaken her, and heard him speak.

He stood, feet apart, as if braced for a blow. Just as she determined that she had committed a monumental mistake, she heard him inhale. "Yes, I'm Jackson Stansfield."

Jackson stared at his wife. A plain bonnet, out of date even in the backwater of Marcher Mills, covered most of her shiny brown hair; her enormous green eyes, shadowed by long lashes, swallowed a face that was all sharp angles, angles reflected in her painfully thin body. Even wearing shoes that had a moderate heel, and adding the upward sloping front of her bonnet, she barely reached his shoulder. Not exactly a curvy armful, but female. Definitely female, and his for better or worse.

She appeared to shrink before his eyes, as if such a futile action would make her a smaller target. He found himself resenting her assumption that he was a brute. Her clothes were worn, but respectable, with no claim to fashion, and of a sensible dark grey. Everything about her spoke of a desperate courage. When he remembered the contents of Ethan's letter, he was surprised that she had even appeared at all. But she had, and he had to control his wayward thoughts. He had whiled away many an evening wondering just what would cause a woman to take such drastic action.

"Uh, umm, Susannah, ma'am, this is Emily and Caleb. Say hello to your Aunt Susannah, children." Jackson cursed himself for his gaucheness.

"Hello, Aunt Susannah," chorused Emily and Caleb, eyes fastened on their Uncle Jackson for approval. "We're very pleased to meet you," mouthed Jackson.

"We're very pleased to meet you," dutifully chorused the children. Jackson decided to ignore the fact that their eyes were still on him, not Susannah, when they followed his instructions.

"Is that the ticket for your luggage, ma'am, I mean Susannah?" *Well done, Jackson, your role as the village idiot remains unchallenged.*

She started as she realized she had been staring at him. "Yes. Yes it is. I just have one box." Susannah thrust the ticket at Jackson, with a command to herself not to blush. As he strode towards the agent to retrieve her luggage, she turned back to the children. A furtive glance over his shoulder revealed that much of the tension had left her body.

"I am so very glad to meet you both. I have a little present for you. It's in my box, and as soon as we get home, I'll give it to you." She smiled at the astonished delight of the children. Tonight, tonight, she promised herself, tonight I'll hear their prayers. Tonight we will eat as a family. Tonight I can tuck them in. Caleb and Emily were worth everything she had to give. She would make this marriage work. Memories of the small amount of time consumed by unpleasant but necessary marital duties would yield a rich reward. Patience and endurance would get her through the act, and he seemed like a reasonable man. She clung to that thought, trying to remember Ethan's oft-repeated assurances about his cousin's kindness. *Please, God, let him be a reasonable man,* she prayed.

"Here we are, Susannah, all right and tight. I'll just put it in the wagon and we can be on our way." Jackson was delighted to have specific tasks to complete. He quickly made space in the back of the wagon and swung the children up to the pile of straw just behind the seat.

"Remember, you must stay seated when you're in the wagon. And Caleb, do not touch the chicken cage." Experience taught Jackson to be both specific and literal when giving instructions to the little ones. Caleb, especially, showed promise as a lawyer or politician. He had the ability to circumvent strictures that provided even the smallest amount of wiggle room.

As he turned to help Susannah to her seat, the hem of her skirt whisked past his eyes. She had seated herself. He compressed his lips in annoyance. He was perfectly able to help his wife, or any other woman, for that matter. There was no need to make him appear unmannerly or careless of her comfort.

"Do you need anything at the store, Susannah?"

She turned her head in surprise. "No, no thanks, Mr. Stansfield, I have all I need." She was astonished to have her needs considered. Fatigued by weeks of exhausting travel, she steeled herself to contain sobs of fear and despair. No matter how many stories Ethan had told of Jackson's kindness, sense of humor and code of honor, experience had taught its lessons in a manner not to be ignored. Ethan had given Susannah the few coins left over from the money that Jackson had sent for her. She thought of the pitifully small amount in her pocket and the vast unknown that lay ahead of her. The prospect of life with her new husband had caused her to spend more than she had planned on decent underclothes, hose and a nightgown. Her enquiries as to possible escape routes availed little usable information, hampered as she was by accessibility and lack of funds.

"Jackson, call me Jackson, Susannah. Mr. Stansfield is my father." He smiled at her, but received only a tiny jerk of her head in reply.

He grunted and swung onto the seat. *Well, that's plain enough. I hope she doesn't think I'm going to demand my rights as soon as we're home. A bed of rocks would be softer— and probably more welcoming, as well. She doesn't have to be eager, but abject terror can really kill a mood.*

As the horses headed toward the Turner's farm, he thought longingly of his dreams of a snug home, loving, responsive wife, and large family. Those dreams died hard and refused to be buried even in the face of a forced marriage and the unforeseen guardianship of two small children.

"I've arranged for Emily and Caleb to stay with a neighbor, Mrs. Turner, for tonight. We'll take them there on the way home." Jackson kept his head pointed forward, but monitored her response from the corner of his eye.

Susannah froze. She was very upset at missing the opportunity to tuck the children in. Furthermore, she regarded them as a lifeline and much-needed buffer in her attempts to cope with Jackson over these first awkward hours of acquaintance.

"Oh. I see." Her voice was flat, in sharp contrast to the warmth she had displayed when she spoke to the children. "Will we get them tomorrow morning?"

"Yes, I thought it would be a good idea for us to have some time to ourselves before we included the children. They've been eager to see their friends and to tell them all about their new auntie." He glanced at the clouds and then back to the horses, still watching Susannah from the corner of his eye. Her body was rigid, as if in protest against some well-known terror.

"I understand," she murmured. The silence burgeoned to include the chickens, whose cackles had finally subsided. Even the horses seemed to walk quietly, the jingle of their harnesses muted by their even gait.

The clouds lowered, and the wind picked up. Susannah, frantic to fill the silence, searched desperately for a topic of conversation before falling back on the faithful old standby, the weather. "It seems as if it will rain quite soon, sir."

"Jackson, please Susannah. Call me Jackson." He realized that his tone was brusque. He moderated his tone and continued. "Yes, I only hope that we can drop the children off and get home before the heavens open. If it holds off for another thirty minutes or so we'll be fine."

Susannah cleared her throat. Anything was better than that dreaded silence. She refused to think of the night to come. *I can do it, I can do it—he can't be worse than Albert. It's over quickly; I can manage for that little time. But oh, I wish the children would be here!* "How many cows do you have...Jackson?"

"I have five who are milking right now, and I expect three more to freshen in August and September." The fear in her face sickened him. Far from demanding his husbandly rights as soon as they were home, he wasn't sure he could even perform those duties, given his current state of mind. He resolutely pushed the idea of a happy home to the back of his mind.

They would have to occupy the same bedroom to avoid gossip. Jackson was under no illusions about the intelligence system that flourished in small communities. He just hoped that Susannah would be amenable to a period of getting to know one another before the physical side of the marriage took place. He desperately wanted to build the same warm and supportive relationship that had existed between his parents: loving, giving and full of ginger. Aware that the marriage had to be consummated to be legal, he determined that his "rights" could be postponed for a short period of time. After all, as a widow, no one could prove the matter one way or another.

"Does that mean you will milk right through the winter? Don't you let them go dry?" Susannah had never heard of this kind of dairy farming before.

"Yes, I don't like to run up bills in the winter to hang over me, so I breed the cows to provide a constant milk and cream supply. Edmund, my friend, had some misgivings about young stock wintering, but I've checked the barn, and they should be fine." Jackson was quite proud of his ability to organize and provide a year-round income, but agreed that this method would require close supervision of the calves in the coldest weather. The two men had discussed the topic at length; Edmund, while unconvinced, agreed to try it for a year. He was loud in his complaints that there would be no sleeping in on cold winter mornings. He admitted, however, that it made sense, especially since the investment in animals, equipment and seed had consumed most of their capital. Searching for a safe topic of conversation, he decided to tell her a little about the Turners.

"The Turner's are our closest neighbors to the east. It's a nice walk in good weather, but not today, with those clouds promising rain, and soon." Jackson desperately tried to end the uncomfortable silence. The children were uncharacteristically quiet, and he wondered if they were up to some mischief. Silence, far from being golden, he discovered, usually preceded a disaster, frequently of epic proportions. He guided the team into a long, winding, bush-lined lane way.

"The little ones are with Mrs. Turner; er, that is, she volunteered to do her bounden Christian duty." Susannah smiled wryly. "When no one else...uh, she took care of the children until I came." Jackson gave thanks for the humidity, for which he could blame the perspiration threatening to trickle down his face. "Mrs. Turner is committed to her bounden Christian duty," he murmured.

"I see." Susannah responded, and was surprised to find herself fighting a grin. She turned to face the box of the wagon. Her skirt brushed against Jackson's leg as she did so. His body's reaction startled him. Perhaps husbandly duties were not as far in the future as he had thought. If she realized that her action brought her closer to him, she seemed comfortable with the fact.

"Did you enjoy yourselves with the Turner's, children?"

Emily said, "yes", just as Caleb, said "no!"

Emily smoothed her skirt, straightened her bonnet and folded her hands. "Mrs. Turner was very kind to take us in. She told us that many times every day." Emily obviously reported only what she heard. "We had chores to do, but it was fun to play with other children." Emily, torn between truthfulness and politeness, hung her head.

Caleb had no such qualms. "Mrs. Turner said I was a holy terror! She washed my mouth out with soap, and she didn't believe me when I told her I just repeated what Henry had told me." Caleb's sense of persecution was still strong. "I think Henry is a holy terror, too. What's a holy terror? I know it isn't good, but I want to know exactly what it is."

Susannah coughed and covered her mouth to hide a smile. It was of no help that Jackson's shoulders were shaking. When she could control her expression she explained, "Well, Caleb, that's an expression that's used to indicate that a person has a remarkable ability to get into mischief. Do you understand what mischief is?"

"Oh, yes," confirmed the unrepentant one, beaming. "It means something that's really fun to do."

Susannah began to appreciate just what the duties of a mother might entail. "That's all very well, but perhaps thinking before doing might avoid some of the trouble." She waited for the response that was quickly forthcoming.

"You may be right, Aunt Susannah, but it's awful hard to remember to think of reasons why not to do something when it's so easy and so much fun just to do it!" Caleb's seraphic expression caused grave suspicion on Susannah's part. It bespoke considerable experience at evading the consequences of his actions.

"Well, Caleb, perhaps we can work on that together." Caleb's face did not reflect unbounded enthusiasm. "Emily, what was your favorite thing to do at the Turner's?" Susannah could see that Emily was not nearly so frank as her scamp of a brother, and she wanted to encourage her to express her opinion. Emily wriggled as if to settle herself for a good chat.

"Well, Aunt Susannah, I liked to set the table and feed the chickens. Caleb and I had to gather the eggs, and some of the hens pecked me. I didn't like that part. Oh, yes, and I liked to wipe off the table and straighten my bed. It made me feel good to make things look pretty. I didn't like the bath on Saturday night. I was one of the last, and the water was really dirty and cold."

Emily, once started, was loath to stop. Her initial shyness subsiding, she was hungry to confide in her new aunt. She suspected that her Auntie could cook a lot better than Uncle Jackson. Uncle Jackson tried, but he did a terrible job. She was sick and tired of scorched porridge and blackened eggs, but she'd never tell Uncle Jackson. She might hurt his feelings. Besides, he always told them he was sorry that he had burned breakfast again.

"I'm glad to hear that, Emily. I like to make things look pretty, too. Did you help your mother in the dairy?" Susannah began to get an idea of the children and their personalities.

"No, she said she would teach me this summer, but then she got sick and, and...." her voice became totally suspended with emotion.

"There, there, Sweetheart." Susannah reached over the seat to pat Emily's hand, so intent on comforting that she was unaware that her breast brushed against Jackson's sleeve. He grinned. *Yes, indeed, those husbandly duties appeared very doable, very soon.* He tried not to rise to the occasion.

A gust of wind caused the dust to swirl just as Jackson called, "Look, children, we're here." His voice projected that note of false heartiness adults assume when they fear a child's tears. "I wonder if their mother cat has had her kittens yet and if they're as old as ours." The children's attention, effectively refocused, promised happier thoughts. Jackson's own thoughts turned to the possibilities of a childless house and a wife who might be more amenable to her own "bounden duty" than he had first imagined.

Susannah looked at Jackson. "I'm sorry, Mr. Stans…, I mean Jackson. I feel terrible that Emily was crying."

"That's all right, Susannah, she doesn't do it often. I think that she might have been told that after all this time, less than four months, mind you, she shouldn't be such a cry baby." Susannah could see that Jackson was upset at such a cold and unreasonable attitude. She agreed with him.

"Well, she needs to cry for her parents, and so does Caleb. Crying helps to take away the pain." Susannah retorted in a whisper. *But not all,* she thought, *not all. I still feel the pain of my loss. The bruises and cuts, and even the broken bones can heal, but it takes the spirit much longer. Sometimes I wonder if I will ever stop crying for my babies. I know I'll never forget them.*

"You're right, Susannah", he agreed, "and here we are at the Turner's. I'll turn the wagon around first, and then we'll take the children inside." Jackson glanced at the sky. "We've just made it in time—looks as if we're in for quite a downpour. We'll stay for a visit when we pick them up." As Jackson drew the wagon up beside the porch, the door opened and the oldest Turner girl, fourteen-year-old Claire, emerged, a harried expression on her face.

"I'm sorry, Mr. Stansfield, but you can't come in. Two of the children are down with fever and spots. My mother thinks it might be measles or chickenpox. She says to tell you she can't leave them, and that she's sorry she can't take Emily and Caleb."

Jackson looked at Susannah with despair, who stared right back, with hope. "Uh, this is my wife, Mrs. Stansfield." Jackson was suddenly aware that this was the first time he said the words "my wife". He felt as if he were hearing his father introduce his mother. "Susannah, this is Mrs. Turner's oldest girl, Claire." Claire nodded.

"How do you do, Claire. I'm sorry for your troubles, and I look forward to meeting you and the rest of your family at a better time. Your mother was so very kind to take in Emily and Caleb until Mr. Stansfield arrived in Canada." Susannah smiled and returned Claire's nod. Jackson was surprised at his wife's charm and ease, given the strained conversation they had shared so far.

"Yes, Claire. I'm sorry to hear that, too. Please tell your mother that I hope everyone gets well quickly." Jackson nodded courteously and tipped his hat. His brain scrambled for a way to cope with this new situation as he released the brake, lifted the reins and clucked to the horses. Claire waved goodbye, and Caleb and Emily returned the salute.

"Why are we leaving, Uncle Jackson? Aren't we supposed to be with the Turner's tonight? I wanted to tell Henry about my new Auntie and see if that cat had kittens." Caleb's voice was perilously close to a whine, and Jackson braced himself for the storm to come. Of the two storms, the weather would be the easier to deal with. By now the gusts of wind were stronger and closer together. Jackson urged the horses to a canter in a race against the rain.

"Yes, Uncle Jackson. I wanted to play with the Turner girls and tell them about my new Aunt Susannah. I wanted to see the kittens, too. I bet they're not as sweet as ours." Emily's voice matched Caleb's.

Susannah knew it was time to change the subject. "Now, children, you heard what Claire said. There's sickness at the Turner's, and it might be measles or chickenpox. You don't want to get that, do you? Besides, Mrs. Turner will have her hands full without two more little monkeys." The voice of reason had little effect.

Susannah could hardly keep the smile off her face. Saved! She would have the children as a buffer between her and Jackson, and could start her new life as a mother immediately. Anxious to prove her worth, she hastily added, "but Emily and Caleb, just think. You don't have to wait until tomorrow afternoon for your presents. You may have them when we get home."

Jackson sighed with relief. What a clever, clever woman—crisis averted. He knew that once started, Caleb and Emily could whine for hours. They never seemed to run out of new ideas. More than one tearful night occurred since he picked them up at the beginning of May. "Thank you, Susannah," he muttered. "You're a savior!" Susannah's cup overflowed. Surely this was an auspicious start to their time as a family.

"I've found distraction usually works, Jackson. The secret is thinking of one quickly enough." She failed to realize how naturally she had used his name.

"When children start to whine there's usually more than one reason." She kept one ear cocked to monitor the speculation about gifts emanating from behind the seat.

"These two have been through a very great deal in the last year. They travelled from England with their parents, lost them to the fever and then lost Edmund, as well. He was their only link to their parents. They don't have any anchors left.

Everyone they loved and trusted has left them." Susannah felt strongly about this, and she could certainly relate to the upheaval felt by the little ones.

"Whatever works is fine with me. They have certainly had a very rough year. I don't think the stay with the Turner's was a bed of roses. Mrs. Turner, while clasping her sacrifices in the name of duty to her ample bosom, does not strike me as one with an abundance of the milk of human kindness. I appreciate that she has a house full without two more children, but she seems quite a martinet. Her husband keeps his cider jug hidden in the barn." Jackson grinned. He had been grateful for that cider jug on the day he arrived in Marcher Mills.

"Now Emily and Caleb, you be good and quiet. We'll be home in just a few minutes, and you can show me where we'll live. Did you know that we're in a race? I wonder if we'll make it home before the rain starts!" Susannah felt it wise to keep distractions coming thick and fast. "You may show me your rooms and introduce me to your pets."

"We don't have any pets, Aunt Susannah, except that the barn cat just had kittens. They're too small to play with, but when their eyes are open, Uncle Jackson said we could choose one for a house cat to keep down the mice."

"That's a great idea, Caleb. I'm sure you and Emily will have a wonderful time choosing which kitten will be the house cat. And then there's all the fun of naming it!"

Susannah glanced at Jackson. "That was a kind thing for you to do, Jackson. The children need a pet to love and to learn about responsibility for animals." Again she failed to notice the ease with that his name rolled off her tongue.

Jackson kept his eyes on the horses. "It just makes sense to have a cat in the house. I'm afraid the mice have already taken up residence. They appear to be well established."

Inwardly, he winced. They turned into the drive, and he braced himself for Susannah's reaction. Unaccustomed to housework or children, under his auspices the house had deteriorated from dreadful and dirty to desperate and deplorable. It took all his time and energy to keep up with the necessary chores, to see what he could next burn for a meal, and try to keep the children safe and clean.

Apparently more than hot water, soap, and a scrub board were involved in cleaning clothes. It seemed to him that the white things had acquired a definite grey tinge. At least they'd stayed the same color since he decided to wash the white things first. His wonderful idea to have the children wear only play clothes didn't apply to their underwear—or his! Also, he'd discovered that clothes worn for several days made the task of dirt removal much harder. He now had first-hand appreciation of sore knuckles and raw, red, hands from wringing out clothes before spreading them on the bushes to dry. He squirmed at the condition of the sheets that he had ignored as not important to this point. He vowed he'd check the price of a washing machine for Susannah.

CHAPTER EIGHT

Susannah blanched at the sight of the neglected yard and overgrown path. It seemed appropriate that the first drops of rain fell as they approached their home. The wagon that had appeared so utilitarian when Jackson had greeted her at the station, suddenly acquired considerable luster. If this was the condition of the yard, what awaited her within?

Emily and Caleb clamored to get down. "Can we go and see the kittens, Uncle Jackson?" Emily begged. "Yes, yes, let's see the kittens!" Caleb seconded the idea.

"All right, you two, but first you must change your clothes." Emily and Caleb darted off, each determined to be the first one back out the door and with the kittens.

Susannah's perusal continued. At one time in the past, judging by stones snuggling amongst verdant weeds, a flowerbed had framed the front of the porch. Withered vines clacked and rattled in the wind—sad reminders of climbing roses that had once perfumed the air and added a touch of beauty.

A large, neglected garden patch, now a vista of undisturbed growth, lay beside the house. Poles to support runner beans leaned drunkenly in all directions. Strawberry creepers and raspberry canes grew unchecked. Currant bushes, planted with an eye to creating a hedge, formed a ridge in a bed of variegated green that gave no sign of rows, hills or method.

Jackson shifted his weight uncomfortably and braced himself for a comment as he prepared to help her down. He was well aware of the depressing sight before her, and cringed at the thought of revealing what lay behind the door of the house.

Don't flinch, don't flinch, keep your chin up. Ethan said he was a kind man. He won't hurt you. Susannah trembled, then braced herself, determined to assume a confidence she was far from feeling. As Jackson's arms reached up and his hands clasped her waist, she took a deep breath and looked him straight in the eye as she placed her hands on his shoulders. She could feel his strength as the muscles bunched and flexed with the motions necessary to lift her off the wagon and place her gently on the ground.

"Thank you, Jackson." She looked at him, then quickly lowered her gaze.

'You're welcome, Susannah." He was amazed that she had met his gaze, for he could feel her tremble in his grasp as she held her body stiff and straight. "I'll just unload your box and some things for the house, then see to the stock. Don't worry about milking tonight, I'll handle it. You go right on in and look around."

Slowly, shoulders slumped and shawl drawn closely to counter a chill that came from within, Susannah trudged towards her new home. The front of the house was the original log cabin. A clapboard addition extended behind and to the right, forming an ell. No curtains masked windows opaque with dirt. Stepping onto the stone that served as a riser to the porch, she inhaled, raised her hand, pushed the door open, and entered.

A small bench held a basin and bucket accented with a limp grey rag, obviously meant to be used as a hand towel, drooping from a nail driven into the wall directly beside the comb case. The fireplace, in dire need of scrubbing, stank of the dead ashes clogging the grate and decorating the hearth. Across the room a large stove stood, shamefaced; rust and grime almost obliterating the nickel trim. Its top was covered with what must surely be every pot Jackson owned; each featuring streamers of dried food. The length of the long table, framed by benches and an armless chair at either end, indicated that accommodating a threshing crew would be no problem. Its surface shone dully with grease punctuated by gobs of some indeterminate and petrified food. One wall had a workbench, with open shelves above and below. Tins, bottles and sacks of foodstuffs with rodent holes evident in the corners, had been placed on the shelves in no particular order.

The pump at the side of the sink and the drainpipe below promised to lighten her work load, saving a great deal of time and energy. A lump of harsh lye soap rested on a cracked saucer; a barely-used scrub brush waited at its side. The meager light coming through the windows revealed a doorway in the far right corner of the room leading to the clapboard section of the home. Cobwebs, thick with dust and soot, festooned the ceiling.

Picking her way carefully through a minefield of clutter and spills, she found herself tiptoeing into the parlor. A rocker and an armchair stood in front of the ash-choked fieldstone fireplace. They bracketed a small and extremely dirty rag rug. Sections of bark-clad tree trunks served as convenient resting places for cups, glasses, etc. One corner of the room held a square table with an empty candlestick heavy with lumps of melted wax. In the opposite corner a ladder provided access to a loft.

The doorway beside the ladder revealed a short hall that led to the bedrooms. The three smaller rooms each had two bunks attached to the walls, pegs for clothing, a bench with bucket and basin, nails above for towel and washrag and a chamber pot underneath. Pallets of sacking-covered straw provided small relief from the boards used in place of ropes. A suspicious rustling could be heard in the room not presently in use. Emily and Caleb's rooms were easily identified by the clothing strewn all over the floors. The largest bedroom contained a wide bed with rumpled covers, once-white sheets, and dirty pillowcases. A washstand and dresser completed the furnishings.

She turned to retrace her steps, gasped, and tried not to flinch as she took a hurried step backwards. She couldn't avoid a betraying stiffening of her body. Jackson was standing behind her with her box in his arms. She was amazed that he had been able to come so close without her knowledge; then noticed that he had removed his boots. The end of each big toe poked through his socks.

"I know it's a mess, Susannah, but it's been all I could do to keep up with the chores and take care of the children." He felt his face getting hotter and hotter. Susannah's paleness, on the other hand, surely meant she would faint.

"I was just looking at the house," she murmured. Color flooded back into her face in a vivid blush. For the first time Jackson saw beauty in his new wife. Her large grey eyes spoke eloquently of fear and courage, and her plump bottom lip quivered.

Husbandly duties really, really might not be so difficult, after all, he mused. *But not now, you dolt. She's just arrived.*

"I'll put your box in our room and get the crowbar." Her eyes widened in fear, and her hand fluttered to her throat.

"I'll need it, and perhaps a hammer, to open your box," he added in explanation. *What did she think I'd need them for?* Appalled at her fear but also admiring of her courage, he quickly moved away to place the box in the farthest corner of the room.

"Yes. Of course. How silly of me," she responded, writhing mentally. To show fear gave power to another, and she fought to remember her vow to never do so again. Also, it was unfair both to her and to Jackson, who had done nothing to indicate that he was anything but gentle and considerate.

"I'll attend to unpacking it later. No, first I want to get the presents for the children." In her zeal she failed to notice that she practically trod on his heels.

Jackson was having a great deal of difficulty knowing how to handle Susannah. A healthy male, he was unprepared to forego his rights for too long, but a woman who eyed him with wariness, flinched if he approached her, and braced her body for a blow if he moved suddenly did not engender passion. On the other hand, when her fear abated, she blushed delightfully. He hoped she would settle soon.

Susannah almost danced with impatience as Jackson struggled to untie the ropes. What she would give for no husband and a good sharp knife she hesitated to think. Finally, the knots yielded to his determination. The hammer and the crowbar make short work of the lid. He stepped aside, winding the rope neatly.

"There you are, Susannah. Do you want me to open it for you?" He waited for her response.

"No, no, thanks, I can do it. I put them right near the top so they'd be handy." She leaned the lid beside the box and pulled out the doll. "There, you see, she's perfectly fine." Absorbed in fluffing the doll's skirts and smoothing its hair, she failed to notice his reaction.

So the way to her heart is through the children! Smiling, he said, "Is that for Caleb? I don't think he'll take to a doll too readily."

"Of course not," she snorted. "It's for Emily, as I'm sure you know very well." She dived into the box again and pulled out Caleb's gift, unaware of his closeness. "Do you think he'll like this top? I was able to buy it from one of the people on the boat. I know it's not brand new, but most of the paint is intact." Anxiously she held it up for his inspection.

He couldn't help seeing the bright paint on the top and the crisp fabric she had used for the doll and comparing it to her own well-worn gown. The material for the doll's dress was a gift from the personal maid of the woman she assisted on her ocean crossing. Mrs. Higginsbottom provided material for a new uniform to the nursemaid, who gave the scraps to Susannah.

"I'm sure Caleb will be as delighted with his top as Emily will be with her doll. When will you give them their gifts?" He waited for her response, guessing that she would say after supper.

"After supper, I think. Or perhaps before? How long do you think they'll play with the kittens?" she inquired anxiously.

"Probably until supper is ready, or almost. The kittens were just discovered today, so they have all the charm of newness."

Smiling, she commented, "Yes, I can remember as a child that the birth of kittens was a very big event, indeed. Actually, we were so enthusiastic that sometimes my father had to hide them until they could survive all that loving attention and had their eyes open."

Expression softened by the happy memory, her gleaming eyes and happy smile intrigued her husband. Sighing, she returned the gifts to their former resting place and turned her thoughts to preparations for feeding her family.

"What food is there for supper? Where is the dairy you spoke of? Where are the cows?" Jackson responded to the only one of her questions he heard. Food, of course! Tonight he wouldn't have to fight with the stove and bear the reproachful stares of two small critics.

"Supper! Well, that is, that is to say, uh, maybe there are eggs! I'm sure there are eggs. I'll just go and check the hens. Between those we brought home and the ones already in the pen there must be eggs. And the smokehouse —I'll check the smokehouse, too." His escape was both rapid and noisy, and he failed to notice his boots were still on the porch until he started down the steps.

I wonder if he's taken care of poultry before. Probably not, if he expects eggs from hens that have been jostled and crammed into a crate. What did he feed the children before I came? Susannah returned to the kitchen, grabbed the bucket beside the basin and pumped vigorously, rewarded with a veritable cascade of water. She found tinder and flint on the mantelpiece of the kitchen fireplace; kindling and logs in the wood box. The old ashes were swept from the grate. As she laid the fire, she promised herself that the kitchen would sparkle very, very soon.

With the fire providing heat for the water and warmth for her soul, she fetched brush and soap from the shelves and looked for a scrub pail. Finally, at the very back of the bottom-most shelf, a dented bucket came to view. Before tackling the stove, she moved the food-encrusted pots to the workbench and realized that the almost bare shelves resulted from every possible pot and pan being pressed into use. The ashes from the fire box filled the metal container used to transport them outside. Noting with relief that the stove had a large reservoir, she resolved to make use of it as soon as possible.

Finally, she stood back to admire her handiwork. No odors of burning food resting on the stovetop would invade her kitchen, and the nickel trim reflected the evidence of her efforts. The warmth of the fire would soon heat the water in the reservoir. She turned to view the array of dirty pots and pans, sighing as she filled them with water and returned them to their former resting place. The only way to get them clean was soaking them in hot water—for a considerable period of time.

Grimacing at the enormity of her next task, she turned her attention to the table. Even using the back of a kitchen knife, she had trouble removing some of the granite-like lumps, going over and over the same spot before bare wood came into view.

I wonder where the eggs are. He's been gone long enough to have laid them himself.

Smiling, she noticed that the second lot of water was coming to a boil. She loaded the dishpan with plates, cups and cutlery, and added enough hot water to cover them. Since Jackson and the eggs failed to appear, she decided to investigate other possibilities. Flour, cornmeal, and salt were stored in tin containers, while glass jars showed four different kinds of beans. Small bottles held peppercorns, baking powder and soda, but she could find no evidence of a pepper mill. Sage, parsley, rosemary and some dried apples were in bags hung from the rafters. The sugar had escaped the attention of rodents and she prayed that ants had not found their way to such largesse. A can of bacon drippings had been hidden in the warming oven.

As there was no evidence of a trapdoor or other entrance to a cellar, she resolved to ask Jackson about vegetable storage when he returned. Just then footsteps sounded on the porch, and he appeared in the doorway, cradling several eggs in his left hand and holding a large ham in his right. He smiled tentatively.

"Ham and eggs won't be too bad, will it?' He smiled. "We have a smokehouse in the backyard. The east side of the house lies against a small hill that has been dug out for storing root vegetables. I'm afraid it's like the house and needs to be cleaned. I'm not really sure just what is there."

"Ham and eggs will be fine", she agreed. "I can make some soda bread, and there might be something in the garden. Are the children all right? Should I have them in the house with me?" He appeared relieved at her approval of the menu.

"No, that's all right. I'll keep an eye on them. You'll have enough to do just making supper." Jackson smiled. Silently agreeing with him, Susannah took a deep breath, daring to feel that she could build a new life in a new land. After all, the chances of meeting anyone she knew, or who knew about her this far from Yorkshire were slim, indeed. She found herself anticipating her first meal in her new home.

"You've already made a huge difference, Susannah. I hadn't realized just how bad that table was. It never seemed to get really clean when I remembered to wipe it off," he mumbled, shamefacedly.

At least he has the grace to be embarrassed.

# # #

"Aunt Susannah, is it time for the presents now? We've waited a long time." Caleb, his attention finally wrenched from kittens, readied himself for new adventures. Susannah smiled. She had enjoyed every minute of this meal, from lovingly preparing the food to setting the table. The hastily-washed-and-not-quite-clean faces of the children filled her heart to overflowing. The face of her husband had quite another effect, entirely. He had shaved and changed his shirt. Jackson Stansfield, she reflected, was quite attractive. Further than that she refused to let her thoughts wander.

"Caleb! You know it's rude to ask for presents!" Emily was horrified at his lack of manners and feared that such behavior might result in no presents at all.

"That's all right, Emily, but you are absolutely correct. It is rude to ask for presents. And you're right, too, Caleb, it has been a long time." Susannah spoke quickly to forestall the censure she saw in Jackson's frown. Let's just clean off the table and then I'll get them." The table cleared in record time, she made sure that the dishes rested in hot water. She smiled as she realized that she had seen more soap and water today than in the past several weeks combined. What, she wondered, would she find in the dairy tomorrow? She also realized, with a jolt, that the preparation of the room and meal, and her anticipation of having the children at supper had pushed all thoughts of the dairy completely from her mind.

Refusing anxious offers of help, she made her way to the bedroom and retrieved the gifts. Holding them behind her back, she entered the kitchen to see two wriggling children hardly able to contain their excitement.

"Choose a hand, Caleb. Which one do you think has a present for you?"

"I know, I know, it's that one" he shouted, pointing to her left hand. Susannah brought her hand out from behind her body. It had taken a bit of fancy finger work, but she managed to transfer the top from her right hand to her left.

"It's mine, it's mine. Look, Uncle Jackson, look. It's a top. I bet it's a whizzer." Prepared to snatch the top, he obeyed the firm hand on his shoulder.

"Uh, thank you, Aunt Susannah. May I please have my gift now?" He leaned closer and closer to the prize.

"Of course, Caleb. I hope you like it!" She laughed at his unbridled enthusiasm. He plopped on the floor and prepared to test his new acquisition.

"Now, Emily, it's your turn. Which hand will you pick?" Susannah put her hand behind her back again.

"That one, that one, Aunt Susannah, I'm sure my gift is in that one!" Emily's eyes opened wider and wider.

"It's a dolly! Look, Uncle Jackson, it's a dolly! They burned mine when Mommy...."

Susannah quickly thrust the doll into her hands in an attempt to forestall unhappy memories. Later she would encourage Emily to speak of her parents and her Uncle Edmund, but not tonight.

"I hope you like it, Emily. I made it for you. I've always wanted to make a dolly."

Emily gave no sign that she heard. Tenderly she smoothed the skirt and stroked the hair. Then, hugging it to her, she flew at Susannah.

"Oh, thank you, thank you, Aunt Susannah. It's the most beautiful dolly in the world." Her arms wound around Susannah's neck and a warm, moist kiss landed between cheek and chin. Susannah held her close and tried to control her emotions. This was a reward, indeed, and one she would treasure forever.

As she put the children to bed, the supervision of face washing and tooth cleaning was as wonderful as she imagined. The best part, though, the part that made her eyes fill with tears of joy, was when, a child cuddled on either side, she told them a bedtime story. The rush of emotion that swept over her as she carefully tucked them in threatened to reduce her to a puddle.

A few hours later, there was no way to avoid the matter. It was time for bed. Susannah fought exhaustion. At Jackson's insistence, they had spent that time in the parlor. He had cleaned the grate and lighted a cozy blaze. A little too cozy, she thought. *I'm sure he'll demand "his rights" at any moment.* She shifted and smoothed the sweater on her lap, pretending to inspect the pattern for errors. *Do not panic, do not panic, do not panic* she chanted silently. *You can do it. It won't take long, God knows, and he doesn't seem brutal.*

Jackson eyed his wife and noted her worried expression, the whiteness of her knuckles as she clutched the knitting needles, and the fine tremors as she smoothed her work. *Why, she's terrified.* Thoughts of passion drowned in a wave of sympathy. *I don't want a relationship based on fear and duty, nor do I expect instant love. We're here for the rest of our lives and there must be respect and passion at the very least.*

Just then Susannah folded her knitting around the needles and thrust them through the ball of yarn. With great precision she placed her work on the table beside her chair.

"Would you like a cup of tea, Jackson? I'll be glad to get it for you. It's no trouble. Really." She turned quickly to hide the fiery blush that suffused her face and, she feared, her neck and ears, too. *Stop babbling—you sound like a ninny.*

"No, thanks, Susannah. Any more tea and I'll not sleep. Would you, that is, uh, I expect you'll be, I mean," *my God, man, spit it out. Everyone makes a last trip outside before bed.* "What I mean to say is that I'll light the lantern for you."

"No, that's fine, Jackson, I can do it." She fled, embarrassed for acting like a schoolgirl faced with her first beau. On her return she started to the stove for some warm water to take with her for her nightly wash, only to find Jackson putting the cups on the shelf.

"You didn't have to wash the cups, Jackson, that's my job," she protested. He turned to face his bride.

"Susannah, we're a family, now. I know it's customary for men and women to divide the work in a manner dictated by tradition, but you've had a very stressful day and must be exhausted. I appreciate what you have done more than you can know. I've had to manage by myself for some time, and am well aware that even a little help can make a big difference." He waited to see her reaction.

Her mouth opened and closed twice, but her brain refused to form a coherent thought. He grinned and grabbed the lantern.

"I'll just check the stock. It takes me about fifteen minutes." He waited to see if she understood the unspoken message. She did.

"Fine. I'll just check on the children and get ready for, that is I'll...." As her voice failed her, her color rose. He took pity on her embarrassment.

"That's all right, I understand. I usually sleep on the side near the window." This last was thrown over his shoulder as he disappeared out the door, grinning. Susannah was too overwhelmed at the thought of what was to come to notice the sudden redness of his complexion. She grabbed the kettle and hurried to the bedroom, determined to be washed, in her nightgown with the sheet pulled up under her nose before he returned. She reckoned that there was enough water for both of them, and she'd make sure the reservoir and kettle were filled against the morning needs, too.

A short time later she peered over the sheet at her new husband as he entered the room. There was no modesty screen in the bedroom, and she would, she promised herself, turn on her side when he began to undress.

Jackson, his bared toes leading the way, grabbed the pitcher, only to find it half full of warm water. To her surprise, she thought not of what would transpire in just a few minutes, but that she really must make laundry and mending a priority. Besides being a poor reflection on her housewifely skills, toes through holes were very uncomfortable.

He noticed the gaze that followed his every move, but was puzzled when it seemed to fix on his feet. The sheet covered her mouth and her eyes crinkled as if in amusement. Automatically reaching for the top button on his shirt, he viewed his wife, or rather her eyes, forehead and hair. He hung the shirt on a nail and picked up the soap and washcloth.

"Thanks for the water, Susannah. It's very thoughtful of you." He turned, careful not to look at either bed or occupant.

"You're welcome. There was lots of water in the kettle." *Now he thinks that you only did that because the water was handy.*

Well you did.

I know, but I didn't have to say it. He was being kind.

You worry too much.

Be quiet. I do not.

Silence. A great deal of silence from that annoying little voice in her head.

Jackson, too, was having a conversation with himself.

Oh, well done. You sound as if you're being polite to the maid.

Well, you were being polite.

Yes, but it sounded pompous.

You're nervous.

I am not.

Are too.

Am not.

He pulled himself up short. Surely he had matured beyond senseless arguments, especially with himself. He flicked a glance at his wife. She turned on her side, her back toward him, and only the top of her head was visible.

Well, there's a message. I suppose she thinks I'm prepared to attack her and demand my rights as soon as I get into bed.

He finished washing, removed his trousers, hesitated, then decided to leave his drawers on. He tiptoed to the unoccupied side of the bed, drew back and slid underneath the bedclothes, hardly daring to breathe, and wincing at the creaking of the ropes.

"Good night, Susannah. Sleep well." He felt her body stiffen even more. *She'll be worn out from trying to imitate a stick.* He grinned ruefully. Not exactly how he had imagined his wedding night would be.

"Good night, Jackson," she whispered. After an appreciable pause he felt the covers move and realized that she relaxed enough to bend her legs and get her shoulders out of her ears. It would be a long, long night.

In spite of her exhaustion, sleep eluded her for some hours. She found it especially galling that her husband snored. It underscored the injustice that he, at least, would be well rested in the morning.

CHAPTER NINE

Dew shimmered on the grass as Susannah walked toward the dairy. Exhaustion from her attempt to balance on the edge of the bed had culminated in a sleep so deep that Jackson had to waken her. Startled by the sound of her name, she tried to jump up quickly. Bedclothes and embarrassment joined forces, and only a dexterous move on the part of Jackson prevented her from landing on the floor. He scooped her up and gently set her back on the bed, appreciating the softness and warmth of her body.

"I brought you some tea, Susannah. I'll start the chores. You come along when you're ready. The children are still asleep, and with luck they'll remain so until we're done. That's been their pattern so far, and I must say I enjoy doing something without help." He smiled at her sleepy confusion and enjoyed the rosiness of her blush.

"Uh, oh, thank you, Jackson. You didn't have to bring me coffee. I mean tea." She was stunned that he would do something so thoughtful. She had never had such an experience before.

"I'm usually up with the birds, but I didn't sleep too well last night." *Drat, now he'll think that I'm complaining about the bed. Or him. Or both.*

"Not to worry, Susannah. I'm not used to company in bed, either." *Damn, that sounds as if she didn't sleep with her husband. Worse, she'll think I'm being sarcastic that nothing but sleep happened.*

"That is, uh," he could feel the warmth suffuse his face. "I'll, uh, I'll meet you at the dairy. I mean the barn. Later." He fled.

Diligent scrubbing in the kitchen revealed a pleasant, though rather Spartan, room. Establishing that same order and cleanliness to the rest of the house would not be nearly so onerous. The condition of the dairy had yet to be determined. She sighed at the thought of even more back-breaking labor to bring the dairy to an acceptable level of cleanliness. No stranger to hard work, the combination of exhaustion from travel and stress plus the sheer drudgery probably still in store caused her to shudder.

Jackson confided that so far he milked the cows in the small pen attached to the dairy and fed the results to the pigs, reserving only the cream and sufficient milk for household needs. The pigs had responded to the unexpected largesse with remarkable weight gains. She wondered at his kindness and insistence on doing the milking last night, mentioning that she must be tired. He was right, but she still could not believe that he would do women's work, now that she was here.

The dairy nestled in the shade of an enormous maple tree. Ethan told her that the winters were colder, the snow much deeper, and it lingered longer than in Yorkshire. He also revealed that the heat and humidity experienced during

Canadian summers far exceeded that to which she was accustomed. The maple's dappled shade would be welcome and help to keep the dairy cool.

Because the door appeared to be only four feet in height, she suspected that the floor was recessed to preserve heat or coolness, according to the season. A broad, flat stone provided a step from the path to the raised lintel. As she opened the door and stooped to enter, she realized that the floor was at least a foot lower. A wide wooden step inside gave easy access to the stone floor.

Some light seeped around the shutters on the windows, and she appreciated the thoughtfulness of such an easy way to adjust the temperature. Opening the shutters and windows provided light and fresh air. She noted that the screens were in good condition, and, after a vigorous scrubbing, would provide a welcome relief in the summer months. The windows, too, needed an application of soap and water. She could hardly wait to enjoy her little kingdom.

The gurgling sound of water led her to a large stone trough placed against the back wall. A spring provided a year-round source of water for cleaning, processing, and cooling the milk and cream. The bottom of the trough featured pillars of different heights to permit the use of a variety of containers.

Turning away from the trough, she was amazed to see a stove. No longer would she have to keep her dress out of the flames of the fireplace, or have her workload increased when ashes floated and settled over the results of her labor if the wind were in the wrong direction. She peeked into the wood box and smiled to see that it held a good supply of seasoned wood, as well as a stock of kindling. When she opened the firebox, she reached for the ash bucket and its small shovel.

Ample fuel was of little use with no air circulation to feed the flames. The grubby goose's wing resting on the floor beside the stove provided an excellent way collect the rest of the debris. She started a fire and looked for a pail to fill the reservoir.

The stone sink had a good extension for draining utensils was located beside the stove. She was pleased to note that a pump promised surcease from endless trips outdoors. Somewhat of a luxury when the spring was already in the building, but Susannah well knew of the tremendous amount of water used in her craft. Although every surface wore a coat of dust, basically the entire area was clean. With the exception of the milk pails, the equipment looked quite new and barely used. She primed the pump with water scooped from the trough, scrubbed a pail found under the sink as well as she could with one of the rags she had prudently stuck into her apron pocket, and filled the reservoir.

Sturdy shelves extended on either side of the front corners of the room. Beside them was a tin of salt-peter for removing the unwanted taste of leeks and other strong vegetation. Sometimes the cattle grazed on such plants, or their milk would have the flavor of the turnips often used for winter feed. A large container of salt rested beside a supply of bowls, pans, ladles, stirring sticks and other tools of her trade. She hastily grabbed a stack of cheesecloth and rinsed it in preparation for cover the milk. The top few inches proved to be lengths already cut to the correct size to cover the pails. Just a few minutes with her scissors would transform the rest of the unwieldy bundle to lengths appropriate for a variety of tasks. The rotary churn stood between the shelves and the sink. It would be a pleasure to work in such a well-equipped space.

The sounds of lowing cattle demanding relief from full udders could no longer be ignored. She grabbed two pails from the shelves against the wall, rinsed them thoroughly, and rushed to help Jackson attend to her four-footed charges. Meanwhile, the two-footed charges appeared to be offering their help to Uncle Jackson. His grand plan to have them sleep through the milking had gone awry. She spared a grin and offered thanks for his willingness to free her a little longer.

As she washed udders and milked, she asked about the names of the cows. If they had not been named, then she and the children would soon provide them with appropriate labels..

"Well, not that I know of, I never thought about it. Guess I've just been too busy with the day-to-day stuff." He wondered, now, at his inattention to such a commonplace matter. Every horse and cow on his parents' farm had a name. Naming the pigs was discouraged, as they inevitably became table food—as did the chickens.

"I'll finish up here, Jackson. Breakfast will be ready in about an hour. Emily and Caleb, you please stay and help me name our cows. They can't all be called Bessie."

"Thanks, Susannah. I'll feed the rest of the stock. Call me when you're finished and I'll show you the way to the pasture. Not that it's necessary. They know the way better than I do. Emily and Caleb usually come with me for company." He lowered his voice. "I don't tell them that then I also know just where they are. Emily is usually quite reliable, but Caleb seeks adventures, as he calls them, with distressing regularity." His grin elicited a shy smile.

He was particularly grateful for the offer to mind the children. They forgot even the kittens in their contemplation of names for cows. Emily scornfully rejected Caleb's offerings of

Racer and Blackie. He hooted at her suggestions of Princess and Flower. The cow naming committee continued their assigned task with enthusiasm.

She hastily placed the pails of milk on a convenient bench inside the door that led to the night pen, covering them with the lengths of cheesecloth. Then she headed for the barn to collect her family. Names bestowed, the duo departed to inspect the kittens.

My family. Yes, they are my family. Mine to love and care for. Shocked, she came to an abrupt halt. *Love? Yes, I already love those two little scamps, but I don't know if I'll ever love Jackson. I'd be happy if I could just trust him not to beat the children or me. Loving the children is safe; loving Jackson is another matter entirely.*

She hurried to complete her errand, including a quick detour by the kitchen to add wood to the stove. Biscuits required a hot oven, and she was sure that by the time all the feet were under the table hunger pangs would be sharp.

CHAPTER TEN

In addition to its usual serving of heat and humidity, July brought an epidemic of influenza. Susannah staggered out of Emily's room, one hand over her mouth, the other at arm's length in an attempt to get the chamber pot as far away from her nose as possible.

I will not get the influenza, I will not. The past three days of hell started with Emily and then Caleb catching the disease sweeping the countryside. Jackson made a special trip to town to get lemons and honey to soothe sore throats. Susannah tried every trick she could devise to get liquids into the children. She remembered with dread how this disease took the very young and the very old first, and recalled that the village doctor advocated the imbibing of as much liquid as possible to replace that lost by vomiting and diarrhea.

Because the children could not be left alone, Susannah and Jackson took it in turns to do as many of their daily activities as they could. They were now down to the most essential chores. Jackson tried in vain to get some help, but those who escaped the ravages of the disease refused to be exposed to it. They heard that old Mrs. Atkinson succumbed, and reports of other elderly neighbors did not bode well.

Susannah barely managed to get to the outhouse in time to lose her breakfast. She dumped the contents of the pot and hurried back to the yard pump to rinse her mouth and the container. Chanting her mantra about not succumbing, she hurried back to the children, refusing to acknowledge that she felt worse with every step. By the time she reached the bedroom where both children remained for the duration, she was bracing her shoulder against the wall and praying that she could make the few steps across the room to replace the pot.

Emily slept fitfully, but Caleb's little voice piteously called for his mother. His face was beet red, and he had somehow managed to throw off the covers, his nightshirt rucked about his hips. The cloth she used to cool his brow was nowhere to be seen.

"Hush, hush, baby," she crooned. "Auntie's here for you. Let's get you more comfortable." She pulled down his gown, frightened by the heat radiating from his body. "Let's get that nice cool cloth back on your head and off the pillow." As she reached down to rinse the cloth in the basin on the floor beside the bed, she used one hand to stop from falling as dizziness threatened to overwhelm her.

I'll bring in another chair from the kitchen and put the basin on it, she thought, as she wrung out the cloth and put it on Caleb's flushed face. Fighting dizziness, she rose slowly and started toward the kitchen, staying close to the wall to prevent a fall. *I'll dump the contents of the basin out the window and bring a pitcher of fresh water with the chair.* Extending her arms to full length on either side of her body, she used the walls of the hall as supports on her seemingly endless journey. As she entered the room, she could hear Jackson on the porch.

"Jackson, Caleb's burning up with fever. I'm just getting some fresh water." He leapt through the door, frightened by her quivering tones.

"Susannah, do you have the flu, too?" Jackson prayed that it wasn't so. The two of them could barely do the essentials. He noted Susannah's flushed countenance and jerky walk at a glance. "Here, sit down. Whatever you need, I'll get it." He crossed the floor in three giant steps and caught her just as she began to crumple.

"I'm fine, really. Just give me a minute and I'll be ready to go."

"Yes, I can see that," he retorted. "Ready to leap like a gazelle, no doubt. You sit right there while I pump some water and get a rag to wet and put on your no-doubt-aching head." He brandished the pump handle like a weapon in his panic and frustration. As the water gushed into the sink, he grabbed a pitcher and held it under the flow, his head turned to check on Susannah, concerned that she might slide off the chair. He snatched a rag from the pile that they were keeping on the table because of the number they were using on a daily basis, wetted it, wrung it out, and slapped it on her forehead with a great deal more force than he meant to.

"I'm sorry, Susannah, I didn't realize just how fast I was moving." He waited for her reaction. She seemed to be of an equable temperament thus far, but illness could wear down anyone.

"Thank you. That's much better. I'll just take a minute and then I'll be fine. I want to bring in a second kitchen chair into the bedroom to put the basin on. For some reason I seem to be a little dizzy when I bend over." She closed her eyes for a blissful minute. *Just one minute*, she promised herself, *and then I'll move that chair.*

"I want my mama. I want my mama." Again and again Caleb repeated the words, breaking Jackson's heart.

He picked up the damp cloth that from the floor. "I'm here, son."

Caleb looked up and smiled. "Hi, Papa. Where have you been? Where's my mama? I want my mama." The tears rolled down his cheeks, but he was too exhausted to sob.

"There, there, little man, Uncle Jackson's here. Let's get you more comfortable." In the time needed for Susannah to get to the kitchen, Caleb's fever turned to chills. His entire body was shaking and his teeth chattered at an alarming rate. Grabbing the bedclothes and tucking them around the boy's shoulders, Jackson's heart began to race. Surely no one could be this sick and recover.

"I'll get you a warm blanket, son." He started to leave to get the sheets heating in the warming oven when he heard a voice from the other bed.

"I'm going to be sick—right now." Emily was right. She vomited all over the bedding, herself and the floor. *At least I won't have to empty the pot this time,* he thought, ruefully. Grabbing the cloth from the basin, he quickly wrung it dry and wiped her face.

"Are you going to be sick again, Emily? Do you need the pot?" Emily was beyond a coherent answer. Her sobs rose in frequency and volume.

"I was sick all over myself, just like a baby." Emily hated to be called a baby.

"Emily, honey, don't you worry. I'll just get some warm water and soap and be right back." Jackson sprinted out of the room, then came to an abrupt halt, whirled around and got the basin. His speed slowed fractionally, but not a drop landed on the floor. As he entered the kitchen, he noticed that his wife was having a nap, her cheek pillowed on the table, the cloth on the floor.

The chorus of sobs and wails from the children's room recalled him to his duties. He emptied the basin down the sink, wiped it dry, and placed a warmed blanket for Caleb and several rags from the table for Emily in the container. Grabbing the kettle of water now kept at the ready, he returned to the children.

"I'll just tuck this warm blanket around Caleb to stop his chills, Emily, and then we'll clean you up." As he endeavored to warm Caleb and clean Emily, he wondered aloud if she had another nightie. He was startled to hear a piping treble inform him that there was one in the chest in her room. Fortunately only the top cover needed to be changed, and he soon had her back under the blankets.

"Sleep, sweetheart," he whispered, praying that they would both nap long enough for him to get Susannah into bed. They seemed to be sleeping comfortably as he tiptoed out of the room with the basin and another armful of dirty clothes to be added to the already impressive pile on the back porch.

Since his wife still slumbered, forehead now resting on the edge of the table and arms straight down at her sides, he decided to get the wash pot going. He wasn't acquainted with the niceties, soon but conquered the basics of hot water, soap, scrub board, rinse and dry after the children came to live with him.

"Susannah, Susannah, wake up. You're falling off the chair. I'm going to help you to bed." One of Jackson's arms circled her shoulders, while the other cupped her elbow as he tried to help her stand.

"What are you doing? I'm fine. I just shut my eyes for a few seconds. The children need to have their wet cloths changed, and Caleb should be bathed in cold water to bring down his temperature."

"Susannah, I've already taken in the other chair, changed the water in the basin and the cloths on the children's foreheads. Caleb's chill has passed, Emily's bed and nightie are clean, and both children are asleep. You've been sleeping in the chair for almost an hour."

In spite of his terror at what the next days would hold, he couldn't resist smiling. She was indomitable. Unable to stand alone, she clung to the back of the chair and tried to lie about what she thought she would do. Whilst he admired her spirit, he felt that such determination boded ill for the chances of having a cooperative patient. Luckily he had finished the milking and feeding before assuming nursemaid duties.

"Why don't you try another little nap on our bed?"

"What do you mean, another nap? I just put my head down for a minute. I'm fine now," she snapped. In spite of her best efforts, her knees refused to cooperate. They kept buckling. She gripped the back of the chair in desperation. "I'll just take this chair along so that we both can have a seat while we watch the children."

Jackson smiled. Guiding his cranky cohort into their room, he flipped back the covers, scooped her up in his arms and placed her on the bed.

"And I'll just get you into your nightgown, Susannah, and then under the covers." Her eyes flew open. She and Jackson were sharing a bed, it was true, but nothing of an intimate nature occurred. She refused to remember that almost every night they were ending up in the middle of the bed, frequently with Jackson's arm around her, and his hand cupping her breast.

"You'll do no such thing. I can perfectly well change into my nightgown," she huffed. "You know you can't take care of the children and the farm by yourself. Give me twenty minutes and I'll be fine. There's still some roast beef from yesterday if you're hungry now, or you can wait until I finish that nap you keep insisting on, and I'll make a meal."

Susannah's speech deteriorated into an inelegant mumble. She keeled over and sighed as her head met the pillow. Jackson removed her shoes and stockings and undid the buttons on her dress. He pushed her petticoats and dress up to her hips and sat her up. Susannah slept on, mouth agape. Sitting beside her, he eased the clothes up over her head, which lolled in a very comfortable manner on his shoulder. Dropping the clothes on the floor, he picked up the nightgown carefully placed beside him and eased it over her head.

"Put your arms in, Susannah. Come on, now. I need some cooperation."

He couldn't help but notice her turgid nipples under the thin camisole. Her drawers, equally worn, hid little. Obediently she shot her arms straight up into the air.

"No, no, Susannah, put your arms in the sleeves!"

Eventually, with a great deal of effort on his part, he tucked her in. Her flushed cheeks made her prettier than ever.

"You're so pretty, Susannah. Have I ever told you that?" He gently stroked her face. She scrunched her nose and brushed away his hand as if it were a bothersome fly. He smiled, sighed, and headed for the wash pot.

Three days later Susannah was able to stagger from her bed into the children's room and take over as the amusement committee. While still in the fever/chill cycle, the children's recovery was at the stage where they wanted constant amusement, sobs and laughter lurking close to the surface. Since she couldn't yet face the odors of cooking, Jackson did his best.

No one's appetite was hearty, except Jackson's, although he noticed he wasn't eating as much as was customary. *Probably the result of my cooking.* He added three cups to the tray he contrived from a cookie sheet and headed down the hall.

For the first couple of days Susannah hadn't cared, in her few moments of lucidity, what Jackson did or what he saw. She was miserable and worried about the children. On the first night her fever was so high it induced delirium. Jackson wept and held her as she keened for her dead babies. He seethed as she tried to dodge the kicks and blows of her former husband and pleaded for him to stop. The next morning, when her fever lessened, she appeared to have no recall of her rantings, and he was careful not to mention them.

Her recovery, while much faster than that of the children, was still not swift. Perhaps the most telling part was her willingness to stay in bed. She insisted on getting up the next day, but after collapsing on the floor in a heap, she agreed to move between the bed and the chair and to use the chamber pot. Only Jackson's forceful exhortations led her to agree that it was less work and worry for him to empty a chamber pot than to wonder if she injured herself by falling on the way to the outhouse. By the third day the fever was gone. She insisted on getting dressed and sitting with the children, forcing herself to eat to regain some strength.

"Here you are my hearties!" Jackson's voice boomed down the hall and he appeared in the doorway with a tray holding a pot of tea, three cups and saucers, and a plate of toast and scrambled eggs. He cut the toast into different shapes for the children to identify. Triangles and squares alternated with toast soldiers and fingers.

"Thank you, Uncle Jackson" Emily and Caleb chorused. They craned their necks to be first to see the shapes. Susannah smiled wanly, pluckily ignoring the burned bits in the eggs and the suspicious removal of crusts on the bread.

"Thank you, husband," she smiled, "you're getting to be quite a cook." His head jerked around and he stared.

"What's the matter?"

"That's the first time you've ever called me husband. I find I quite like the sound of it." He gave her that devastating grin that always caught at her heartstrings.

"Well, nothing unusual about that," she retorted. "You *are* my husband," she continued, vainly trying to control the color rising to her cheeks. He continued to grin and enjoyed the blush that bathed Susannah's face with its rosy glow.

The next day she was able to make the meals and do the dishes. Jackson was adamant that she venture no further than the porch to sit on the bench to enjoy some fresh air and sun. The children were also allowed to get dressed and join her. They grumbled at the adults' insistence on a morning and afternoon nap, but slept soundly for two hours each time. By the end of a week the patients were well on the way to their usual robust health.

Susannah viewed her family with pride as they gathered around the supper table. The children's cheeks sported roses once more and even their squabbling was a welcome sound after the eerie quiet that invaded their home for those few anxious days. The worst of the epidemic seemed to have passed, and life for the Stansfields, as well as for their community, settled back to normal. School was due to reopen on the coming Monday. The adults decided to wait one more week before they attended church. The children were not at their peak, and she still had the remainder of a stubborn cough.

As her gaze travelled around the table once more, she noticed that Jackson's face was white, and beads of perspiration stood out on his forehead. Refusing to believe the evidence of her eyes, she inquired, "So, who's for some apple crisp for dessert? Caleb, you clear the plates while Emily removes the serving bowls." The children bustled importantly to complete their duties.

On her way to the warming oven, she remembered the buttered biscuit left on Jackson's plate at lunch. He failed to exhibit his customary vigor and urged her to complete the evening chores earlier than usual.

She turned from the stove just in time to see him collapse. His body slowly bent forward, his forehead hitting the table with a thud that made her wince before he toppled sideways and landed on the floor.

"Uncle Jackson, Uncle Jackson" the children screamed, terrified that their strong uncle was dead. "He's dead, he's dead!"

"Shhhh, shhh, children, it's all right," crooned Susannah, placing the dessert on the table and putting an arm around each of them. "He's just sick with the flu."

Inwardly she quaked. Jackson, the backbone and center of the family was the latest victim. She felt his forehead, noticing that he was burning with fever. "Emily, bring the chamber pot, and quickly!" Emily returned at a run, the chamber pot in her hands.

"Now put cold water from the pump in the basin and get a rag to bathe his head. Caleb, run and turn down the bed." The children hurried to their assigned tasks.

She moved the chair and knelt on the floor, raising Jackson's head and shoulders.

"Jackson, Jackson, can you hear me?" A mumble was her only response. "Jackson, you'll have to help me get you to bed. Try to stand up. I'll give you a hand."

Shifting to her knees, she raised him to a sitting position, pulling the chair to his side to help him rise. The heat radiating from his body was frightening.

"Jackson, the chair's at your side. Grab it and use it to get up." He groaned, and felt for the edge of the seat.

"Just let me get on my knees. I think I can make it from there." Slowly, with him pulling and her pushing, he succeeded in kneeling, his upper body stretched across the seat.

"I don't think I can stand up, Susannah, and I know I can't open my eyes because the room won't stop spinning," he wheezed.

How could he be so sick so fast? She trembled at the possible ramifications of this sudden and strong onset of the disease.

"That's all right, dear, just push the chair and crawl, and I'll keep you on track." With agonizing slowness they inched across the kitchen floor, down the hall and into their bedroom.

"Quick, the chamber pot." She grabbed it from Emily and pushed it under his head just in time. He retched and retched to the point of dry heaves, moaning piteously between spasms.

"The bed's ready, Aunt Susannah, do you need me to help?" Caleb's voice wobbled. He had never seen his tall, strong uncle anything but in robust health.

"My daddy was like that...." His voice became suspended in emotion.

"There, there, Caleb, Uncle Jackson will be fine. I guess it's just his turn for the flu! Why don't you get him a glass of water so he can rinse his mouth?" Susannah's try at a cheery voice fell far short of its goal, but Caleb seemed to derive some comfort from her attempt as he dashed off on his errand.

"Aunt Susannah, I've put the basin of water on the chair so you can move it beside the bed," whispered Emily. Tears rolled down her cheeks.

"Should I make the cloth wet like you did for Caleb and me?"

"Yes, dear, that would be wonderful. Your Uncle Jackson will be so glad to feel that coolness once we get him tucked in." Putting the chamber pot in the hall, she helped him crawl the last three feet to the side of the bed.

"Just one more effort, Jackson, and then you don't have to move."

He slowly and painfully shifted his torso from the chair seat to the mattress. It felt as if the bed were five feet off the floor. "Straighten your legs, dear, and you'll practically be there. One good shove will do it."

As she supported his torso, slowly his legs stretched out. He bent one knee and put it on the bed. Susannah pulled on the back of his shirt and used her body as a brace to prevent him falling. He sprawled face down. He sighed when a cool cloth touched his face. Jackson was down for the count.

"Now, children," Susannah said, "We've tucked Uncle Jackson into bed and left him with a cool cloth on his forehead. Sleep is the very best thing for him. Thank you both for all your help."

Her small audience, seated in their accustomed places at the kitchen table, chorused, "You're welcome." She stifled a smile before continuing.

"I know you remember how sick we felt when we had the flu, and how long it took us to get better. We'll have to work together to help Uncle Jackson, and this means with his chores, as well as taking care of him." Two small heads bobbed in agreement.

"Emily, you'll have to help with some of the cooking, just like we practiced. Caleb, I'm going to need you to keep your mind on your chores and to help Emily and me inside, too."

"I'm very strong, Aunt Susannah. I can feed the cows and horses," piped Caleb.

"And I could probably cook all the meals, Aunt Susannah. You know I can boil eggs and make toast," boasted Emily.

"You know I'll count on both of...."

"Susannah! Chamber pot! Quick!" Jackson's voice, its volume weak, but its tone urgent, floated into the kitchen. She leaped from her chair and ran down the hall, two small shadows trailing behind.

"It's right beside the bed, Jackson. Just reach your hand down and you'll have it." She rushed across the floor, grabbed the pot, and made it just before Jackson erupted.

"Sorry, so sorry...."

"Now that's just enough of that, Jackson Stanfield. Who was there for me when I was so ill?" Caleb handed him a glass of water to rinse his mouth. She placed the lid on the pot when he was finished and turned to take it to the outhouse to dump it. "Emily, you bring the chamber pot from your room, just in case you uncle needs it. I'll be back in a minute."

"Here's a new cloth for your head, Uncle Jackson," Emily piped. Susannah and Emily made sure that Jackson was as comfortable as possible. Caleb returned from his errand.

And I'll cover you up nice and warm, Uncle Jackson" he volunteered.

"Thank you, children." Jackson smiled weakly. "I have to sleep." He closed his eyes and heard two small pairs of feet tiptoeing out of his room.

"Now, children, where were we?" Susannah had her crew back at the table to continue their aborted discussion. "Oh, yes, we were talking about the chores. Caleb, could you feed and water the chickens, as well as gathering the eggs?" Susannah held her breath. Caleb's least favorite place on the farm was the chicken coop.

"Sure, Aunt Susannah, I can do that just before I feed and water the horses."

"Well, as to that, Caleb, I know that you are growing every day and getting bigger and stronger, but perhaps you and Emily could work on that together? Then, if Emily washes the cows' udders for me, and helps strain the milk, I think we can manage." Solemn nods greeted her suggestions.

"Because your uncle is ill, I'm going to read your bedtime story now. You get ready for bed and come right back.

The children were finally asleep. Constant reassurance that Uncle Jackson, the lynchpin of their world, would recover, finally lulled their fears.

Jackson spent a restless night with alternating chills and fever. He finally seemed to be over the retching and could tolerate small sips of very weak tea with sugar. Susannah sat in the chair pushed in from the kitchen, alternately bathing his head when the fever struck and bringing in warmed sheets to help combat the chills. Finally, shortly before dawn, she crawled into bed beside him and fell into exhausted slumber.

The children took turns caring for their uncle; Emily bathed his head, Caleb smoothed the covers, brought a pitcher of water, and filled the glass. Then all three headed out to do the morning chores. Breakfast was a quiet meal, with all the participants subdued by their concern for Jackson.

Later, Susannah checked that the children were busy adding hay to the horses' mangers. They gave their solemn promise that they would leave the watering to her. She felt confident enough with their promises to creep back into the house to check her patient. The covers were on the floor and he had curled into a ball, shaking with a chill. She carefully replaced the blankets, fetched another from the warming oven, put a glass of fresh water beside the bed, and returned to the dairy just in time to hear her name.

"Aunt Susannah, we've fed all the horses. Would you like more help with the cows? I've washed their udders. Caleb and I can take them to the pasture when you've finished milking." Emily preened with satisfaction at the big job completed with such effort. Caleb's smile faded when he heard his sister offer their services for even more chores.

"I'll check on Uncle Jackson, Aunt Susannah," he volunteered craftily.

"Very well, Caleb, but don't go into the room and disturb him, just peek in from the doorway." Caleb agreed, but on his way to the house he resolved to take very good care of his uncle and to surprise his aunt. Fortunately, before he could do much more than push a chair over to the pump to get yet more fresh water, Susannah and Emily came in. Emily smugly put the basket with the eggs on the table. Caleb had gathered them, but forgot to bring the basket to the house.

"Caleb, how did you find your uncle? Were the covers on the floor? Was he shivering?"

"I checked just like you said, Aunt Susannah, and now I'm getting some fresh water for him. He was shivering and he wanted his toothbrush and powder." Caleb continued to pump with vigor.

"Well done, Caleb. I'm proud of you. I'll just be sure he's well covered while you get the things he needs." Susannah and her eager helper headed for the bedroom. Alone in the kitchen, Emily took some warm water from the reservoir and washed her hands. If she hurried, she could have the table set before they returned.

Later that night, when the children settled down to much needed sleep, Susannah prepared to bathe Jackson. Cleanliness was an integral part of her weaponry in fighting this disease.

Noting that he was free of chills, she opened the window a crack to air the room before she began to assemble her supplies. She put a fresh nightshirt over the back of the chair beside the bed, and added a couple of towels on top. The soap dish and a washrag were placed on the side of the chair before she went to the kitchen for the basin and some warm water. She slipped a small bottle of olive oil into her pocket. She had prepared it earlier when she noticed that Jackson's lips were chapped. This would soothe and heal them.

When she returned he was beginning to toss his head from side to side and mumble. Recognizing signs that the fever was rising again, she quickly closed the window. Her hand rested briefly on his forehead to see how warm he was. She wished she dared to put her face next to his, as she did with the children. Dipping a cloth in the warm water, she began to wipe his face, lingering over each pass across his forehead and down his cheeks.

"What are you doing, Susannah?" Jackson's eyes opened to slits and he frowned as he tried to focus. "No, no, leave me alone," he muttered, pushing her hand away. This was a repeat of his behavior of the night before; moments of lucidity interspersed with longer periods of delirium.

"Jackson, it's me, Susannah. Your fever is starting to rise again, so I'm going to bathe you. You'll feel so much better." She caught his hands in hers, noting that they were warm, but not hot. "Come, now, you've been in this nightshirt since yesterday, and you need a fresh one. I'll change the bed when we've finished with your bath." She put his hands at his sides and reached for the buttons at his neck.

Jackson's eyes popped open. "So, you want to play games, do you?" Her mouth dropped. He'd been cranky and cooperative by turns during the night, but never playful.

"Jackson? I'm just giving you a bath because you're ill."

"Of course you are, Susannah, but you don't have to play games. I've wanted you for a long, long time." Her heart began to race. Increasingly she was compelled to find excuses to touch him, disconcerted by her inability to breathe properly when he was near. His hands slid up her back, one stopping at her shoulders and the other continuing its upward sweep to cradle her head. He moved so quickly that there was barely time to register the minty scent of toothpowder and the warmth of his body.

This man was so gentle. Even as he restrained her, she knew she could break free with very little effort. Soft, soft kisses rained on her eyelids, her nose, her chin and then her mouth. How had her hands ended up behind his head? She had no memory of their wayward trek.

Now his lips grazed hers lightly, like the caress of a butterfly's wing, and his tongue probed the seam of her lips. This was magic. She felt her breasts swelling and the nipples peaking as moisture gathered between her legs. Her hands now rested on his shoulders. Suddenly, she realized that only one of them was participating in this delightful exercise. Jackson was asleep.

Blushing furiously, she fastened his buttons and crept out of the room. This must be why Miranda lusted after Michael. The incredible sensations that flowed through her at his loving embrace were a revelation. She wanted more. Her hands trembled with a heady combination of delight and frustration.

Three days later Jackson was finally able to get dressed and sit up for an hour or so at a time. Because of a terrible cough, and Susannah refused to let him out of doors. No protestations on his part moved her. She was adamant that he recover fully before resuming his duties. The toll this disease could take on those who regarded it lightly was frightening. Not just the old and young were at risk, but strong men and women in their prime could be struck down with complications from the disease.

As she started the fire under her wash pot, she gave thanks that her little family survived intact.

Wife Seller!

CHAPTER ELEVEN

Susannah and Jackson stood side by side, surveying the kitchen in the morning light, the children's voices audible through the screen door. The sultry days of July encouraged the opening of all windows and doors to catch every breeze. Thoughtfully regarding his wife, he noticed that she no longer jumped when he addressed her or trembled when he helped her on and off the wagon on their trips to town. Her death grip on the edge of the mattress had relaxed to the point where, upon waking, he frequently found their bodies spooned. Whilst undeniably a most pleasant way to start the day, the effect on his ability to concentrate for quite some time after he banished the physical evidence of his desire was disconcerting. Also, the fact that she no longer leapt from bed as soon as she wakened, even if she didn't linger, offered proof that progress was being made. Although she kept her back to him as she hurried to put on her wrapper to make her first trip outside, he knew she was blushing by the color suffusing the nape of her neck. And surely a smile caused such a delightful curve to her lips yesterday?

Jackson reflected on his momentous decision to court his wife. It was getting harder and harder to control his passion. He wanted a loving relationship. They might never be in love, but love could grow by way of affection, caring and companionship. He was convinced that the four of them were becoming a family, and not just in appearance. In an effort to address his physical needs, he concentrated on deepening the relationship with Susannah. Wooing his wife into his arms seemed a good start.

They had, purely as a theoretical exercise, talked about formally adopting Caleb and Emily. Now he was ready to make theory fact. Two children represented a satisfactory start, but more would be welcome. It was the begetting of those additions that posed the problem at the moment. He didn't want submission through duty. He wanted passion and eagerness.

Usually a man expressed his regard with candy or flowers, walking the favored one home from prayer meetings or church, and then dining with the family. They, however, had married before meeting and dined as a family every day, not just for Sunday dinners. If he couldn't follow the well-trodden path of tradition, he could show his regard in more practical ways. His hunger for a fulfilling relationship increased daily, as did his determination to win his wife's affections.

"Susannah, is there anything that would make your job easier in the kitchen? Something that I could do or make that would help you?" Having decided that this unique courtship encompassed more than flowers or candy, then surely making her life easier or more pleasant would provide an excellent start. Because it was several years since he considered any thoughts of a permanent relationship, he lacked confidence in devising a plan of attack. Courting a wife was not in just the usual way of doing things, but then neither was buying a wife.

Greatly daring, her clenched hands the only outward sign of trepidation at extending a tendril of trust, she offered, "Well, cupboard doors would make things look tidier and keep the dishes cleaner. I wouldn't have to dust or wash them before I use them." She thrust her hands in her apron pockets.

Jackson was afraid to look at her. This was the very first time she ventured an opinion or indicated that something could be improved or changed to make her workload lighter. He noticed a gradual lessening of tension when they stood close to each other, or worked together on a project—a welcome shift from the blank face and board-like body so evident when she first arrived. Sometimes, as now, she stood within hugging reach if he were to extend his arm. He clasped his hands behind his back and turned to face her.

"That's easily enough done, then. I'll get Zeke Marshall to pass the message along to Amos Weatherby. He does good work and is always ready to add to his bank account."

Susannah returned his smile. "Isn't he one of the regulars at Zeke's store? The one who's notorious for telling tall tales to see if the gullible will swallow them?"

He grinned. "The very same. However, his carpentry work is second to none. You think of just what you want so you can tell him when he comes. Since we're putting in new cupboards...." Jackson was fascinated by the play of emotions that flashed across her face. She so rarely allowed her feelings to show except with the children. He sometimes thought she would melt with tenderness as she brushed Emily's hair or straightened Caleb's collar.

"New cupboards?" she gasped. "I thought you were just adding doors to the shelves. I can make do, Jackson, there's no need to spend good money just to save a little work." Susannah was stunned. Not only had Jackson considered how hard she worked, he saw her as worthy of consideration. The fact that he was willing to replace what could perfectly well be used as it was defied description. Astonished to find her hand resting on his arm, she discovered she had no memory of placing it there. Even more astounding was the realization that she felt no inclination to remove it or to try to devise a seemingly innocent reason to do so, thus causing his hand to drop. And why hadn't she noticed that he was standing so close? Their shoulders were practically touching!

It took all his control to lightly cover her hand with his when he wanted to clasp it tightly and raise it to his lips. Although his touch was firm, she could easily withdraw if she wished. "Susannah, in addition to having all the work of keeping up the house and garden, you also provide very valuable services in the dairy. Not to mention the time and effort that goes into caring for Emily and Caleb." Jackson saw the look of shock on her face and was puzzled. Her hand still rested on his arm. He hurried to reassure her of his affection and esteem.

"You're my wife. It is my duty as your husband to take care of you." Would she ever respond to him freely and without fear in her eyes?

"Your duty," she echoed, slipping her hand from under his to tuck it back in her apron pocket.

"Yes." Desperate to put her at ease again, as well as to emphasize his regard, he continued. "Even if we weren't married, a worker who is exhausted doesn't perform as well and is much likelier to have accidents that result in serious injuries." Jackson felt that if he put this on an impersonal level she might be more receptive to the idea.

"Serious injuries could mean loss of services for a considerable time." Susannah ventured to offer an opinion, albeit one that reinforced her belief that Jackson valued her mainly as a worker. Only in her most secret thoughts did she think that he might like her—or that she might like him. Her lessons in the danger of offering trust had been shattered too many times. She wondered that she could entertain such thoughts again, even for a moment.

"Exactly," he responded heartily. His plan to lighten Susannah's work load and indicate his appreciation for her contributions proceeded apace. She responded well to his justification of reduction of possible injuries. A great deal of thought and effort were a small price to pay for such a victory.

He remembered the day the washing machine arrived at Zeke's store. Manufacturing a reason to go to town, *sans* family, taxed his powers of inventiveness, but the look on her face when he escorted her from the dairy to the kitchen to display his prize was one he treasured. And one he wanted to see again. The amount of laundry the family created during their bouts with the flu appalled him. He vowed that his wife would have the best machine available to help her with such an onerous task.

Susannah, too, was lost in thought. *Duty. Injuries that might cause loss of work.* She stepped back, increasing the space between them. He was just being considerate of his worker. There was nothing personal in this offer. Of course. *How could I be so stupid!* Jackson took good care of stock and equipment so there was no reason he wouldn't extend that same management to employees, as well. What a fool! She frequently noted his kindness to both the children and herself, so why did her eyes burn? Confident now that Jackson would never brutalize her, hope of a closer relationship burgeoned. What could she expect? A mature (she dismissed the word *old*) woman and not a young girl with silly notions, she should be appreciating the warmth that already established between them. The children, ever dearer, would have to fill her heart to the exclusion of romantic impossibilities.

But, her treacherous mind insisted, *a man who buys a washing machine might think in terms of less time washing and more time for other duties. Or pleasures.* However, cupboard doors, let alone new cupboards were an entirely different matter. He could have agreed to pay for fabric to make curtains. While not as effective as doors, they would still provide an excellent deterrent to dust and dirt. Of course, if she didn't have to wash the dishes before they were used, then she'd have more time for other household tasks. That must be it.

Noting her withdrawal, he endeavored to regain her lost enthusiasm. "I'm responsible for you, Susannah. Your well-being is very important to the children. I don't know what we'd do without you."

"Oh, yes, the children," she murmured. The flush of pleasure that suffused her face faded, and he saw the stony visage she offered when she arrived, one he now realized hid fear and uncertainty. He waited for that wonderful, warm smile to light up her face.

"You're responsible for me." Susannah felt a fool. The joy that had flooded her heart receded more with every indication that she was a duty, a responsibility, a valued worker, and, probably, just one more thing for Jackson to oversee. The fact that his body leaned toward her added to her grief. His scent was dear to her. Sometimes, when she knew that he was asleep, she ventured to touch his hair—softly, lightly. At first, such contact filled her with tenderness, but lately passion was taking its place.

"Yes, well, of course." Susannah pasted a smile on her face, confused by Jackson's reaction. His body straightened, and while this made it easier for her to think, she was unprepared for the feeling of loss.

What's happening to me? I know he's nothing like Albert. He's really much more like Michael. When he loses his temper he yells, but then he apologizes afterwards. And Jackson's never struck either me or the children. Well, there was the incident of Caleb gluing his tools to various surfaces the day he found the work shed door unlocked. The spanking, while forceful enough to deter further incursions into forbidden territory, fell far short of brutality. She gradually became aware that he was waiting for more.

"Thank you, Jackson. Please make arrangements for Amos. I shall look forward to our new cupboards," she replied, certain that this was the response he wanted. His smile faded, and his demeanor became formal.

His body straightened and pulled away from hers. "Is there any time that would be more convenient for you, Susannah?"

Why was his voice so cold? Just a minute ago it was warm. He shifted so that their bodies were no longer touching. It must be her fault; something she had said or done. Sometimes she despaired of making him happy.

She knew the money made from her dairy products provided a significant addition to the farm's income and that he relished the warm and welcoming atmosphere permeating their home. This was not the first instance where Jackson's mood had changed from eager and enthusiastic to withdrawn and stilted. She failed to understand why he was upset, since she merely repeated the salient points of their conversation

What did he want? If she knew, she would do her level best to provide it. Jackson's happiness, along with that of the children, was the goal toward that she strived. *Well, I do know that when he comes up behind me and I don't know he's there, or if he raises his hand suddenly, I flinch. But neither of those things happened here, so what could the problem be?* She hastened to respond to his latest query.

"Any time is fine with me. Thank you for your thoughtfulness." No, that was wrong, too. Not only was Jackson no longer smiling, but he was on his way out the door.

She felt like a fool. When Jackson asked for some way he could lighten her work load she was shocked, but pleased. It had been so many years since anyone offered to consider her that she was, quite literally, short of breath. The happiness flooding her added to her amazement. He almost caused her heart to stop beating when he told her that she would have new cupboards, not just doors on the existing shelves. By now she knew that he refused to have anything slipshod or shoddy. Those cupboards would have their own special significance, not only in her kitchen, but in her heart. Then he uttered words that took all the light from the room: duty, responsibility, injury causing an inability to work.

What did it take for her to learn? Just because she no longer feared for her life, or even thought that a careless slap would come her way didn't mean that his feelings for her were more than an acceptance of her value as a worker.

Lately, with increasing regularity, she awakened in the middle of the night to find herself cuddled against his warmth, but her care in easing away ensured that he didn't know she lost her grip on the side of the bed. Those times that he sought her warmth in sleep she banished as meaningless. They reflected nothing, except that he felt cold. Even the fact that his arm circled her waist, or his hand rested on her breast could be rationalized as the unconscious movements of sleep. She refused to contemplate that waking to find his arms around her was fast becoming the norm. Or that she found the experience far from unpleasant.

Shocked, she realized that her feelings were completely different. From fear and resignation, through a slowly-building trust, she found her attitude one of acceptance and liking. Further than liking she refused to go, even in the privacy of her own thoughts. She decided to check on the activities of the children as an antidote to this fruitless self-examination.

By supper time Jackson seemed to have recovered his composure, but his actions, whilst perfectly correct, lacked the spontaneity and humor that were so much part of his personality. When he held his mouth in in just that way it was a sign of emotional withdrawal. She now realized that he did so not to punish her, but to protect himself. The children, too, were subdued.

The dishes were done, the floor swept, and her kitchen back in order. Caleb and Emily were occupied with the checkerboard. Emily expounded on the rules of the game as she understood them. Caleb demanded an explanation and justification for each rule, and an uneasy truce reigned. Jackson worked on farm accounts at the other end of the table, seemingly unaware of the looming threat of warfare.

Susannah grabbed a lantern and muttered an excuse about checking on something in the dairy. "I'm going to the dairy for a few minutes," she mumbled. While she probably didn't need the lantern, it gave her something to do with her hands. The dairy always soothed her. Scrupulously clean and in perfect order, there were really no chores to be completed. She adjusted the alignment of her equipment by infinitesimal amounts and checked the state of the wood box.

The single trip to and from the wood pile completed, checking on the stock was next. The cows were all lying down chewing their cuds. Obviously Jackson filled their trough with fresh water before supper. She remembered being surprised when he agreed that the trough should be emptied, scrubbed with a brush and warm water, rinsed and filled anew each day. He even listened with interest to her suggestion of augmenting their winter feed to include warm mashes as an aid to increase winter milk production. Albert scorned such notions as being unnecessary and a ploy to make more work for him. Susannah could never understand this argument, since he refused to have anything to do with the dairy at all.

She had devised several ways of coping with the heavy tasks because of Albert's refusal to set foot in her workplace. Jackson's endorsement of her plan to keep milking at five in the morning was another pleasant surprise. This meant they could complete the night milking early enough for family time after supper. He confessed he had started milking so early in an attempt to accomplish the chores before the children rose.

Inspecting the supplies on hand, she reminded herself to get more saltpeter for the winter. They had an excellent crop of turnips, and a little saltpeter added to the milk would remove any residual flavor of the strong winter feed. The cloths used for straining and wrapping cheeses were boiled and scrubbed before they were wrapped in paper. The stone floor exhibited a degree of cleanliness greater than many a kitchen, and the metal utensils glowed dully in the warm lantern light. As she passed the barrel churn she gave it an affectionate pat. It represented the elimination of many arduous hours in the butter-making process. She merely drained the buttermilk, storing it in jars to be sold at the market, and then rinsed the butter in the churn until the water ran clean.

The space reserved for the special butter press was now occupied by a fine example of its kind. She and Jackson agreed that the symbol of a rose for the white rose of York was appropriate. Every time she used that rose press she smiled to see a bit of her old country in the new one.

Her plan to coax the cows to come for the night milking to the sound of a horn proved successful. They could be sure of two things: salt and relief from the pressure of full udders. Emily and Caleb quarreled loudly over who would blow the horn. After several instances of confused cows and an unholy racket, she found a place of hiding that defeated even Caleb. The horn now rested in one of the cheese presses, high on a shelf. Out of sight, perhaps, but by certain expressions on two little faces, definitely not out of mind. Only the sternest strictures that the dairy was out of bounds unless Susannah invited them in provided adults and cows with any relief.

Earthenware pots, aligned with military precision, waited to receive the salted butter destined for market or the local store. Jackson had installed special shelves especially for this purpose. The cleanliness of her workplace and meticulous care of all parts of the processes contributed in no small way to the escalating reputation of their dairy products. The large, shallow bowl and broad paddles used to work salt into the butter were highly valued, and the pots and pans she used to heat the milk and cream to the correct temperature for making cheese rested, scrubbed, inverted, and ready for use, in their allotted spaces.

As she surveyed her kingdom she mulled over the Cupboard Situation as she called it. Over and over again she tried to determine what happened. Jackson had been smiling, eager and affectionate. She knew that he offered her the cupboards as a generous gift. So what went wrong?

At first she felt herself blushing like a young girl given a gift by her chosen beau. Jackson's earnestness was evident. He evinced none of the meanness, so familiar to her, of offering a carrot only to snatch it back and give a cuff instead. With the exception of that well-deserved spanking of Caleb for meddling with, if not ruining, the tools, he struck neither human nor animal. His patience seemed boundless, and she often wished that she had an equal amount.

Whether it was helping her in the dairy or the house, or minding and instructing the children, he was a major force in melding four very different people into a family. The man was amazing.

She knew the cupboards would be installed as soon as possible, and that she would be an integral part of the planning process. But what created those warm feelings, that treacherous glow that threatened to mow down her defenses and melt her hard-won strength? She was well aware that the increasing intimacy in daily living, and especially during the night when guards were down, could plunge her from affection and liking, to love. Loving, she knew, meant pain and disillusionment. No matter how precious it might be at the start, living with someone for years and years was fraught with peril for hearts and emotions.

Jackson watched his wife scoot out the door as if pursued by the hounds of hell. He analyzed the conversation that deteriorated from joy to reserve. At first she was clearly thrilled and amazed that he would give her new cupboards, and not just doors for the shelves. Why was she always so stunned, and often reluctant to accept, when he made a contribution to their home?

His mother and sisters weren't backward about coming forward when they perceived a need. In the case of his sisters, it might be a desire to have some labor-saving tool or an attractive piece of furniture or clothing. As a child he merely accepted that these things happened, but with adulthood came the realization that his father got as much, if not more, pleasure from giving something to make his women happy and acknowledge their contributions to the family's success as the recipients did. So what happened this morning?

"Caleb, I've told you and told you that you can't move your pieces like that unless they've been crowned."

"I can, too, Miss Bossy. I can move my men wherever I want." Caleb's lower lip jutted in an ominous manner. Emily's expression assumed that degree of superiority guaranteed to drive a younger brother to mayhem.

"That's enough from both of you! If you can't get along, the checker game will be put away for the next two weeks."

The combatants subsided. When Uncle Jackson spoke in that tone of voice it was best to do as he said. He never made idle threats.

The children made promises of exemplary behavior, and Jackson returned to his thoughts. As he recalled the conversation, practically word for word, he began to realize that Susannah's withdrawal and dampening enthusiasm seemed to march hand in hand with his rationalization of why she should have the cupboards. Every time he tried to apply logic to the situation, she had retreated. There was no understanding the fair sex.

CHAPTER TWELVE

Susannah stood at the kitchen door, scrub pail in hand. Pressing her hand to her lower back, she straightened, wiped her brow and admired her handiwork. The floor was as clean as sand and soap and hard work could make it. Curtains, starched to crispness, parted to reveal gleaming windows. The table glowed softly with beeswax and elbow grease, and the chairs waited on the porch, drying in the sunlight. No specks of dust, strips of bark, or bits of wood marred the floor surrounding the wood box. Tantalizing smells wafted from the pot of stew simmering on the back of the stove, its pristine appearance and bright nickel work another testimonial to determined effort.

Carefully closing the door on her morning's work, she picked up the pail of dirty water preparatory to flinging its grey contents onto the lawn before rinsing both pail and cloth at the outside pump. "Aunt Susannah, Aunt Susannah, look at what we found!"

"Yes, yes, Emily. I'm coming. What have you discovered now?" She wondered again at the amazing turn in her fortunes. Except for her fear that her bigamous conduct might become known, a fear she found increasingly easy to push aside, her life was as close to perfect as she could imagine. Two wonderful children—and a husband whose appeal increased daily—far exceeded her expectations.

Emily and Caleb's unnaturally good behavior was giving way to the mischief and mishaps common to children who felt secure and loved. They were particularly fond of the jungle, formerly a garden. It was their current location for noisy and mighty adventures. Susannah had plans for that garden next year, and for the flowerbeds in front of the house. Georgina Turner promised some bulbs and cuttings. In her mind's eye they were already in bloom.

"It's a baby snake. Well, lots of baby snakes! They're so sweet."

Repressing a lifelong aversion to anything that squirmed and slithered, Susannah prepared to admire the latest discovery, mentally noting that she would have Jackson remove the monsters at the first possible opportunity. She crossed the lawn to the garden with lagging steps.

"My, there are a lot of them. And so wriggly! Let's leave them for their mother to find. I'm sure she's not far away." The clutch on her skirts tightened as she eased them a little further up her legs. Modesty came a poor second to safety, and she was convinced that each one of them had plans to slither under her skirts and bite her. She rejected categorically the image of them climbing her legs.

"Oh, Aunt Susannah, they're so sweet," Emily repeated. "Couldn't we keep some as pets? Uncle Jackson says that they eat mice and moles and all kinds of garden pests. I bet they could eat house pests, too!"

Silently cursing Jackson's enthusiastic natural history lessons, Susannah searched frantically for a caveat. Inspiration struck.

"That's true, Emily, but remember the kittens will soon be able to catch mice and crickets. Caleb, put it down. Right this minute! However, their mommy has to teach them how to catch all those pests, so.... Caleb, I said put it down, not in your pocket. So, we should leave them until they're older and know all the snake tricks. Caleb, if you do not put those snakes down right now there will be no dessert for the rest of the week!"

Susannah counted as Caleb returned four snakes to the garden. He did so with reluctance and a distressing lack of regard for their longevity. Assessing the glint in his eye, and armored with knowledge garnered from painful experience, she demanded, "Turn out your pockets, young man." The last two snakes joined their siblings. His look of longing plucked her heart strings, and she hastened to make amends—anything to keep the wildlife in the garden and out of the house.

"Caleb, they're a family, and you know how important it is to keep families together. Their mommy would be very cross with you." Emily, never one to miss an opportunity to pontificate, drew herself up in her most contentious manner. Caleb's lower lip jutted ominously. Susannah stepped behind him and surreptitiously patted his back while simultaneously putting her finger to her mouth as a signal for Emily to hush. He still became very upset at any mention of his family, and nights often echoed with his screams.

Searching desperately for a way to deflect the looming storm; then remembered a promised treat.

"Are you ready for our picnic lunch? You were very, very good children to play quietly while I scrubbed the kitchen floor. Let's wash our hands, fill the water bottles, and be on our way." Susannah reached into her apron pocket and removed a small piece of soap. They cleaned their hands under the pump, and with the jars of cold water nestled in the lunch basket that had reposed in the dairy to keep it cool, they set off for their favorite spot.

For the first time since her youth, she enjoyed the opportunity to eat her lunch under a tree. This particular tree was a chestnut, and its location beside a wide and shallow part of the creek, designed for picnic outings. Minnows and frogs provided good, if damp, entertainment. The creek, very shallow at this point, contained several quiet pools and just enough stones to let it chuckle. It was a favorite spot, and promised many good times ahead. Emily finally admitted that the kittens did not enjoy wading, minnows notwithstanding.

Susannah could hardly wait to see their faces tonight wen Jackson brought home a puppy from the Smitherson's place. Caleb was quite vocal in his support of the great good a dog could do on a farm. Jackson, with happy memories of hours of fun and companionship with his own dogs, had discovered a neighbor who had lab-collie cross puppies. Jackson felt sure that it was a lab-collie-every-dog-within-ten-miles cross, but the bitch was quiet and affectionate, and the puppies accustomed to small children.

Susannah was beginning to believe that his actions reflected his personality, and were not a diabolical plot to lull her into a false sense of security. His unfailing kindness to the children and small courtesies to her contributed to her growing trust. She didn't know what to think of his encouragement and insistence that their home should be a place of warmth and love and laughter.

She still remembered the day that he glowered and growled until she agreed to buy material for kitchen curtains.

His clinching argument, did he but know it, was that he was not a poor man, and a few paltry yards of material would not break him. Susannah could see the kindness behind his sound and fury, and his real desire to have a home, not just a place to live. Although he roared, he did not threaten her, either verbally or physically, nor was there that sly behavior that foretold a beating later. From buying curtain material to buying yard goods for clothing for the children was an easier step, but it still required all her courage to purchase fabric and notions for herself. The biggest spur was concern that her dowdy appearance might reflect badly on him.

Jackson lifted his hat and swiped his brow with the sleeve of his shirt. He could just make out three figures under the chestnut tree by the brook. His little family often gathered there on hot afternoons, or for picnic lunches. He was on his way to fetch a replacement for a broken trace, along with the requisite tools to complete the job. As he neared the house, he noted the chairs lined up in military order on the back porch, a sure signal that Susannah was cleaning. The rag rug that usually resided just inside the door hung on the clothesline, drying rapidly in the sun and breezes.

Jackson's stomach growled when the aroma of stew wafted out of the kitchen's screen door. Surely just a small helping wouldn't be noticed. A very small helping. Just one spoonful. Or two. He would use a serving spoon; after all, he was a big man. Or, on second thought, perhaps a smaller spoon would be better. He could hide it quickly if Susannah returned unexpectedly.

Checking to ensure that he was still alone, he carefully removed his boots and brushed his trousers. No trace of his presence must be detected. He tiptoed across the shining floor, swiping a spoon from the table caddy on his way. He abandoned the quest for a larger spoon in favor of speed and stealth. The aroma of the stew was pulling him closer and closer, and he was unable to resist its siren call. He dipped his spoon into the pot, blew on the mixture to cool it and prepared to enjoy. It was delicious.

Just as he reached for a second spoonful to verify his opinion that it was ambrosia, not stew, he heard Caleb and Emily. They appeared to be arguing over the time it took for snakes to learn how to catch garden pests. Caleb held firmly to his opinion that an afternoon was more than enough time. Emily knew that they needed at least a day. Susannah's voice rose in volume and register as she reiterated that snakes needed at least a year before they were sufficiently skilled.

By the time they arrived at the house, Jackson had hidden the spoon in his pocket and was industriously bringing the chairs from the porch to the kitchen table. Susannah found the spoon on her next laundry day and smiled as she recalled a suspiciously helpful husband cheerfully helping her put the chairs back.

"Thank you, Jackson", she muttered. It made her extremely uncomfortable when he performed duties she felt were hers. It was almost as if she were cheating him in more ways than one.

"You're welcome. I smelled the stew on my way to the barn for some leather to mend a broken trace." He waited for an invitation to test it.

"Would you like some cold water? I'll be sure to have tea ready by six tonight, as I know you're busy after supper."

"Yes." He sighed. The stew continued to tease and entice. "Do you think I'll need any help on my errand? Why don't we all go? You've not had a chance to visit with Betsy, yet, and Smitherson's children are about the same age as Emily and Caleb," he offered, pretending to be very busy drinking and watching the children. "Jason said everything would be ready by seven." He waited for her response. Her confidence increased daily, and that beautiful smile brightened her face more and more often.

Susannah drew a deep breath, failing to notice the admiring glance her husband bestowed upon her heaving bosom. Thus far Jackson meant precisely what he said, with no hidden meanings. Was this a way to catch her for not staying home and working? Or did he want to present a normal front to more members of the community? Certainly he wasn't indicating a preference for her company, although he did seem close to the children. She noticed that he made a special time for each of them after supper, and showed remarkable patience during the day. On occasion, he even offered to keep an eye on them while she milked or was busy in the dairy. *Stop it! You are destroying your happiness with all this second guessing. Albert was the exception to the rule; Jackson is exactly what he seems.*

The silence was becoming uncomfortable. Caleb and Emily regarded her with hope. They missed having children to play with, especially after the time they spent at the Turner's farm.

"Uh, um, yes, Jackson, the children and I would love to come with you to visit Mr. and Mrs. Smitherson. I, too, seem to remember that their children are very close in age to ours."

Jackson wondered if she realized what she said. No hesitation marred the statement. It was offered simply as fact: they were a family: mother, father, son and daughter.

Emily and Caleb were thrilled. Barring one or two trips to the store and regular visits to church, they had not left the farm meeting Susannah at the station. The children were acquainted with both Amy and Eddie. Emily was anxious to see baby Carl. Caleb planned to tell Eddie about the wonderful family of snakes they found.

"Uncle Jackson, we found a whole family of baby snakes in the garden today." Caleb shouted, anxious to be the first to tell the news.

"I found them, Caleb, not you!" Emily waxed indignant that Caleb was first with such a momentous announcement. "They were just sweet, Uncle Jackson. We thought they could come in the house and catch mice and other pests, just like you told us they did. Aunt Susannah said that they had to learn snake things. How long do you think that would take?"

"Uhhhhh...." Jackson looked at each of them in turn and then at his wife. The frown she sent his way strongly reminded him of his mother glaring at his father when the right answer had better be forthcoming.

"Caleb thinks they can learn it all in an afternoon, but I think they need at least a day. Aunt Susannah thinks they need a whole year. What do you think, Uncle Jackson?" Emily piped.

Jackson put his best efforts into giving an answer that would please everyone. "Well, Emily, babies don't learn everything in a day, or even, Caleb, in an afternoon. Perhaps Aunt Susannah's idea of a year is well taken." Although the faces of his wards did not reflect unalloyed approval, Susannah's smile convinced Jackson that his answer was the right one. Unfortunately, in an effort to bring smiles back to the children's faces, he continued "Why don't we keep an eye on them, and see what happens."

The children's smiles warmed his heart. Then he realized that his softness to the children resulted in an entirely wrong answer for his wife. Belatedly he recalled her aversion to earthworms. If an earthworm engendered a shudder, then her reaction to a snake was best left unexplored. His caveat that snakes had no place indoors, or, indeed, anywhere but on the ground, was blithely disregarded by the children and discounted by Susannah.

"I hope you realize what you've just done." Susannah stopped abruptly and clapped her hand over her mouth. Any sign of resistance or non-compliance in the past met with a blow or kick at the very least. She hunched her shoulders and waited. She couldn't believe that those words had come out of her mouth.

He puzzled again over her apparent fear after she delivered a delightfully spunky retort. Her hand covered her mouth, her body shrank into itself, and she braced as if to withstand a blow. He was beginning to realize that Susannah's natural spirit had almost been beaten, or at least scared, out of her. She no longer always walked with her head down and shoulders hunched. Occasionally she forgot to keep her back to a wall and her position near a doorway when he was in the room. Jackson resolved to write to Ethan in an attempt to learn more about his wife's background.

Susannah saw that the children were holding hands, a sure sign of stress. She noticed this behavior whenever they perceived that everything was not exactly as it should be in their little world. Traveling from their home and relations to a foreign land, losing their parents and then Edmund destroyed their feelings of safety. Realizing that their security meant a stable relationship between her and Jackson, she searched frantically for a way to defuse the situation.

"Well, children, when we think about it carefully, snakes and animals don't really belong in the house. They are much happier outside. Kittens and puppies, of course, are quite different." Observing Susannah out of the corner of his eye, he waited for a reaction.

"Does that mean we're getting a puppy, Uncle Jackson?" shrieked the children. A heated argument over suitable names, and gender of the puppy then ensued—a sure sign that the children felt safe once more.

"Yes, Jackson", Susannah responded pointedly, "Does that mean we're getting a puppy? One that is trained?" She waited for the answer, no longer fearful of his reaction.

Jackson blew out a breath. "Well, I guess I stepped into that one." He grinned. A man could do worse than a saucy wife and two rambunctious children.

The visit to Betsey and Jason Smitherson and their young family was particularly satisfying. The children played with the puppies while the adults visited. Emily was thrilled that she was allowed to hold the baby all by herself.

Jason Smitherson's interest in garden produce as a cash crop had been piqued by Edmund's foray into such a venture. The Smitherson's orchard, one of the best in the county, tended to produce bumper crops when other orchards were damaged by frost. Jason had plans for a significant increase in the number and variety of trees he wished to plant.

Betsey and Susannah gossiped freely over cups of coffee and pieces of pie. Susannah demonstrated a new crochet stitch, and Betsey gave Susannah the recipe for a cheese that her grandmother used to make. Only the fading daylight cut the visit short.

"It was so kind of Betsey and Jason to have us for dessert, Jackson. We must invite them to come and see how the puppy is doing in a few weeks." She adjusted her shawl, smoothed her skirts, monitored the activity in the back of the wagon, then turned her gaze back to Jackson.

This was the first time that she suggested having company. "You're right, wife. We certainly must. Jason is very interested in seeing the new harrows I purchased. Didn't I hear you and Betsey discussing some of your cheese recipes?"

"You did indeed, husband." Susannah smiled warmly. Very warmly. Jackson's interest escalated from polite to focused.

"Yes, indeed, indeed," he responded, his answering grin promising future delights. The next step in wooing his wife was quite recent. He would drop a kiss on the nape of her neck, and when she whirled around to confront him, give her a kiss on the mouth. These kisses were increasing in frequency and duration. He and Susannah started exchanging good night kisses. At first they were merely a peck on the cheek. Last night he felt passion in her response. Those kisses generated considerable heat between the sheets. Tonight his patience would finally be rewarded. He whistled softly between his teeth. Susannah's smile faded into a knowing smirk as she rested her shoulder against his.

Meanwhile, in the back of the wagon, certain conclusions and decisions as to gender and name resulted in female and Spooky, as the puppy was a grey and black brindle mix. Jackson also thought she qualified for some kind of award for the frequency of her ability to squat and sprinkle. Maybe they should have called her Sprinkle. He knew that Piddle Queen wouldn't get past Susannah, though he felt sure that Caleb would agree wholeheartedly. As shrill barks and squabbling over whose turn it was to hold and pat Spooky subsided to blessed silence, he caught his wife's eye. The sparkle and slow smile indicated a willingness to map hitherto unexplored territory as soon as they had the children and animals settled.

He left Susannah and the children at the porch, then found himself smiling like a fool as he drove to the barn. With the horses stabled, the harness wiped down, and an eager woman waiting, he hurried to the house. He was confident that she would have the children in bed.

Alas, in his zeal to examine the pleasures of their ripening relationship he forgot the inevitable result of separating the pup from her siblings and mother. He and Susannah agreed that dogs should never be allowed on beds or, indeed, on any furniture. His agreement resulted from the correct interpretation of the blood in his spouse's eye if he argued for any arrangement other than the dog would be allowed in the kitchen, but no other part of the house. He even constructed a barrier to put across the doorway and thus confine her to the kitchen. Susannah found a box, lined it with an old rug and put a warmed brick under one corner. Certainly Spooky was not hungry; her stomach still bulged from the eagerness of her new owners to ensure that she was as full as she could hold—and to curry favor with their new pet.

Spooky, however, had different ideas. Box and brick notwithstanding, her new friends no longer stroked her soft coat or scratched behind her ears. Even the big people were deserting her.

Surely this abandonment was an oversight. Such kind people could not possibly mean to leave her alone in this big, dark, cold place. Without people, her mother or litter mates, the loneliness overwhelmed her. Whining having proved ineffective, she raised her voice in song, its volume increasing in direct ratio to her distress. Just as she paused for breath, she heard footsteps. Tumbling out of the box, she scooted across the floor to greet her visitor, only to find her way barred by a wall. The footsteps continued to approach. She waited. The steps came closer and closer. Spooky rushed back to the barrier to offer an eager welcome.

Sharp yips of pain died down to the occasional whimper. How could she possibly have known that people couldn't see very well in the dark? After all, it was her tail that was throbbing, not his. Jackson swore under his breath. Stepping on the pup's tail caused him to jump away quickly in an effort to ease her pain. The resultant loss of balance flung him against the corner of the table. The table survived bruise-free. Would he could say the same.

Scooping up Spooky and cuddling her to his chest, he petted her, scratched behind her ears, made sure that the brick was still warm and deposited her back in her bed with an admonition to be a good girl. Susannah giggled when she heard the dog singing, but Jackson was determined to recapture the mood. He had waited too long to let three pounds of wiggle come between him and this long-desired goal of making love to his wife.

Spooky, while willing to cooperate, apparently failed to convey her displeasure with Jackson's arrangements. How could he be so kind and pat her so gently, know exactly how to scratch her behind the ears, and then leave her all alone again?

She indicated her suffering with energy and volume. Firm footsteps once more approached the now dreaded barrier. If she could just get past that, she could follow her nose to the smaller humans and be warm, comfortable and not alone. Her instincts told her that the big humans, while willing to provide warmth and food, were incapable of understanding the inherent need of a small pup to be with those who understood her so well.

This time Jackson was prepared for the tripping hazard. Carefully sliding his leg over the barrier, he tapped the floor with his toes before putting his weight on his foot. Success! He was safely in the kitchen and both he and the pup were uninjured. A wet nose pressed against his ankle, and small, sharp claws followed. So much for remaining unscathed. Spooky received considerably less cuddling and scratching. He plunked her in her box, demanded that she be quiet and go to sleep and strode to the barrier.

Who in the hell moved that chair he grumbled as he rubbed his knee. Limping slightly, his pace increased with every step as he answered the siren call of bed and wife.

Susannah had the pillow over her mouth. Tears rolled down her cheeks, but she failed to fool her husband. He knew hilarity when he saw it. Mirth had vanquished seduction.

Just as he bent to blow out the light the dreaded canine aria began again, followed by a loud bang! Turning angrily, he retraced his route. *I'll throttle her,* he threatened, knowing perfectly well that the pup was safe. *The little bugger has managed to push down the barrier.* He knew when he was beaten. The last few steps resembled an inelegant shuffle. His toes found the end of the barrier. As he reached to set it upright and to one side of the door, he felt a furry tail brush his wrist.

No fool I, he thought. *She'll head straight for one of the children's rooms.*

Returning to his room, he prepared once again to blow out the light. Susannah made no effort to hide the tears streaming down her face. She was laughing so hard that she held her stomach and rocked from side to side. Jackson kissed her cheek, tugged on a lock of her hair and said good night. Dog one: man nothing.

Wife Seller!

CHAPTER THIRTEEN

Jackson sighed as he inserted the last hook into the ceiling. His two lookouts were far more interested in observing and critiquing his activities than in keeping an eye out for Susannah's return from the garden. He often saw her check her step as she entered the kitchen to gaze at the new cabinets, or absently run her hand over the smooth counter top while speaking to him or the children. He especially treasured the little smile when she admired her cupboards. *Courting a wife involved a great deal more thought than flowers or candy,* he mused, *but the experience and the results were exhilarating!* After last night, he had plans to guarantee a puppy-free period.

Caleb, the self-appointed supervisor of the project, already objected to the location of the hooks.

"But Uncle Jackson, bigger hooks would hold up the quilting frame, too. Then we could use them to swing from in the winter, or even in the summer during storms. Why, we could even hang stuff up on them." Just in case the first two vital reasons failed to sway the decision in his favor, he was sure that the last offering would clinch it.

Caleb failed to understand the concept of quilting frames, and was convinced that the use of larger, and therefore stronger, hooks would facilitate a crackerjack swing for stormy winter days. Realizing that his arguments were failing to achieve the desired results, he slumped onto a chair, crossed his arms over his chest and projected his lower lip to an amazing degree. Spooky dropped the piece of wood she was chewing into splinters and jumped into his lap. Slowly his arms relaxed. One hand cradled his friend, and the other stroked her soft fur.

Jackson and Emily ignored him. Their animated discussion about the exact placement of the hooks to maximize the benefit of the fireplace and lights from either the window or the hanging lamp over the kitchen table continued unabated.

Susannah and Emily had conferred about the intricacies of making a quilt for Emily's bed. A special piecing bag to collect scraps of material nestled in the sewing basket. Emily could choose any pattern she wished, providing she learned to stitch well enough to make up some of the squares. They also planned to host a bee when the top was completed and the quilt assembled. Conversations about borrowing frames led to discussions between Emily and Jackson for a surprise for Susannah.

Susannah banged her boots against the log set beside the back steps for just that purpose. With the worst of the mud removed, she placed them neatly beside the door. She hitched the pan of vegetables from the garden a little higher on her hip and entered the kitchen. As a special concession to Jackson and Caleb, she planned to add a cheese sauce to the cauliflower. Thoughts of coaxing Brussels sprouts down reluctant throats had convinced her of the efficacy of the "everyone may choose one thing they don't have to eat" theory. Fortunately there was always enough food to fill empty stomachs.

No one was in the kitchen, but the heat exuded by the stove indicated that its firebox had just been replenished. Susannah plopped the pan on the workbench. She removed her shawl, checking for twigs or leaves that might have clung to it, and hung it on one of the hooks by the door. She slid her feet into her house shoes, picked up the pan and started for the sink.

"Surprise!" shouted three voices, two of them piercing trebles. She jumped and whirled to face them, one hand on her chest as if to calm her tripping heart. Surprise? What surprise? Knowing the children would be disappointed if she failed to discover their secret, Susannah let her gaze travel slowly around the kitchen. From the corner of her eye she kept Jackson and the children in her view, hoping for a clue. Finally, she had to admit defeat.

"We know, we know," chanted the children. Just then, Susannah noticed that Jackson was holding quilting frames in his hands.

"Whose frames are those, Jackson? Where did you get them? Are they Georgina's?" she asked. His grin spread from ear to ear. "They're yours, Susannah. I made them for you."

Her mouth formed an O as three voices chorused, "Look up!" It was then that she noticed the four sturdy hooks secured to the ceiling. Swiftly gauging their position in relation to sources of warmth and light, she realized that a quilting frame would be placed to receive the maximum benefit of both. She laughed shakily as she wiped away tears of joy.

"Oh, oh, oh myyyyyy! What a wonderful surprise. Thank you, thank you, thank you! Now we'll all have warm covers this winter." Years of practice let her control her voice, but her eyes refused to cooperate. She knelt and spread her arms to hug the children.

"Aunt Susannah, I thought you liked our surprise!" wailed Caleb.

"I do, Caleb, I do! It's the most precious gift that you would think to make my work as easy and pleasant as possible." Susannah hugged Caleb and reached for Emily.

"Then why are you crying?" Caleb was distressed.

"Look closely at Aunt Susannah's face" soothed Jackson, "and you'll see her smile through her tears." Caleb dutifully stared at Susannah's face.

"You're smiling and crying at the same time, Aunt Susannah. Can't you make up your mind?" Caleb's anxiety that his beloved Aunt Susannah might be sad overwhelmed him.

She managed a wobbly laugh. "Caleb, when ladies are really, really happy, they cry." She gave them a squeeze and dropped a kiss on each little head.

"That doesn't make any sense at all." Caleb needed to be convinced.

"You're right, Caleb, it doesn't, unless you're a woman. So, we men just have to understand that it happens." Jackson's grin threatened to split his face. Their surprise had really stunned Susannah. He well remembered the women of his family laughing and crying when they were moved.

Susannah groped in her apron pocket for a hankie. Quickly wiping her cheeks and eyes, she kissed the children again. "There, you see, no more tears."

"Ahem." Jackson cleared his throat, looked hopeful, and leaned towards her. Susannah, correctly reading the warning in his eyes, and the hope on the faces of the children, quickly planted a hearty kiss on his proffered cheek. Their gazes met and important messages were exchanged silently.

Susannah's regard for her husband was blossoming into deep affection—very deep affection, she admitted. She refused to acknowledge that affection had slipped into love, but she did wonder how much longer she could remain on her side of the bed. Jackson's careful wooing had created a willingness to explore the chance of a satisfying physical relationship. Her nipples puckered in response to her thoughts. She became painfully aware of the friction of her dress when she shifted her stance, and a blush suffused her body.

Jackson's breath caught in his throat. His wife's eyes made promises he was determined she would keep. That kiss had been given willingly. He noticed Susannah leaning toward him even before he had offered his cheek. If they had been alone, he would have turned his face, pulled her into an embrace, and proceed to show her just exactly how this husband kissed his wife. In an effort to control his physical reaction, he addressed the children.

"Let's all help Aunt Susannah get supper ready. Afterwards we can set up the frames to be sure that everything is just as we planned." As he finished his suggestion, Jackson's arm snaked out and grabbed the straps on Caleb's overalls. Bowing to greater strength, Caleb stomped over to the washbasin for the constant hand washing that Aunt Susannah always insisted precede activities in the kitchen, particularly those involving food. Just as he prepared to dry them, two large hands appeared on either side of his, one holding a cake of dry soap, the other protecting the towel. He sighed, accepted the soap, and with resignation began to wash his hands for the second time.

"Hurry up, Caleb. We ladies have to get the supper ready."

That night, assured that the children were asleep, Jackson slowly removed the brush from Susannah's hand. Their eyes met in the mirror. As he turned her and drew her into his arms, she raised her hand and cradled his cheek. Her thumb brushed his bottom lip. He lowered his head, one hand behind her shoulders and the other pulling her hips towards him.

The soft kisses drifted across her forehead. They continued down her cheek and found just the right spot under her jaw. Her breath caught, half sob, half gasp, then exhaled slowly in anticipation.

The hand cradling his cheek drifted to his ear. Its mate grasped the nape of his neck.

"Yes," she breathed. "Oh, yes!"

Not until the next day did Susannah speculate about what would happen to this wonderful little family if her secret were discovered.

CHAPTER FOURTEEN

Susannah and Emily viewed the items on the table. Together they chanted: "Bread, butter, salt, pepper, plates, knives, forks, spoons, castor set, cups, saucers, glasses, napkins!" Napkins were the newest addition to their standard table setting. Susannah taught Emily to check that everything was ready before they served the food to avoid jumping up and down during the meal.

"Do you think Uncle Jackson will guess that I made the apple crisp, Aunt Susannah?" Emily enjoyed learning to cook and bake almost as much as Susannah enjoyed teaching her. Each new skill was greeted with lavish praise from the adults, although Caleb could be distressingly frank.

"Let's not tell him until he's eaten some of it, Emily. Won't that be a good joke?"

Giggling like a pair of schoolgirls, the ladies went their separate ways. Emily scurried to tell her pesky brother and beloved Uncle Jackson that supper was ready. Susannah began putting food on the table. She treasured mealtimes, especially supper, when, the majority of the day's work completed, they came together as a family and shared stories of their activities. Lately she noticed Jackson's periods of quiet reflection. This usually signaled the mulling over of plans and possible changes. She bided herself in patience, knowing that he would share his ideas when ready.

She acknowledged that her reputation was well earned as she placed the cottage cheese on the table. It was creamy and rich by itself or provided the perfect complement to flavorful vegetables, spices or fruits, whether fresh or preserved. None of the cottage cheese offerings at the market came close to hers. If she and Jackson completed the proposed addition to the dairy to permit her to age cheddar, they could begin selling it within the next year. She looked forward to proving that her cheddar would make their dairy produce the most sought after in the county.

Supper proved lively with the children badgering the adults with questions and suggestions for picnics. They brushed aside the caveat that chores would, or even should, come first. No assurance that the picnic was work prevailed. Caleb's assertion that they could fish and might catch enough for a meal fell on deaf ears. Even pointing out that Spooky could have a good run, and then they could wash her in the creek failed to move the adults. Picnics were shelved for the immediate future.

Emily pressed on: "Well, then, Aunt Susannah, we could sew a cushion for the kittens. You said that we could each have one as a house cat when they were weaned, and next Tuesday the six weeks will be over. I found a basket in the parlor that we could use." Emily smiled seraphically, sure that this suggestion would be embraced.

"Emily Grace Farnley! You know perfectly well that that basket holds my knitting. It will most certainly not be used to house kittens. But your idea about making a cushion for them is quite good. We've some material left over from your quilt. Let's see what else my scrap bag might have in it." Susannah smiled at Emily and touched her gently on the nose.

"Can we do it right now, Aunt Susannah?" Emily was developing quite a taste for stitchery, and anxiously awaited her aunt's verdict. Susannah insisted that she learn plain stitching first. Emily hoped that if she did an outstanding job on the cushion, perhaps she would learn embroidery stitches for the pillowcases her Aunt Susannah promised.

"Not just this minute, Emily. We haven't finished our first course, let alone dessert—and you love apple crisp!" Susannah knew that Emily not only loved apple crisp, but that she was bursting at the seams to serve some to Uncle Jackson. The sewing project was successfully, if temporarily, abandoned.

"Oh, yes, Aunt Susannah. May I serve the dessert?" The ladies cleared away the food and dishes from the first course. A stack of dessert bowls, flanked by the apple crisp and a large spoon, waited in front of Emily. She carefully put a large spoonful in one of the bowls and passed it to her uncle. Receiving a meaningful stare from Susannah, he made sure to express his appreciation of how good it smelled, looked and tasted.

"This is the best apple crisp you've ever made, Susannah. Did you do something different to it?" He directed his gaze to Susannah, but monitored Emily from the corner of his eye.

"I made it, I made it!" Emily all but shouted. Aunt Susannah watched me so I didn't make any mistakes, but I did the whole thing myself." She waited eagerly for his response.

"I bet you didn't put it into the oven or take it out, Emily. So there!" Caleb found Uncle Jackson's praise for Emily's cooking efforts, no matter how terrible they tasted, very tiring. While it was true two servings of the apple crisp had disappeared down his throat, not all of her efforts tasted this good.

"Caleb, that's a very rude and hurtful thing to say. You know that Emily isn't tall enough to use the oven safely. You aren't allowed to, either. Please apologize to your sister." Susannah presented a stern face, but was hard pressed not to laugh. She knew quite well that Caleb was jealous of the attention that Emily reaped from her cooking efforts. He lowered his head and mumbled what might have passed for an apology.

"Oh, no, young man. That's not how we apologize. Do it again, and look at your sister when you're speaking." Caleb, with a mutinous expression, glared at Emily and said "Sorry". Susannah decided to let the matter rest.

"Well, Emily, you're going to put your Aunt Susannah out of business if you continue to bake like this. She'd better watch her step, or you'll be taking over in the kitchen and the dairy! Jackson reached across the table and stroked Emily's hair. Susannah caught her breath at the tenderness of the gesture. Even more amazing, Emily leaned into his hand, a loving smile on her face. No fear of blows or abuse here; just perfect trust in the loving kindness of her uncle.

"Uncle Jackson, if they're going to sew, what are we going to do? Are the calves big enough for me to ride? I bet they're almost as good as a pony." Caleb, ever hopeful, temporarily laid aside his campaign for a pony to concentrate on the calves. They had, in his eyes, the double benefit of being meant to be ridden and much more accessible.

"You said you didn't want to keep all the bull calves, so maybe I could practice on one of them. That way, if something happened, it wouldn't cost so much money." Caleb was gradually realizing that the farm animals and produce represented money for things they needed.

"And you said that Emily and I could each have one of the bull calves for our own. Surely I could ride my very own calf."

"Caleb, I did say that you could each have a calf, but that money was to start your bank account. When you get older, you might want to buy a farm or get some training. This way you would have the money to do that." Jackson offered the sensible-to-an-adult answer. Caleb remained unimpressed.

"Also, Caleb, calves are not meant to be ridden. You could be thrown and hurt yourself very badly." Caleb ignored the statement and hurried to further his case.

"But Uncle Jackson, they aren't old enough to be sold yet, so I could ride them until they are." Caleb was nothing if not tenacious. The grip of a bulldog and Caleb's persistence were equal in strength and endurance. "Not only that, you said that handling them was good so that they would be used to people."

Jackson groaned silently. How like Caleb to remember every argument in favor of his chosen activity, but forget to gather the eggs. Caleb remained oblivious to such non sequiturs as the danger of a calf bucking him off, causing him to break an arm or leg or be trampled by the reluctant steed. He knew his riding skills more than equaled that of any calf on this farm or any other. His friend, Henry Turner, had twitted him one time too many. Henry frequently took unfair advantage not only of the six-month difference in their ages, but also that Caleb was younger than Emily, and thus the baby.

Jackson thought desperately of an activity that would equal the status and thrill of riding calves. Finally, inspiration struck.

"Caleb, you may come to the workshop with me when we're finished supper, and after you have filled the wood box. We'll decide on the type of wood and the pattern you'd like to have for a treasure box." Jackson remembered his own treasure box from his boyhood days. He still had it, though papers replaced shiny stones and petrified frogs. He waited patiently for Caleb's answer.

"Very well, Uncle Jackson, I guess that would be a good thing to do." Caleb, reluctant to abandon his Wild West adventures, submitted to the inevitability of an adult's plans superseding his own. Besides, if he just happened to lean across the back of one of the calves when he was petting it to get it used to being handled, well, who knew what would happen?

"Susannah, after the children are in bed, I'd like to discuss some plans for the farm." Susannah felt a jolt of pleasure. While not the first time that he asked for her opinion, she continued to find it both heartwarming and confusing that he considered her ideas had worth.

"I'd like that, Jackson. Perhaps after the children are asleep would be a good time. Now that the days are getting longer, they don't always settle down as quickly as they might," Susannah agreed. She knew that he planned to extend the market garden next year. Strawberry plants were now in the field closest to the house. He made sure the fences were in excellent order before he began the new bed. No more than she did he plan to have all his hard work go for naught due to sloppy preparations. She shuddered at the mental picture of the cows making themselves at home in the garden—all that work for nothing. As her two men headed for the workshop, she heard a piping treble badgering Jackson.

"What's a treasure box, Uncle Jackson? I've never heard of one of those before." Caleb began to remember the results of his only other foray into the workshop as they headed off to begin the promised project. His exploration of the tools and glue resulted in an explosion of truly monumental proportions. He recalled clearly the smarting smacks on his derriere, and assiduously avoided the building now. Uncle Jackson, whilst generally understanding, brooked no interference whatsoever in that area.

Completing the clearing of the table, the ladies discussed the merits of various types of stuffing for the kitten cushion. Hay, straw and wool each received careful consideration. Emily was in favor of wool, as it would be the softest for the kittens. Susannah finally agreed, providing that they had enough to do the job.

As the knitting basket was deemed out of bounds for a container, the ladies decided, once they finished the dishes, to check for a box in the barn. Emily was careful not to mention that Spooky's bed could be used. Spooky bunked with the children. She carefully and silently padded down the hall and into her bed in the kitchen as soon as she heard movement in Susannah's room. Spooky and Susannah had an unspoken agreement that if she didn't see a dog in one of the children's rooms, then all was quiet on the domestic front.

"Oh, look, Aunt Susannah, there they are. Aren't they just so cute? Watch, they'll come when I call." Emily tore after the kittens, intent on collecting all of them in her apron to let her aunt see just how adorable they were, and how big they were getting. She soon returned with all three.

"They certainly are cute, Emily They know you and how gentle you are. See, they aren't the least bit afraid." Susannah cuddled the tabby, while Emily endeavored to keep his twin and the soft gray one in her apron.

"That one is yours, and that is Caleb's? Have you finally decided on their names?" Many heated discussions about the thorny issue of just the right names had occurred.

"Yes, the soft gray one is mine, and I'm going to call her Shadow. Caleb wants the tabby you have, Aunt Susannah, and he's going to call him Sam. I think that's a dumb name for a cat, but he won't change his mind." Emily frequently deplored Caleb's actions and ideas. Her birthday was almost here and she would be a grown up seven, as well as, however briefly, three years older than her sibling.

"I think those are lovely names. Have you given the other kitten a name?"

"Well, I wanted to call him Stripey, but Caleb wants to call him Butch. We're still deciding." Emily's attention was mostly devoted to crooning to Shadow.

"What about calling him something to go with his mother's name? Since she's called Hissy because she has hissy fits, you could call him Mouthy, because he has the loudest meow and the loudest purr." Susannah smiled at Emily, storing up yet another memory.

"That's a good idea, Aunt Susannah. I'll tell Caleb, but he might not agree." Emily had no faith in Caleb's willingness to compromise, even if it was Aunt Susannah's idea.

Barn and dairy were inspected with care, but a kitten box was nowhere to be found. As a last resort, they decided to ask Jackson to build one for them, and returned to the house to inspect the contents of the scrap bag. Remnants of two old shirts of Jackson's provided enough fabric for the bottom, and they would use strips of the other fabrics and sew them together for the top.

In the meantime, the men first checked the stock and then headed for the workshop. Caleb, still chastened from his last venture into his uncle's domain, hung back at the door.

"Come on in, Caleb. You're welcome here if you're invited and I'm here, but not allowed to even open the door if I'm not." Thoughts of the mayhem wrought by eager and inquisitive hands surged to the front of Jackson's mind. Shortly after he brought the children back to the farm, Caleb found the magical work shop. By the time Jackson made his own discovery, the culprit had glued every tool he could reach to a waiting surface. Climbing the ladder to the loft resulted in a torn jacket. Nails protruded from the floor at various levels, indicating a commendable ability to stick to a project. The nails also created a formidable tripping hazard. As his hand shot out to grasp the work bench when his foot met the crooked row, it landed on a sharp chisel, adding blood to glue and sawdust.

"Yes, Uncle Jackson." Caleb replied. He stepped over the doorsill and into a magical world of tools, redolent of the wonderful smell of freshly-cut wood.

"Pull up a stool, son, and we'll sketch some ideas on paper before we begin." Jackson smiled, remembering almost the same words said to him many years ago by his father. "Do you want it to be the same size as mine? What do you think you'll put in it?" He swiveled on his stool to face Caleb, leaned his head on one hand and waited.

"Oh, yes, Uncle Jackson, it should be the same size as yours. I'm going to get my treasures and put them there. Henry and I found three wonderful stones. Two are like magic. They look dull when they're dry, but sparkle if you spit on them and hold them in the sun." Caleb could hardly contain himself, imagining his very own treasure box. Henry didn't have one, and he didn't think that anyone in Henry's family did, either.

"I'll bet those Turner boys don't know about treasure boxes. Just wait 'til I tell old Henry. He'll turn green!" Gleefully anticipating his friend's envy, Caleb wiggled on his stool, then mimicked Jackson's pose.

Very well, Caleb," Jackson said, rubbing his upper lip to disguise a grin, "we'll make it the same size as mine. Now we'll have to draw a picture and put the dimensions on it. Do you know what dimensions are?" He waited for the answer.

"Nope, Uncle Jackson, but I bet they'll look great!" Caleb's enthusiasm increased. Turning his head and reaching for a ruler, Jackson's grin expanded. What a little snorter this boy was. Into trouble up to his neck on one day, and charming the pants off his uncle on the next.

"Dimensions are measurements. We have to know how wide and long and deep, or tall it will be so that we know which pieces of wood to use." Jackson quickly sketched the box and jotted down the measurements.

"What kind of wood will we use? Does it matter? Is one kind better than another?" Caleb was anxious to get to the good stuff—sawing and hammering. They seemed to be taking a long time doing nothing but talking.

"Well, cedar or apple wood smell good. Oak is hard to work with when it's been aged, but it lasts forever. Pine has a beautiful grain and is soft. Let's see what we have against that wall." They moved to the far side of the shop. "Look at this cedar. Doesn't it smell good? This would make a fine box." Caleb, sensing that the saw was almost in his hand, agreed, barely glancing at the board.

"Now, let's see if we have enough." Jackson unfolded his wooden ruler and measured the board. Leftovers, sawn into small pieces and sanded, would be sewn into sachets to protect linens and clothing. As he hefted the board and turned, he almost tripped over his enthusiastic assistant.

"Why don't you sit on that stool, Caleb, and hold the ruler for me while I get this ready to saw." Jackson foresaw the need to devise many small and seemingly important tasks to satisfy his helper. Measuring completed, he began.

"I bet I could do that, Uncle Jackson. I bet I could do that real good," chirruped a voice at his elbow, jaw in perfect alignment to be struck on the next back stroke.

"OK, Caleb, why don't you put your hand on mine so that you can get the rhythm? Then, when we have some smaller pieces to cut, you can help." Resigned to an overly eager and helpful co-participant, Jackson sighed. He quickly completed cutting the pieces for the top and bottom. He braced himself for Caleb's first foray into woodworking—the first supervised foray, that was.

Just then the door of the shop opened and Susannah and Emily appeared. "We were wondering if you could make us a box for the kittens' cushion. It should be about this big." Susannah's hands drew the dimensions in the air, trusting that Jackson would know what she wanted.

"Sure, Susannah, that's about two feet square, and about six inches high?"

"Yes, thanks, that will be perfect." She turned away from the door, careful not to intrude on the men of the family. She appreciated receiving the dimensions from Jackson. It would never do to have the cushion and the box different sizes.

"Emily and I are taking our sewing to the arbor—it's a shame to be indoors on such a beautiful day. We'll be back later to see how the box is coming along."

"OK, then, Caleb. Now we're ready for you to cut the sides. The first thing we have to do is measure the wood. We want them to be four inches high and ten inches long, and we need one for each side.

"I've been learning my numbers, Uncle Jackson, and I can show you on the ruler where the number four is and the number ten." Caleb's chest expanded with pride. Just wait until Henry heard that not only was allowed back in the work shop, but that he could saw some of the wood for this wonderful treasure box.

"That's good, Caleb. Now, show me where they are." Caleb complied, and was set up with a small stool on that to rest the wood. Jackson curled his body around Caleb's, enjoying the smell of small boy, and carefully guided his hand and supported the lumber. "I can see you're going to be a fine carpenter and a good farm worker when you grow up." His small helper beamed and lifted his head, striking his uncle's nose with unerring accuracy. Jackson's eyes watered as he cautiously dabbed his nose, fearful of finding blood.

"As soon as we sand the pieces, we'll glue and clamp them and leave them to dry." They settled down in perfect amity, sandpaper-wrapped blocks of wood in their hands.

Later, with the children asleep, the adults each took a cup of coffee and settled on the veranda.

"I really enjoy these times, Jackson. Our work is done, the children are asleep, and a kind of peace enfolds the end of the day." Susannah rocked gently as she sipped.

"Me too. When I sit on my front porch or go for a walk, I can't imagine living in a town and surrounded by buildings. Here I can see my fields and plan. Or, discuss with you, as I've been intending to do, hiring a farm couple and the changes that will mean." Jackson watched his wife rest her head against the high chair back as she continued to rock and sip. He contrasted the relaxation of her body, looking practically boneless, with her wariness when she arrived. Every time she smiled or leaned into him, he gave thanks that at last she was overcoming the brutality in her past.

"Well, we've discussed the expansion of the dairy so that I could have a room to age my cheddar. Do you see both of them working on the land and me in the dairy and watching the children, if they have any? The house that Caleb and Emily's parents used only needs a good cleaning—it's perfectly sound." She straightened slightly, but the rocker's rhythm remained unchanged.

"I'd like to get a couple around our age, with children." he continued. "The wife will take over the kitchen garden and have at least basic skills in the dairy. The husband and I would handle the market garden and the farming. I'd also like to expand the orchard, so if he had skills in that area it would be good." Jackson eyed her carefully. Their relationship was deepening every day, enriching his life beyond all expectations. He was anxious to ease her burden.

"That would be excellent, Jackson, and I'd certainly enjoy the company. If we ate lunch together it would save time. They could still have breakfast and supper by themselves. Where would you advertise? Here in Marcher Mills, or in Toronto and Hamilton?"

"All three places, in the hope of a fast response. I also wrote to Ethan some time ago and asked him to keep his eye out for a likely couple. More people are emigrating. Ethan's shop acts as a clearinghouse for local gossip. With any luck we'll have our couple in place before winter."

He shifted on the chair and smiled complacently. This was the stuff of dreams: a loving wife, two lively children and an established foothold in the community. His foresight in bringing more cattle with him, especially the young bull, proved to be particularly astute. He had received a number of inquiries about just when he would be offering the bull's services.

Susannah's heart pounded. Only the sternest admonitions that the likelihood of Ethan's ability to find a couple before someone local applied for the position permitted her to keep a semblance of calm. She admonished herself to remember that worrying about something that might happen was useless.

Reaching for Susannah's hand, he raised it to his lips, gently nipping her knuckles before kissing them softly. His reward was a rosy blush. She took her back slowly, eyes downcast.

"Come, wife, time for bed." He laughed as he felt her hands pushing him toward the bedroom.

Wife Seller!

CHAPTER FIFTEEN

Susannah carefully closed the kitchen door, admired her flowerbeds on the way to the buggy, and eyed her small family with satisfaction. Caleb and Emily were neatly attired, with stout shoes and shining faces. Her own dress and bonnet were additional reflections of Jackson's generosity and the farm's prosperity. A feeling of feminine satisfaction warmed her—stylish clothing made of good fabric gave her a confidence not experienced for many years. The children's demeanor reflected pride in their new clothes, and her husband's crisply-ironed shirt and well-brushed coat and pants completed the picture.

Jackson's pride in his little family surprised him. It was his duty, he reflected, to provide for his wife and children, but this went beyond duty. He felt that they were a family, a unit.

Susannah counted over the items on her shopping list. In addition to sugar and starch, she needed thread and some yarn to knit warm clothing for the coming fall and winter. Christmas had entered her thoughts lately, and visions of caps, scarves and mittens for all the members of her family expanded to include that of a dark blue sweater to match her husband's dark blue eyes. Those pleasant summer breezes would soon become cold and sharp—reason enough for warm and sturdy clothing.

She stubbornly refused to admit any softening in her attitude towards Jackson in spite of their growing physical intimacy. Trusting a man, even one like him, was difficult. She knew that Albert's behavior was responsible for her fear, but it didn't make the trusting easier.

Jackson's demeanor could not be faulted. He was unfailingly courteous, even helpful. He seemed to have a real appreciation of the backbreaking labor involved in scrubbing, rinsing, boiling, starching, spreading or hanging garments to dry, and then bringing them in, only to be dampened and ironed. Over the past weeks they developed into a team—he to start the fire and fill the washing machine, scrubbing and rinsing tubs while she finished the breakfast dishes and started something for the nooning.

She refused to remember how she awoke to find herself plastered against his back, or even worse, his front. That was just a natural progression of the fact that they frequently made love. Feelings of affection were a far cry from love. Love meant vulnerability and a lowering of defenses. The momentary shortness of breath and jolt her heart experienced when seeing him unexpectedly was not love. It simply indicated surprise. Constantly striving to find ways to please him was just good manners given his helpfulness towards her —nothing more.

Her introspection was interrupted when a warm little hand wormed its way beneath hers. Then a small, light body relaxed into her side. Emily's acceptance grew steadily, but spontaneous signs of affection were few. Susannah cherished and counted over each one, like a miser counting his hoard.

Caleb rebuffed her attempts at hugs, but would permit her to smooth his hair. Occasionally. Reluctantly. His preferred method of indicating approval was the inclusion of Aunt Susannah in his activities. While she could, with fortitude, admire the pretty colors in a caterpillar, or enthuse over his ability to lead the calves with confidence, she paled at snakes, mice or rats. Her Herculean resolve not to flee, scream or kill the horrible things went unnoticed and unappreciated.

Jackson enjoyed the sporadic brushing of Susannah's shoulder against his arm. She appeared to be totally unaware of either the contact or the fact that she felt relaxed with him. Just relaxed. Well, actually quite relaxed. Relaxed to such an extent that she no longer stiffened and pulled away. He admired the gentle curves that were appearing as her appetite improved and her nervousness decreased.

A pocket of his vest contained a very special list. He anticipated her eyes widening and her breath catching, with that accompanying and exciting lifting of her bosom, when she unwrapped her Christmas presents. They would select presents for the children together, but his personal gifts to her must be a complete surprise. While very aware of Susannah's gradual acceptance of him, the children, and her new home, he failed to recognize the same signs in himself. Pleasing her was simply the welcome duty and pleasure of a caring husband.

Planning for Caleb's ongoing education in farm husbandry and equipment had become such second nature that he couldn't remember not arranging his life in such a manner. Nor did he think of himself as a sacrificial goat when Emily "surprised" him with a special treat from her cooking. No matter what happened—too much of one ingredient, forgetfulness of the passage of time and the subsequent charred bits—Jackson consumed them with every indication of enjoyment, and much praise for a blushing young cook. Provisions for Emily's future were also an integral part of his plans. She would be able to choose teaching or nursing. She might wish to be a librarian. Whatever she wanted to do, there would be money for her education.

He reveled in the beautiful late summer day and an outing with his family.

"Susannah, has anyone told you of our fall fair?"

"No, is that somewhat like a church fete?"

"More like a harvest fair, really. People bring the best of their stock and produce for judging. Everyone can participate, and there are events for the children—foot races and such. The women enter their quilts, knitting, preserves, dairy products and baking. There's even a box lunch, with the proceeds going for the church, or school or some other community project."

"What would you enter, Jackson? Your cattle?"

"Yes, and some of our produce. I'd also like to take one or two of the cows I brought from England. Ayrshires don't seem to be well known around here, although several people inquired about that young bull I brought with me. Why don't you enter some of your cheeses? And your butter? Your butter is acquiring a glowing reputation at the market. People are asking for it at the general store." Jackson was quite sure that her confidence would let her to participate in a contest, but he kept an eye on her reaction.

She was amazed. "Oh, Jackson, do you think they're good enough? I could only enter the cheeses that ripen quickly, or that don't need to ripen at all. Maybe next year some of the cheddar would be ready if we add that room to the dairy." She thrilled at the idea that Jackson considered her products good enough to be entered in such a contest.

Next year, Jackson thought. *Next year sounds very comfortable indeed.* "Those quick cheeses you make are the best I've ever tasted. Besides, it's only good sense to introduce the cattle and some of their produce at the same time. They even have a category for best pets, so the children could take one of the kittens and the puppy. What am I saying—make that two kittens and no puppy." They smiled at each other. "As for the produce, the pumpkins, oats and barley were particularly good this year, so I'll enter them, too."

Next year, Susannah thought. *I said next year and didn't even have to think about it. It just came out, and sounded grand.*

Smiling and sneaking glances at each other out of the corners of their eyes, Jackson and Susannah took their little family to town. Her bubble of happiness popped when, as they passed the first signs of the town, Caleb leapt up, waved his hat in the air, and screamed, "We're here and we're the best. Country people are better than town people."

The adults turned simultaneously to view the rebel in their midst. Jackson pulled the team to a halt.

"Where did you hear such drivel?" Jackson thundered, pulling Caleb back down onto the seat.

"Caleb, I'm ashamed of you. Where are your manners?" cried Susannah at the same time. She was appalled. What would people think of her if she couldn't control her charges any better than this? The acceptance she received from the Ladies Sewing Circle and her inclusion in the church's Women's Circle were very precious to her. She looked at her husband to see how he would handle the matter.

Caleb, unrepentant, proudly reported that his good friend (and fellow troublemaker), Henry Turner, told him that townies were soft, and the country fellows had it all over them. "Indeed.! snapped Susannah, "Did he bother to mention that the town boys might think the same thing about the country boys?"

"He said they might try to fool me, but that they were the fools and that we country boys were the best and the ones to beat and that we could beat them to flinders without even...."

"Caleb." One word, spoken quietly, but it had an amazing effect on the would-be warrior. Caleb settled his hat on his head, hitched his trousers, lowered his eyes, and replied in his softest voice "Yes, Uncle Jackson."

Susannah braced herself for Jackson to discipline Caleb. One part of her recognized this as an automatic reaction developed from years of living with abuse. The other part was ashamed. Jackson had proved himself over and over again, and he never acted harshly. Still, she was shocked to hear him say:

"Caleb, do you really think that's true, or are you just repeating what your friend said?"

Silence. Susannah saw Emily try to stifle a giggle with her hand, and gave her a nudge.

"Be quiet, Emily. This is serious," she whispered. Immediately Emily put her hands on her lap and straightened her back. Her face was solemn, but Susannah detected an unquenchable glimmer in her eye.

"Caleb, I asked you a question." Jackson eyed his charge with a stern look.

"Yessir." mumbled Caleb, his head drooping towards his chest.

"Yessir what? I asked you a question. Do you know for a fact that what you said was true, or were you just repeating what someone else said, without thinking about whether or not it was true?"

Susannah thought this too difficult for a little boy not yet five, but she held her tongue. Jackson had shown himself to be unfailingly fair to the children, and he was never cruel. However, she still thought that the question was too difficult.

"I jes' said what Henry did, Uncle Jackson. He said that he heard the older boys at school say that, so it must be true." Although muffled by his chin-on-chest position, the answer was clear.

"But do you know that it's true, Caleb? I believe Henry said that, but it still doesn't answer my question about whether you think it's true." Jackson's voice remained level and his manner unthreatening, but the implacable tone in his voice indicated that Caleb must answer his question.

"I guess I really don't know if it's true, Uncle Jackson, but I thought Henry would know, 'cause he's a big boy." Caleb's voice was very soft and his eyes bright with unshed tears, but he lifted his head and faced his uncle bravely.

"Well, then, Caleb, maybe you should check your facts first. You can always ask me. A man always makes sure of his facts."

Caleb hung his head again, trying in vain to hide his red face and teary eyes.

"OK, Uncle Jackson, I'll make sure of my facts the next time. It's just that I don't know what facts are." Caleb's voice trembled with suppressed sobs.

Jackson put his hand on Caleb's shoulder. "Good boy, Caleb, I'm proud of you. It takes a real man to admit he might be wrong, and an even bigger one to say out loud that he'll try to do better. To know if something is a fact means to know if it's true." Caleb lifted his head and leaped at his uncle, practically strangling him with a hug.

Susannah was stunned. She couldn't believe what she had just seen and heard. Jackson handled the situation in such a way that Caleb felt good about his promise to get the facts first. Their relationship just added another brick of trust and mutual respect to its foundation. She contrasted this with the authoritarian upbringing of her own youth and with the hell she endured in her marriage.

"That was so well done, Jackson," she murmured. "Now he knows that he did was wrong, but, more importantly, he knows why it was wrong. I hope I can do as well as you when my turn comes."

Jackson mused over such praise. Caleb was his to care for and love, and he handled the situation as his father would have.

"Thank you. You handle the children so well, too." They continued to face each other until Susannah felt the color rise in her cheeks. She pretended to smooth her skirt and straighten Emily's bonnet to give her complexion a chance to cool. Jackson grinned as he turned the rig into an empty space in front of the mercantile.

CHAPTER SIXTEEN

Susannah reminded Emily that she was to wait for Uncle Jackson to help them down—just like real ladies. It required considerable time and effort on Jackson's part to convince Susannah that he regarded this as both a privilege and a right. Susannah, accustomed to doing things herself if she wanted them done at all, had a hard time complying. Finally, when he started speaking between clenched teeth, she acquiesced. Now, she realized, she waited as a matter of course. Emily, torn between wanting to be a big lady and an overwhelming zeal to check out the candy jars, jigged in place. Jackson grasped her around the waist and gently set her on the sidewalk with a grin and a reminder to just look, but don't touch. As he had learned to do through painful experience, he lined the children up and made them repeat, "If it isn't yours, don't touch." They obeyed without question. This was just something Uncle Jackson always did. They knew as soon as they repeated the words, they could investigate the candy counter.

Stepping back to the wagon, he used his thumb to push his hat back on his head. He admired his wife as she rearranged the strings of her reticule on her arm before leaning forward to place her hands on his shoulders.

"Do I have to remind you about touching?" he said with a sly grin. She was shocked at this blatant reminder of last night, and lowered her head to hide her blush, refusing to answer. A smile tugged at her lips. Jackson, his reward the telltale color still high on her cheeks, relented and assisted her to the ground. While tempted to slide one arm under her legs, the other behind her back and carry her right into the store, he felt it prudent to forego what would certainly bring on a blistering scold. As their relationship began to ripen, Susannah's fears decreased as her trust increased. She exhibited a delightful sense of humor as well as a strong sense of propriety that was his pleasure to ruffle. Recognizing his teasing as a sign of affection, she had yet to initiate love play, but her responsiveness continued to grow.

Susannah busied herself with resettling her reticule and brushing out her skirts, refusing to look at Jackson until her blush had faded and her composure returned. Then, lifting her head and looking her tormentor straight in the eye, she suggested, "Shall we meet at the restaurant when we've finished our chores? I'll be awhile, as I want to discuss selling some of my jams and jellies to Zeke. He indicated an interest, and it's a good way to get the name of your farm known to more people."

"That's our farm Susannah, and don't you forget it." Jackson's smile had faded. This ongoing struggle showed no signs of a quick resolution, but some progress was being made. Susannah insisted on referring to his house, his barn, his cattle and his farm. However, he noticed that she claimed the children as her own, unless they had been naughty, when they reverted to being his.

"Our farm, Jackson. Sorry." Susannah bit the inside of her cheek to keep from smiling. Comfortable enough in the relationship to recognize his sincerity, she couldn't help herself. He always rose to the bait, and hadn't yet realized that her insistence on the "his" part of her remarks was a ploy. She knew that his outrageousness in offending her sense of propriety was largely assumed, and this was her subtle revenge.

"Very well, then. Yes, let's meet at Sampson's in an hour and a half. Will that be enough time? I'm sure Moira will still have pie, no matter what time we get there. After I unload the wagon I want to speak with Marvin Sanderson at the livery. We have a bumper crop of hay this year, and he might be interested. Also, I want to make arrangements for some iron work." Jackson had long since decided that his home and farm would be as fine as he could manage. He wanted to order hinges for the planned addition to the dairy that would match those already in place, as well as some special items for Christmas.

"I'm sure that'll be enough time, Jackson." Susannah turned and hurried after the children. Admonitions notwithstanding, young minds soon forgot rules when faced with temptation.

As she entered the store, Susannah pulled out her list and a jar of strawberry jam. She had taken some pains to determine that it was Zeke's favorite. His wife, Doreen, claimed she had no time to do preserves, which was probably true. The Marshall's had a thriving business, with their store open for long hours, especially on Saturday nights.

First Susannah checked that Caleb and Emily were engrossed in deciding on which candy they would choose. It had become tradition to treat them each time they came to town. She placed the jar on the counter. One or two customers were browsing, but Zeke hurried over when he saw her.

No matter how many times she came to the store, Susannah was amazed at the complex scents and incredible amount of merchandise gathered in one place. With dry goods on one side, produce on the other, and a variety of implements dangling from the ceiling, it was a treasure trove. She noted a particularly colorful display of yarns and made a mental note to inspect them thoroughly before she left. The pervasive and delicious scent of freshly ground coffee drew her toward the counter where the shiny cash register stood beside the coffee grinder. First she had to address the matter of selling jams and jellies to Zeke and Doreen. Then she would broach the subject of including her pickles, in addition to the jams and jellies.

"Here it is, Zeke, as we discussed. Lovely bright red strawberry jam, made with our own berries. I also have plum, peach, raspberry, blackberry and red and black currant, as well as crab apple and other jellies." As she spoke, she opened the jar and pulled the string imbedded in the wax to reveal the contents. "Perhaps you'd like to taste it," she continued, smiling. She pulled a spoon from her pocket. "The proof of the pudding, you know...."

Zeke whipped the spoon from her hand and scooped a large dollop of the jam and popped it into his mouth. "Mmmmm, just as promised, Susannah." The spoon swooped jam-ward again "Yes, Doreen and I have decided that we'll take ten jars of each kind you have and see how they sell. Will you take the proceeds in kind, or do you prefer cash?" The spoon continued foraging.

Susannah, reflecting that her hoard of coins was pitifully small, responded. "I'll take half in kind and half in cash, Zeke."

"Well done, Susannah; let's shake and seal the deal." He reached across the counter to take her hand. "Did you have any purchases in mind today?" Then he smiled and whispered "Of course, that's in addition to the candy that I notice always walks out clutched in two sets of no-doubt grubby hands!"

"Indeed I do, Zeke. Here's my list. While you're filling it, I'm just going to look at those beautiful yarns that Doreen promised me she'd ordered." Leaving her list on the counter, Susannah walked briskly toward her goal, pausing only to remind the children not to touch anything in the store.

"Yes, Aunt Susannah," they chorused dutifully, but she was not totally convinced they had heard her. The yarns made her fingers itch for her knitting needles. Quickly calculating how much she would need for sweaters, scarves and mitts for each of the children, she picked up enough navy blue to make a sweater for Jackson. As she placed her selection on the counter, she leaned across and, speaking softly, requested Zeke to lay aside enough of the bright yellow and dark green for the children.

"I'll pick it up when I bring in the jam. I don't want them to see what I have." Giving her a wink, Zeke made a note on a pad and promised to have the package ready when she returned. "I'll just check the fabrics. I need a particular shade of red for the blocks I'm doing for the church quilt." As she headed toward the bolts of fabric, she reflected on how her life had changed. Her circle of friends had grown to include people from many different parts of the community. They considered her an integral part of projects as a matter of course. What she didn't notice was that her spine was straight, her shoulders back, and her chin tilted at an angle that betokened confidence.

Jackson pulled out his watch. He had become so engrossed in conversation at the smithy that time had flown. His plans in place for sled runners and fancy hinges as part of his Christmas surprises, he had just enough time to meet Susannah and the children at the restaurant. He shook his head when he remembered Susannah's initial reaction to "paying for someone else to cook". She was appalled that he would "waste" money on such an extravagance. Now she no longer demurred, but frequently mentioned how nice it was to eat something someone else had prepared. He treasured each small step in her growing ability to enjoy a healthy, giving relationship.

CHAPTER SEVENTEEN

"And that's how the little lamb was saved." Susannah looked down at Emily and Caleb. They were sitting on the hearthrug, immersed in the tale of the lamb that tried to find adventure but was so happy to be safely home again. She became aware of a painful lump in her throat and a burning sensation in her eyes. So many, many times she pictured herself in just this role—her children at her feet, the house in order, and trust and happiness enveloping the whole family.

"Aunt Susannah, why didn't the lamb have more adventures?" asked Caleb. "I would have. When I get big I'm going to have lots and lots of adventures and not be a cry-baby and run home and I'll be brave and strong and...."

"Caleb, Caleb, take a breath," advised Susannah, smiling broadly. "You'll choke on all those 'ands' and lose your voice."

"Oh, he's just full of himself," scorned Emily. "He's always saying he'll grow up and have adventures, but first he has to stop being afraid of the dark."

"I am not afraid of the dark" declared Caleb, stung by the truth of her statement.

"Are, too," retorted his sister. "That's why you always want to come into my bed when you wake up in the middle of the night. You're just a baby." Emily smirked in that particularly irritating way of older sisters, knowing that this would raise Caleb's ire to new levels.

"I am not a baby," roared Caleb. "And I'm not afraid of the dark or anything. So there!"

"Now, now," Susannah soothed. "Let's make some fudge for a treat. Don't you think that your Uncle Jackson will like that?"

"Yes, yes," chorused the children. The argument dissolved into a serious discussion of whether the walnuts should be placed carefully on top of the fudge, or cut up and included in it.

As Susannah organized her cooking assistants, striving desperately to find chores that sounded very important and did not involve working near the stove or using sharp utensils, her thoughts returned to her past. Somehow events had swept her into a maelstrom, and she failed to see any way to resolve her dilemma without causing serious problems for every one of these precious people. Jackson would be shamed before the community. She would definitely go to jail. The children would carry the stigma of her actions with them throughout their lives.

Sometimes she could pretend so hard and so well that pretense became reality. She was a beloved wife and mother. The place she created in the community was one of respect. Her efforts in their dairy and home rewarded her with happiness, confidence, compliments from Jackson, and a considerable addition to the family exchequer. The children praised her cooking, offered hugs and kisses, brought her their little woes, and regarded her in the light of a mother.

The snake in this burgeoning Garden of Eden flicked its tongue from time to time. The community had many and varied ties to the outside world. The railroad made travel between Marcher Mills and Toronto commonplace. England was generous with its emigrants, most of whom, Susannah was convinced, settled in Marcher Mills and its environs. Sooner or later there would be some from Yorkshire, perhaps even from her village, and all would be revealed. Determined to save her little family, Susannah had started to squirrel away coins whenever possible. While she now had enough to purchase a ticket to Toronto, Burlington or Hamilton, she was beginning to realize, as she became better acquainted with her neighbors, that escape would not be easy.

Thoughts of changing her appearance occupied her as she scrubbed Jackson's trousers, mended Caleb's shirts, or whipped lace onto a petticoat for Emily. Cudgeling her brain for a way to disappear and save her loved ones, she considered cutting or coloring her hair, learning to limp, and never working in a dairy again. Her skills in the kitchen were adequate, but would not earn her a job as a cook in any truly respectable establishment. The drudgery of a life as a chambermaid appalled her. Being the housekeeper of a medium-sized home was well within her purview but held little interest. Increasingly she enjoyed the loving exchanges with the children, and fought hard to resist Jackson's attractiveness.

"I love you," trembled on her tongue, but she ruthlessly fought down the emotion that threatened to overwhelm her and make her blurt the words. She loved Jackson. Had done so for quite some time, she admitted. But somehow, if she kept the words to herself, then maybe he would be able to find someone else. Even thoughts of leaving her shawl on a riverbank as to indicate her demise in the swiftly-flowing river occurred to her, but the knowledge that she could swim was bound to come out.

"Aunt Susannah, isn't the fudge ready yet?" Caleb's attention span, always notoriously short, would lead to mischief unless diverted.

"Let's test the fudge to see if we've reached the softball stage," Susannah suggested.

"Yes, yes," enthused her fudge-making team. "Let's test for that!"

"First we need some really, really cold water. We'll pump until it's just the right temperature."

A heated discussion on the merits of boys versus girls as pumpers ceased when Susannah handed each of the children a glass and instructed them to take turns testing for coldness. She knew they would get as much water on themselves as in the glass, but peace reigned. Finally the self-appointed experts declared themselves satisfied, and two half-full glasses made their way to the table. They each received some of the fudge. After a discussion on the merits of its readiness, excess water carefully poured off and spoons issued, a blissful silence ensued.

Susannah removed the candy from the heat, added some vanilla, a dollop of butter and chopped walnuts (a compromise of walnuts being necessary both in and on the fudge having been negotiated), and prepared to finish the candy. Her helpers soon left to follow other pursuits, leaving her the thankless task of beating until her arm threatened to drop off. When she poured the candy onto a greased plate, she found herself the sole member of the decorating committee.

Carefully scoring, then cutting the fudge and testing the requisite piece, she realized that she had too much time to think.

Jackson's steadiness, loving kindness to the children, and care and consideration for her had combined to heal her soul and help to restore her faith in men. As her energy and confidence increased, so did her libido. For the first time in her life she was discovering the joys of a healthy relationship.

"Susannah, isn't that fudge ready yet?" The voice was perilously close to her right ear. Her treacherous body listed toward the source of warmth and excitement. She jerked away, trying to camouflage the move as a turn. Hardly an improvement, as she now faced her nemesis, her nose mere inches away from the third button of his shirt. The longing to lean against his strength, even momentarily, almost overwhelmed her.

"I, I, yes," she stammered.

Jackson laughed. "I, I, yes? What kind of statement is that?" His control over his voice was admirable, but Susannah noticed that somehow that same button was almost pressed against her nose, forcing her to look into the face of her delightful tormenter. She tried to step back, but the table blocked her path, resulting in an embarrassing posture that thrust her hips towards him. She could feel her face flushing, and wished for a shawl to draw across her breasts. Part of her was still shocked that any man or situation could cause these pleasurable feelings. Another part feared his realization of her vulnerability that might cause him to take advantage.

"Have some fudge, Jackson. It's ready now."

"Uh, Susannah, you've probably noticed that I'm becoming more interested in non-food activities. Perhaps you should just hand me a piece of fudge." Susannah glared.

"You are perfectly able to control yourself enough to back up and get some." No sooner were the words out of her mouth than she realized the *double entendre*. Her husband, feet glued to the floor and a gleam in his eye, began to grin.

"Stop that this instant, Jackson Stansfield. Just behave yourself. You know exactly what I mean." Unrepentant, grin broadening, he leaned closer, his breath stirring the wisps of hair that drifted around her red face.

"No! Do I? I'm not sure why you're so hot and bothered, wife. I only asked for a little piece. Of candy. Fudge. The stuff on the plate." His voice, its very softness exaggerating the sibilants that moved those tickling tresses, continued. "And after all, it was just one piece. Of fudge, that is. Not many pieces. Of fudge, of course."

Susannah's embarrassment, tempered by unwanted laughter, was waning. "Behave yourself! I'm calling the children right now." Not giving her spouse further chances to breach her defenses, she called, "Caleb, Emily, the fudge is ready." Desperately, she grabbed the plate and thrust it between them, stepping to one side. Caleb and Emily ran into the kitchen, eager for the treat.

Jackson snatched a piece of fudge, then kissed her on the cheek. His merry whistle followed him out the door. Susannah stood as if frozen. It had been such a loving gesture. She realized that the fudge plate had been used as a barrier, not in fear, but as a method of controlling her own treacherous body. Enjoying each other in bed, in the dark, was one thing. Casual demonstrations of affection, in public, in daylight, even in front of such incurious viewers as the children, were quite something else again.

"Aunt Susannah, please may we have some fudge?" She looked down at the two happy faces.

"Of course, lambkins, but only one piece each or you'll spoil your supper." As Emily and Caleb argued over which pieces were the biggest, Susannah tried to stop trembling. She was shocked to realize that passion, not fear, had caused her reaction.

Wife Seller!

CHAPTER EIGHTEEN

Jackson lifted the last box of preserves and nestled it carefully in the bed of straw covering the floor of the wagon. Emily and Caleb ran from the house, followed by Susannah, who carried her carefully wrapped quilt. She was plagued by worries about her entries in the various categories. From her attendance at the local interfaith women's meetings she understood that the ranking at the end of the day affected not only personal pride, but had an immediate effect on the status of both the farm and its owners. In spite of the high praise received for her dairy products—and it was her dairy, in spite of the fact that Jackson owned the farm—she realized that anything less than a stellar showing could be disastrous. Her self-esteem, affection, and respect for her husband had increased daily. It was thus vitally important to her that she not merely place, but win, especially in the dairy categories.

He encouraged the children to sit down on the blankets covering the straw just behind the seat. He was anxious to get his family to the fair and their exhibits in place so that he could check on the milch cow and young bull he was entering in their respective classes. They appeared to be settling well when he took them in earlier. He would feel much more comfortable, however, when he could keep an eye on them. Also, he anticipated a day with his family and friends. The fall fair was more than a pleasant family outing: it was a celebration of a year's work. He, too, realized that a good showing at the fair ensured higher prices for his produce, as well as recognition and status in the community at large.

Caleb and Emily chattered excitedly. They were entering their kittens in the children's section. Uncle Jackson's reaction to the pleas that Spooky be included in the contest convinced them that the kittens were as far as their uncle would go when it came to pets taken to the fair. Emily resolved to enter a sampler next year. This was their first Canadian fair and the Turner children had proved particularly vociferous and enthusiastic in their detailing of the various entertainments provided by the carnies who travelled from town to town.

"I hope we do well, Jackson. I'm very nervous." Susannah adjusted her bonnet and swallowed audibly.

"So am I, Susannah. I have great hopes for that young bull of ours. If he does well at the fair, I'll be able to increase his stud fee. The quality of our dairy produce is already recognized, and Daisy will reinforce my claims for the Ayrshire breed." Jackson thought of the joy in their relationship. He and Susannah were truly married and worked together like a well-matched team to create a home. Lately he had begun to think in terms of a son or daughter of his own.

She paused to reflect that she felt comfortable in volunteering a subject for discussion. In the months since she arrived in Marcher Mills to meet her new husband and family, her fear for her own safety had virtually disappeared. Now the fear was for him and the children should her secret be discovered. She welcomed passionate embraces and lively conversations equally. The fact that Jackson consulted her about her requirements in the dairy, in addition to soliciting her opinion about various matters, no longer surprised her.

As she turned to check on the children, their voices rising in argument about whose kitten would win in the pet contest, she smiled with joy. Emily and Caleb had occasionally referred to her and Jackson as Mummy and Daddy, and she treasured each instance of their growing confidence. Just yesterday Jackson suggested adoption, and she agreed. They would truly be her children in law, as well as in affection.

"Are we there, yet?" Caleb's voice, perilously close to a whine, came floating over the seat.

"Almost, Caleb. Just a few more minutes." Susannah turned again to view their little family. Emily, of course, was picture perfect—not a curl out of place. Caleb, on the other hand, had a smudge of dirt on his cheek, his hair was standing on end, and one of his shirttails dangled down the front of his pants. She sighed. No doubt hers was not the only young lad who became dirty and disheveled while sitting still, but it was small comfort to have all her efforts put to waste before they even arrived. She took her handkerchief from her reticule, directed him to spit on it, and cleaned the smudge on his cheek. Experience taught that it did no good to give Caleb a comb, so hair and shirttail would be addressed when they arrived. Then Emily screamed.

"The kitties, the kitties! They're out of their box!" Jackson sighed and pulled the team to a halt. He knew exactly who engineered the escape. A curious and bored four-year-old "just checked to see if they were all right". No thought of asking for assistance crossed Caleb's mind. The lid was now tilted a drunken angle against the erstwhile cage, and two small kittens were exploring their new environment with vigor and no thought to safety. With the escapees retrieved, Jackson prudently placed the box on the seat between him and Susannah, giving her a droll look.

"You're not helping, you know. Even covering your mouth and looking straight ahead can't hide the fact that your whole body is shaking with giggles."

Susannah, mopping her eyes with her shawl, cast a glance at her husband. Attempting to steady her voice, she replied. "That's a fact, Jackson. That's a fact." She noticed that he bit his cheek in a vain endeavor to control a grin, and his shoulders, too, were shaking.

"Thank heaven we didn't bring the puppy. I shudder to think how long it would have taken to catch her as she investigated every interesting scent along the road!" Susannah reveled in her new life. Jackson displayed all of Michael's good humor and gentleness. His anger was never used to punish or humiliate. The incident of the glued-to-everything tools was, in her opinion, the ultimate test.

"Did you know they had over three thousand people attending the fair last year? They think they'll exceed that number this year. Given this wonderful weather, that just might happen. I'm glad I didn't have to take my animals more than a couple of miles. One year only half of the exhibitors showed up due to a bad storm." Jackson had been filling their ears with facts and stories about the fair for the past month. She knew his hopes for his young bull were high indeed, and he felt the milch cow they entered had an excellent chance of placing in the top five in the county.

"Look, children, there are the Turners. As soon as we get your kittens in place, you may visit with your friends, but you must be in sight of either your uncle or me. It's all too easy to get lost in such a big crowd."

She feared her warnings fell on deaf ears. Only her firm grip on Caleb's arm kept him in the wagon, the kittens' fate of no interest whatsoever when his best friend and partner in crime waved to him. She noticed that Mrs. Turner's grasp on Henry's coat had turned her knuckles white with the force she exerted to keep her son in place. Jackson drew the wagon to a halt beside the Turners.

"Hello, Georgina", said Susannah. "I've told the children they may be with their friends, within sight of their uncle or me, as soon as we've established the kittens in the pet area. Have you put your goods in the judging section?"

"Hello, Susannah. Yes, we have. I'm just on my way to be sure they're labeled correctly. They're unloading at the back of the building, Jackson." Mrs. Turner eyed the bundle in Susannah's lap. "I see you've decided to enter your quilt after all. When did you finish it?" Little escaped that gimlet gaze.

"Early this morning. I'm still not convinced it's good enough, but, nothing ventured, nothing gained. We'll see you inside in a little while."

Jackson made a brief detour to the pet section and delivered the kittens, making sure they had enough milk and a sand box. Susannah and the children were anxious to get back to the exhibit area. He knew she was nervous about her dairy produce, but his conviction that she'd take all the honors in that area never faltered. His concern centered on her knitting and quilting. Nothing he could say would get her to enter the socks and mitts she provided for her family. They just weren't good enough, she thought, and that was that. Jackson resolved that next year, if she still proved so obstinate, he would enter them on her behalf.

Hiram Turner and his two oldest children met them at the back door, ready to help. Hiram, too, had entered a young bull. He showed keen interest in Jackson's Aryshire cattle. They arranged to visit the animal pens as soon as the wagon had been unloaded. A caveat that children would be in danger near the animals was unsuccessful. The two men resigned themselves to a gaggle of young boys getting into every possible bit of mischief.

Meanwhile, Susannah and Georgina, accompanied by Elizabeth, Carol, Sally and Emily, confirmed that their entries were labeled and placed properly. As they compared their submissions to the others, Susannah, felt that her quilt would not shame her. She thought an honorable mention might be possible. The dairy entries still gave her fits and fidgets.

Georgina made a point of commenting on each entry, complete with a rundown of their standing in last year's fall fair. By the time they left this area, Susannah was desperate to visit the animal pens and find Jackson. While he might be distracted by profound conversations with the other entrants and observers, he would not regale her with depressing information about last year's formidable contestants.

Just as she spotted Jackson and Hiram Turner, she heard their voices raised in fear and exasperation.

"Caleb, get back here this minute."

Simultaneously, Hiram roared "Henry, get over here right now!"

Susannah thought both boys had been gored when she realized that they were in the section devoted to the bulls. She picked up her skirts in one hand, clutched Emily's wrist with the other and ran toward the commotion. She pushed her way through the crowd of shouting men and arrived in time to see Jackson and Hiram pull the boys over the side of the pen. The biggest bull Susannah had ever seen pawed the ground and bellowed. She refused to believe that any pen, no matter how sturdily fashioned, could contain all that rage. Just then the officials in charge of this section began to urge the crowd to disperse.

Jackson, red of face and breathing heavily, tucked the obviously terrified Caleb under one arm and grabbed Susannah with the other. Emily, tethered by her aunt's iron grip, was hard pressed to keep up.

"Let's get out of here, Susannah. My heart can't stand much more of this."

"How did it happen? Both boys? With you and Hiram right there? I don't think you were careless, Jackson, but how could they get in that pen without someone seeing them?" Susannah began to pull back from Jackson's grip, not from fear, but from lack of breath.

Emily sobbed in fear and frustration. She stumbled as she tried to keep up with the mad pace set by the adults. At least Susannah's progress, slowed by the number of men surrounding the pen, had enabled her to trot along and keep up without fear of falling. Now, with more space and Jackson leading the troops, she was in danger of falling.

Susannah became aware of the pull on her arm. "Jackson, Emily can't run this fast." She deliberately slackened her pace. "I'm sorry, Emily. I didn't realize we were going so quickly."

"That's all right, Aunt Susannah. It's just that Uncle Jackson can go so fast." Puffing, Emily regarded her aunt with remarkable complacency as she wiped her eyes on her sleeve.

"Emily, I'm very sorry," Jackson said, "I was just so intent on getting away from there that I didn't think about how fast I was going. We'll slow down now." Emily beamed forgiveness.

"Why don't you and Aunt Susannah check out Daisy and see if she's settled in with the other cows?" Jackson congratulated himself on an excellent ploy to get the ladies out of the way while he dealt with Caleb. Then he looked at Susannah. Chin up, shoulders braced, nostrils flaring, the glint in her eye boded ill for him when they were alone.

"Come along, Emily. We'll make sure that Daisy is all settled in, and then we'll meet the men of our family for a cup of tea in the pavilion." With a meaningful glance, she turned smartly and led Emily away.

"And now, young man, we're going to find a quiet spot and discuss your conduct. What made you and Henry do such a dam fool thing? You both know better." Jackson cast a fulminating glance at the small culprit.

"I'm sorry, Uncle Jackson. Henry told me that the big boys were afraid to get close to the bulls and to enter their pens. I thought that we could get in our bull's pen, 'cause he knows me. Henry didn't think that would count, so we decided to get into a big bull's pen. We were only going to touch our feet to the ground and then climb right out, but we got caught." Caleb bravely looked his uncle right in the eye, ignoring the tears running down his face.

Jackson, torn between discipline and parenting on the one hand, and a soft heart for a little boy trying so hard to be grown up on the other, tried to walk a middle road.

"Caleb, you knew that it was wrong to go into that pen, didn't you?"

Caleb, chin on chest, replied, "Yes, Uncle Jackson, I did."

"Then why did you do it?"

"Well," muttered the miscreant, "I knew it was wrong, and so did Henry. But it seemed so exciting and easy that Henry and I thought we could do it and no one would know. I guess we were wrong."

"I guess so, too, Caleb. You know I'll have to punish you for this, don't you?" Caleb gulped and nodded. "I guess we have to go to the woodshed, don't we?"

"I don't think that the woodshed would answer nearly as well as something else. For one week you have to stay in your room except for chores." Jackson waited for a reaction.

"Even for breakfast and dinner and supper?" Caleb was appalled.

"You may eat with the rest of the family. When you're in your room, you can think about what happens when you don't listen to your conscience."

There was a small pause; then, "What's a conscience, Uncle Jackson?"

"Your conscience is that voice inside of you that tells when you are doing the wrong thing." Jackson maintained a stern demeanor, but anticipated sharing this conversation with Susannah.

"Oh. That voice." Small feet shuffled as a grubby paw rubbed his head. "Yes, sir. I understand." He and Henry had many plans for building a fort and trying to ride Mr. Turner's new young ram. Then there were the kittens in the barn to be checked, and the fish in the creek were surely big enough to nibble on a hook. He sighed.

"Good. Now let's go and find your aunt and sister." Jackson took Caleb's hand and turned toward the pavilion. The penitent recovered enough to ask "What do you think will happen to Henry? Do you think he'll pay a visit to the woodshed?"

"That's between Mr. Turner and Henry, and none of our business." Jackson tightened his grip on Caleb's hand and prepared to join his womenfolk.

"Yes, Uncle Jackson, I understand." Caleb began to compare the various advantages of a painful, but quick, woodshed visit to hours and hours in his room with nothing to do.

Susannah and Emily maintained a fast pace on their way to the tea pavilion. Part of Susannah shuddered to think of how she had looked at and spoken to Jackson. Her amazement was not so much for her actions, but that she feared no reprisals. Over the months their relationship had developed to an extent that permitted the fullest expression of emotions.

How have I been able to build trust so quickly? After Albert I could not imagine any overt expression of my dislike of a situation; yet now I don't hesitate to speak right up. The other day I even yelled. And he accepts it. Accepts it and respects that I have feelings and ideas. His encouragement for entering my produce in the fair is nothing short of remarkable and he nagged and nagged until I gave in and entered my quilt.

While Susannah's rumination continued, her anger and fear about the situation with the bull subsided. She resolved to order Jackson a piece of his favorite pie. Emily chose monkey face cookies for her and Caleb. Just as their food arrived at the table, the missing members of the party approached.

"Is everything all right, Jackson? Are you hurt at all Caleb?" Susannah eyed them with concern, tempered by the fact that no blood was visible and that their progress from the door to the table, brisk.

"I'm all right, Aunt Susannah." Caleb was quite subdued. Even the appearance of the monkey face cookies brought no more than a small smile.

"We're fine. Perhaps we can discuss this when we're in a less public place." Correctly interpreting this as a directive to ignore the ramifications of the bull pen episode for the moment, Susannah poured him a cup of tea and nudged the pie a little closer to him.

"My favorite pie. Thanks, Susannah. But aren't you having any?"

"I've already had two cups of tea. I couldn't possibly eat anything. Do you think the judging is finished?" Her voice was tight with fear and anticipation.

"Probably, so why don't we go and check right now? I've finished both tea and pie." Jackson stood and offered an arm to each of the ladies.

"Caleb, you take your Aunt Susannah's other arm. We have to protect our ladies." The closer they got to their destination, the more Susannah's steps lagged. Finally, unable to put it off any longer, she took a deep breath and prepared to enter the building, only to be all but bowled over by Georgina Turner.

"Susannah, you must come. Your quilt got an honorable mention, and you topped everyone in the dairy entries—firsts for butter and cheese, and seconds, thirds or honorable mentions in everything else. Congratulations! No one has ever taken that many prizes before." Gasping for breath and dabbing at the perspiration on her brow with her lace-edged handkerchief, she couldn't be more pleased if she won herself.

"Oh, Georgina. Really? I can't believe it!" Turning to Jackson she squeezed his arm. "Did you hear? I got an honorable mention for that quilt you had to force me to enter."

"I did, indeed, wife. Now maybe you'll agree that I know a little about quilts. I'm so proud of all your accomplishments. But to win first with both butter and cheese, and seconds, thirds or honorable mentions with all the rest— we'll have to up our prices." The grin on his face belied the price jacking, but there was no doubting his joy and pride in his wife's success.

"Let's see and then check on the livestock. They must have finished judging them by now." Holding hands, the Stansfields rushed into the pavilion to admire the first place ribbons.

Caleb and Emily were happy that their beloved Aunt Susannah had so many pretty ribbons. The pet section was much more interesting. They discovered that their kittens escaped three times, the last time when Jackson came to collect them for the trip home. Their antics amused the onlookers. Jackson kept the swearing under his breath. One of the judges had remarked that their energy, even for kittens, was remarkable.

Jackson was pleased with his results. His livestock took a first for the cow, and honorable mention for the bull. Three different farmers approached him about arrangements to have the bull available the next time their cows came into season. The family had fared well in their first Marcher Mills fall fair.

Wife Seller!

CHAPTER NINETEEN

Susannah smiled as she listened to the children's voices. The weather was typical for late October in southern Ontario. Days were frequently warm. Mornings and evenings were harbingers of the colder weather to come. The sky's color was so intense that it practically hurt to look at it. Sales of her jams and jellies at Zeke's store increased weekly. Orders for cream, butter and cheese were on a first come, first served basis. She applauded Jackson's foresight in having cows producing year-round.

Caleb had agreed to play house. He and Emily were busy making pies, tea and all manner of things from mud and leaves. The arbor that Jackson built for her was a favorite place to play. She smiled and shifted basket of vegetables to her other hand in order to open the kitchen door. They would add flavor and interest to the stew. The custard cooled on the counter. She put out the bowl and ingredients for biscuits. Fresh berries and whipped cream would top the custard for a hearty and easy supper.

How different things were from when she first arrived. Now that they were truly husband and wife, she revelled in the intimacy they shared. She trusted Jackson. Only one worm lived in the heart of her rose—a small worm at present, but with the potential to destroy all their lives. No amount of rationalizing eradicated that tiny canker. She thrust it into the back of her mind, determined to wring every drop of joy from the present. Her capacity for ignoring the possibility of bigamy charges increased with each day. Life's tasks and rewards filled her heart, her hands, and her hours. Life proceeded so smoothly that the spectre of her greatest fear dwindled to a feeling of unease, and at longer and longer intervals.

As she heard Jackson's footsteps behind her, she smiled and continued to wipe the counter. Astounded that she welcomed his closeness, she tilted her head to one side. Jackson had a most delightful habit of nuzzling her neck as his arms stole around her waist. He wasn't always as careful as he should be about where the children were when those same gentle hands rose to cup her breasts.

Did he notice that they were bigger and that the nipples were a little more sensitive? She refused to acknowledge her suspected pregnancy, even while her treacherous mind returned to the frightening and wonderful possibility. She and Jackson had yet to discuss having a family, but his ease with and affection for Emily and Caleb proved he would be an excellent father. Any man who could recover from having the majority of his tools glued to various surfaces and not beat the culprit was destined for fatherhood, if not sainthood, in her mind. She still marveled at his forbearance.

"I have some good news, Susannah" Jackson whispered as his arms encircled her and he gently bit her ear. "Your work load is about to get lighter. With more help we can quickly build that storage room you need to produce the cheddar." She heard the children playing in the garden, even as she turned in his embrace.

"Really, Jackson? Why would you say that?" Her arms circled his shoulders, as one hand stole up to run through his hair. "Have some new people come to town?" Suddenly she remembered the letter Jackson sent to Ethan about finding a couple to help on the farm. "Have you heard from Ethan?" Her hands pushed against his shoulders, her mood altering as a sense of foreboding assailed her.

"Yes, my lovely wife. I just got a letter from Ethan. The couple have two small children. You know I've been encouraging him to pay us a visit—with, of course, a view to having him settle here, but he's still running a bit shy."

Resolutely rejecting all thoughts of impending doom she exclaimed, "That's wonderful! You'll be able to increase the size of both the market garden and the herd. The extra income will more than pay their wages. I'll start cleaning their house today. Will you put up a couple of window boxes? It's too late to transplant or even plant annuals, but they'll be ready for next spring. How old are the children?"

Jackson gazed at Susannah's face, which glowed with enthusiasm. He reflected yet again on his good fortune in acquiring a wife he could love and who loved him. A wife who was strong and worked for his and the children's good. A wife who stinted neither labor nor affection. How so much good could come from the grief and shock of finding his friend dead and himself in charge of two small children still bewildered him.

"If you think that news is good, Susannah, wait until hear where they're from. Yorkshire! From the village where Ethan found you!" Jackson tightened his grip and whirled her around. "Now you'll not only have company, but someone from home! As for the ages of the children, well, you know Ethan. I'm surprised he even noticed that they were little!" He ended his spin with a playful smack on each buttock.

Susannah froze in shock. She couldn't believe her ears. Jackson's joy in sharing the news of a couple with a young family shone in his eyes. Her arms dropped away slowly as she groped for the counter. Her legs threatened to give way beneath her.

"You'll be glad of some assistance, sweetheart. The woman will help in the dairy and the house or garden. The man is a good worker, but doesn't have a great deal of initiative. That's not a problem, really. I'd rather have a good steady worker who does what he's told, and who can be relied upon to do so, than someone brilliant, but erratic."

Susannah couldn't get past the news that the couple came from Yorkshire. Not only from Yorkshire, but from the town where she was sold. A town perilously close to her old home. Jackson reached into his pocket for the letter and failed to notice her panic. He unfolded the papers, oblivious to his wife's rigid body and death grip on the counter.

"Susannah, listen to this: it says that the woman particularly enjoys gardening, and I know that that's not a favorite of yours. Isn't this wonderful? She's also skilled in the basics of dairy work. Their names are Harold and Martha Brown, and they'll be here in about a month."

Bigamist! Dirty bigamist!! The enormity of her crime and the attendant horrors that would affect her little family caused her to move her grip from the counter to the back of a chair. Her knees refused to hold her erect. *A month. One month to cherish her happy family. One month to love Jackson. One month to hold the children close. One month to decide whether to tell Jackson about her pregnancy. Just one more month!* It was as if two voices fought for supremacy in her head. One reiterated the old, almost-forgotten litany of *bigamist, dirty bigamist, shame on you, your husband, your children and your unborn child.* She clutched her head in a vain attempt to think. Jackson, still reading the letter and interjecting happy plans, failed to notice his wife's plight. Her thoughts whirled, frantically.

Where would she go? She still had some coins left from her voyage. Jackson insisted that she keep a generous portion of the proceeds from the dairy and all of the income from her dealings with Zeke. Her work was outstanding, but few farmers wished to hire a woman, and never at the wages paid to a man. None would hire a pregnant woman. They would resent the time it took to take care of a child. Also, she would have no one to vouch for her skills.

Toronto offered the largest number of possible destinations, and a choice of train, stagecoach or boat. If she started out before dawn, she could walk to the next stage stop, saving money and covering her trail. She was too well known in the community to chance taking the train. Or perhaps she should go in the opposite direction. Hamilton's burgeoning population would provide several venues for her to explore. Susannah almost began to wish that she hadn't conceived, much as she wanted a child. *It's not fair* her heart cried. But life wasn't fair. The few months of happiness with her little family were almost over. One month was such a short time to taste the joy she found.

"Susannah, what's wrong?" Jackson's anxious query jerked her back to the present. She willed the tears away.

"Nothing, Jackson." She forced enthusiasm into her voice and her face to reflect the same emotion. "I was just wondering if I know them and thinking how wonderful that extra help would be. The children will enjoy having playmates right here. Have you told them?"

Her thoughts returned to her predicament. How would she escape? At the very least, she owed Jackson the truth. And the children. The children. Already she felt her heart tearing from the anguish of losing these precious little beings.

"Aunt Susannah, Uncle Jackson!" They shouted at the top of their lungs, each determined to be the first to present their case. Susannah heard their voices as from a distance. Desperately she wrenched her mind from its fruitless meanderings and focused on the youngsters.

Emily, by virtue of longer legs, reached her designated target first, throwing her arms around Susannah's waist. "Aunt Susannah, he...."

Caleb, behind by half a step launched himself at Jackson's legs. "Uncle Jackson, she...."

"Stop it right now!" Jackson had learned from experience that the person with greatest volume had the floor. "What is the meaning of this behavior? Look at the mud on your shoes, and on your Aunt's clean floor. Both of you outside right now and remove those shoes. Caleb, you clean the shoes, but only on the outside. No water in Emily's shoes, young man. Emily, you get the broom and dustpan and clean up this mess. Your Aunt Susannah and I were having a conversation.

"But...but" sputtered the children.

"But me no buts," roared Jackson, albeit at a lower volume. "Now, outside the both of you, or into your bedrooms.

If you choose to go outside, you either get along or play separately. Now scoot!"

Recognizing the futility of rebuttal, explanations or excuses, the children fled. Their Uncle Jackson rarely raised his voice, but when he did, playing least in sight was the best thing to do. He seemed to have forgotten about the cleaning up part, so they turned and ran, banging the screen door in turn.

"Now, my darling wife, where were we? Oh, yes. You seem upset, not delighted, with my news. This isn't like you, Susannah. Please tell me what's wrong." Jackson's eyes bored into hers as he reached down to grasp her hands. She evaded his grasp by making a business of smoothing his collar as an excuse to avoid meeting his eyes.

She paid grave attention to her self-assigned task and manufactured a smile. "Really, I'm thrilled, Jackson—just so surprised. I know you've been waiting for this news, but even so, it seems a little overwhelming. In a good way, I mean." She hastened to add, "You're right about the garden—I'll be delighted to hand that over—at least the vegetables. It'll be fun to have someone to share the flowers with. And more help in the dairy means that we are well on our way to adding cheddar to the different cheeses we can offer at market." Susannah prayed that she had covered her slip. "While you check over their house for repairs, the children and I will clean it. Do you think we should put up some curtains, or would it be better to let Martha choose the fabric?" She desperately tried to redirect his attention to safer topics.

"Oh, let's give her the fun of choosing her own curtains, Susannah. But I'm sure I saw fear in your eyes, my darling. Please tell me what's wrong." Jackson kept a firm grip on her waist. While she schooled her expression to match her words, her body told a different story. It was stiff, and he could feel a faint trembling.

"This isn't the first time that you've been frightened, Susannah, but I thought we'd progressed to a point of trust, to sharing our concerns with each other. Don't try to distract me with curtains. Just tell me what's wrong."

She was frantic. There didn't seem to be any way out of this except to tell Jackson the truth. She thrust the thoughts of bigamy and all its ramifications to the back of her mind. The imp who took such perverse pleasure in jabbing her with the sharp points of her conscience, she consigned to perdition. Drawing a deep breath and clutching her courage in both hands, she began.

"Jackson, I am frightened, terrified really, but it's more for you and the children than myself. You know that Ethan purchased me. What you don't know is that he was the wrong man."

"What do you mean the wrong man? How could there be a right man?"

"Please, Jackson, just let me explain, and then I'll answer all your questions. I was running for my life, running from an intolerable relationship. My husband....'

"Husband! What do you mean husband? How could you marry me if you already had a husband?" Jackson's voice vibrated with emotions he struggled to keep under iron control. Susannah flinched when she saw the pain in his eyes.

"My God, Susannah! That means, that means...."

"Yes, Jackson, I'm, that I was, that is I am already married. This has been my terrible secret." The familiar and hated litany of *bigamist, dirty bigamist* strove for supremacy once again. She subdued it with a mighty effort. Susannah locked her knees and willed herself not to cry, unaware that tears trickled down her cheeks. Her voice threatened to become totally suspended in emotion.

"I cannot believe you would lie." Jackson staggered to the table and collapsed onto a chair, his face raised to that of his wife. She stifled the sobs that threatened to overwhelm her, and continued.

"Jackson, please, please let me explain." Receiving no response, she continued.

"My family coerced me into marrying Albert Ashton, the only son of prosperous dairy farmers who lived close to us. It seemed to be the sensible thing to do: his parents were dead and I had excellent skills in the dairy. I didn't love him, I didn't hate him, and I didn't put up much of an argument. There was no one else who interested me, and I knew that I was one more mouth for my parents to feed. My sisters and friends were all married. As you know, a woman's worth is judged on her ability to catch a husband, and by that same husband's place in the community. If a woman is unmarried, then there must be something lacking, as no man desired her. Also, I wanted children. If I had to marry Albert to get them, then so be it."

"But, Susannah...."

"Please, Jackson, if I stop I may never start again." She drew a shuddering breath and continued. "At first things went quite well. I worked hard, and the Ashton Farm butter and cheese began to develop a reputation for quality. As recognition of my skills grew, however, Albert became very jealous. It began with him spending increasing amounts of time in the local pub and neglecting the farm. Not all the time, mind you, but frequently."

"As the farm began to deteriorate, he became discouraged and then enraged. He blamed me. It was my fault. I was lazy. I was trying to belittle him. When I confessed that I was pregnant, he hit me for the first time, and stormed out of the house. Later that night he came back and apologized. I had to understand that a man's emotions were extremely powerful. They were so powerful, that they sometimes caused him to act in unacceptable ways."

"I tried to understand, and thus forgave him. Occasionally my own father slapped my mother. He, too, always apologized, and my mother seemed to accept his behavior as normal, if not appreciated. Little did I know that that was just the beginning. Slaps and foul language led to punches and kicks. He took particular pleasure in hitting or even kicking me in the stomach when he knew I was pregnant. Over the next few years I had several miscarriages and two still births. The frequency and severity of the beatings increased until I realized that I had to flee or face certain death."

Jackson stopped staring and kept his gaze on the floor. His body was stiff, braced as if to withstand the pain inflicted by her words. *Oh, Jackson, I wish I could take away your hurt and make everything better.* She took a mighty breath and continued.

"My only friends, Michael and Miranda Knowles, persuaded Albert to let me try selling our dairy products in a town several miles away. They said that the higher prices more than made up for the extra time and effort. It was there that Miranda discovered that it was legal for a husband to sell his wife. As you can imagine, money was getting scarcer, and Albert agreed. Michael made a special trip and posted a Wife for Sale notice in the town's largest tavern." Susannah paused to regain control of her voice.

"But Susannah...." Jackson grasped her hand.

"Please let me finish while I have the courage. I'm almost done." She seemed unaware of the tears still coursing down her cheeks.

"Michael agreed to pose as my husband. He arranged for his cousin, Daniel, who lives in Sussex, to buy me. Pretend to buy me, that is. Daniel's neighbor has a large dairy farm, and I would be employed there. This way Albert wouldn't be able to find me. He didn't want me. He had a mistress whom he displayed to all and sundry. My friends could write to me care of Daniel, and he would send my letters to them. If anything terrible happened to my family, or if Albert were able to trace me, I would know."

The bitterness in her voice was ample proof of the hurt she had suffered. "He only wanted my work in the dairy. By this time, it was our single source of income.

"I don't know what happened. Maybe Daniel's wagon broke down. Maybe he changed his mind. Maybe he wasn't even able to come because of an emergency. I do know he planned to take the train most of the way, then hire a wagon for the last leg of his journey. That way he would blend in and no one would connect us with the train. We tried to plan for the worst, even as we hoped for the best. The crowd was becoming ugly. The auctioneer was threatening to have the law on us. We had to go through with the sale. You know what happened after that."

Jackson nodded, still refusing to look at her. His voice was flat. "Yes, I know what happened next." The space between seemed like a canyon.

She stifled a sob. "I was terrified when Ethan purchased me. Then, when he explained that you would wed me by proxy, and that I would emigrate to Canada to help you on a dairy and market garden farm, as well as help to care for two small children, I thought I was saved. Surely no one could find me more than three thousand miles from England, posing as a wife and with two little ones."

"You can see how wrong I was. I determined that if you were the least like Albert I would take the little money I had, plus what was left over from the funds you gave to Ethan to outfit me, and disappear."

"But Jackson, it was the children. My arms ached and ached to hold a child against my breast, to sing lullabies, to care and love them. I felt I had already experienced the worst in husbands, and only if my life were in danger would I disappear." Susannah swayed with exhaustion and grief. Jackson reached out to support her, but she avoided his grasp. "Even my name would be changed." She mopped her eyes and blew her nose.

"Instead, when I arrived, you greeted me with a wagon containing a rooster with his head sticking out of a crate and two small children. At first, I was terrified, but you had so much patience for me and the children. You wanted to make my work easier in the dairy and in the house. You encouraged me to buy things for the children, for our home, and for myself. You took care of me when I was ill. You helped to care for the children. You even built me an arbor. An arbor! Not because we needed it, but for its beauty and my enjoyment. At that point I admitted I was coming to love you. As my fear decreased, my affection for you increased. I love you. I'll do whatever I can to clear up this mess so that it doesn't rebound on you or the children." She inhaled determinedly and bravely looked him right in the eye.

"I'm so sorry. You'll never know how sorry. Let me know how you want me to vanish from your life. What do you want me to tell the children? I'll do whatever you want. I will always love you."

She staggered to the table and slumped onto a chair. He remained sitting, elbows on the table, his face in his hands and his body braced as against a blow. The silence burgeoned, filling the room. They became conscious of their breathing. Of cloth touching skin. Of the soft rustle of fabric caused by an inadvertent movement. A log shifted in the firebox, causing them to jump as if at a sudden clap of thunder. Not even the voices of the children intruded. The far, faint clang of a cowbell sounded softly in the enveloping stillness.

Jackson lifted his head and looked at her for a long time with no discernible expression on this face. He heaved his body from the chair. Trudged outside; head down and shoulders slumped. She noticed his hat, still hanging on its peg beside the door. He never went outside without his hat. Susannah covered her mouth with her hands in a vain attempt to contain her sobs and ran into their bedroom. She cried until her eyes burned and her cheeks were stiff. Finally, she fell asleep, her head burrowed into the damp pillow and her hands covering her face.

Plans for the family farm crowded Jackson's thoughts: adopting the children, enlarging the market garden, building a room to age cheeses, perhaps adding pigs and beef cattle. Now those plans rested in ashes. He dipped his hands in the water trough, flicked off the excess moisture and pressed damp fingers to burning eyes. Nothing had prepared him for such a blow. Try as he might, he could see no way out of the quagmire except to sell and leave.

Susannah, Emily and Caleb were his life. Frantically he tried to think of solutions. They could establish themselves in another community, perhaps even change their names. Somehow he and Susannah would sort out this mess. He knew in his heart, even before she gave him the words, that she loved him and the children. Now, faced with this crisis, he realized that he loved them to such a degree that he would do anything in his power to protect them. Could he trust her again? Only time would tell. His love remained steadfast. He turned and headed back to the house to tell her of his decision.

Bigamy was a serious criminal offense. It was also a social solecism of monumental proportions. If they fled this community, they would have to acquire a different name and history before they settled in another one. Jackson wasn't even sure that it would be safe to stay in Canada. Perhaps emigration to Australia or New Zealand might be in order.

The kitchen was empty; the stove barely warm and no children within sight or sound. They were probably in the barn playing with the kittens. Instinctively he moved down the hall. She slept heavily, tear stains visible on her cheeks, her hands folded under her cheek. He turned and quietly retraced his route, reaching the kitchen just as the children burst through the door. He placed his finger to his lips in a shushing motion.

"Your aunt is resting, so you must be quiet and very, very good. She's not feeling well. Perhaps we could surprise her and make supper if she's still asleep." The children, memories of Uncle Jackson's attempts at cooking still vivid, blanched.

"I could hold her hand, Uncle Jackson," piped Emily.

"And I could whistle a lullaby for her," offered Caleb.

"Perhaps later. Right now she just needs to rest. I'm going to put a cool cloth on her head. Why don't you get a story book and I'll read one story for each of you." This was a special treat. Uncle Jackson rarely read to them. They whispered as they tiptoed to the bookshelf, intent on selecting their favorite stories.

He returned to the bedroom with the cloth in his hand. Just as he placed it over her eyes, she started to sit up. He gently pushed her down and replaced the cloth. "You rest, Susannah. I told the children I'd read each of them a story. I'm sure they'll be the longest ones they can find. Try to sleep. We need some time and space before we start making plans."

She squeezed his hand in gratitude, amazed anew at her good fortune in having such a wonderful husband—but for how long? Not only was her crime serious in and of itself, but the severity of the ramifications to her family would be horrendous.

The shame and condemnation of the community encompassed not only the guilty parties, but the extended family, as well. Did the penalties apply to the innocent party as well as to the guilty? She wondered how she could find out. Perhaps she could take the train to Toronto and consult with a lawyer, using a false name. Would Jackson still want her? What would happen to the children?

She turned onto her back, hands pressed against her roiling stomach, grateful for the cool cloth that soothed her eyes. Emily's solicitude when she placed it so carefully on her adored aunt's forehead increased Susannah's anguish. Her fingers still tingled from the love Caleb conveyed with his death grip on her hand.

She awoke to a silent house. It felt like her heart: empty. Removing the cloth from her head, she straightened the bed and headed outside. Automatically her steps took her into the dairy. Her legs were shaking so badly she felt in imminent danger of falling. Things had been going so well with her little family. Her heart and mind were one in their love for Jackson, and for the children. She had sworn never to trust a man again; but Jackson put those fears to rest and encouraged her loving nature to reassert itself.

As Jackson's wife and an expert dairy woman, her stature in the community had increased steadily. Caleb and Emily sometimes called her Mummy instead of Aunt Susannah, and her heart burgeoned with love at each such instance. Long had she hungered to hear childish voices address her. Now the realization of the price she would pay for her fleeting happiness weighed heavily. Far, far more than that, the pain and shame that Jackson and the children would have to endure because of her actions overwhelmed her.

Finally, she reached their favorite family spot beside the brook. She hurried to the far side of the tree and sank down, bracing her back against its wide and sturdy trunk.

Memories of time spent with the children and of picnics that included Jackson tumbled through her mind. She remembered that Caleb always managed to fall down in the water at least once. He craftily aimed the results of his biggest and best splashes to fall onto Emily. Emily, invariably with a family of dolls, plucked grass and collected stones for dishes as she served afternoon tea to her little family. She and Jackson came to know each other in many different ways as they watched the children and shared ideas and plans.

Now, that world had crumbled and she tasted ashes. She would not permit him to jeopardize his business or his reputation. Three weeks, just three more weeks, and she would leave. That meant that he would have to cope with the children and dairy for only a few days before the Browns arrived. Her portmanteau would more than suffice for the few things she would take with her.

She had her strength and her skills. She refused to give the problem of her pregnancy room in her mind. If she kept the wedding ring, she could pass herself off as a widow and avoid any stigma attaching to the child. She decided that either Toronto or Hamilton would provide a sufficiently large community in which to disappear. Perhaps she could find a position as a housekeeper for a few years. If Jackson did hunt for her, he would concentrate on farms with dairies. As a housekeeper, living in the city, she could blend with the population and achieve invisibility.

But how could she bear the pain of parting with her family? In a few short months they had twined themselves into her heartstrings. "Not now, not now" she chanted. "Now I'll feed my family and do the evening milking. Tomorrow is soon enough to make plans." Shoulders back, head high, and heart heavy, she returned to the house.

Wife Seller!

CHAPTER TWENTY

The crisp breeze rustled the bright leaves, lifted the horses' manes and caused Susannah to smooth the tendrils it teased free of her chignon. Puffy white clouds in a blue sky added to the picture of sylvan bliss. Goldenrod danced and bowed in the ditches, adding its rich color to the chicory, Queen Anne's Lace and cool green grasses along the banks of the road. Surely the horses' pace increased with each step. They appeared to be walking, but she felt as if they were galloping, bringing her fate closer much too quickly.

Time had alternately dragged and flown on this most fateful of days. The oven took forever to heat sufficiently to bake the biscuits, but breakfast was over in a flash. Making beds and sweeping and tidying the kitchen telescoped into scant minutes; but the dairy work dragged interminably. It seemed as if twenty cows, not seven, occupied the dairy, each lowing to be milked. The finishing touches of welcome on the couple's house consumed but a moment. Washing and dressing the children seemed to take hours. And over all, in spite of busy work, Susannah's fear fought for supremacy.

The wagon, swept and garnished with piles of hay to provide soft seating for the Brown and Stansfield ladies on their trip back to the farm, bore small resemblance to the conveyance used to bring her to her future home just a few short months ago. To keep her mind off the impending arrival of their promised farm couple, Susannah surveyed her family.

Jackson, of course, wore his suit, tie and stiff collar with both grace and resignation. His complaints against the outmoded tradition that required a man to chafe his neck and be in danger of strangulation were loud and eloquent. The children, when swung onto the wagon with squeals of mock terror, had been spick and span, from Sunday hats to shiny shoes. She suffered no fear that Emily would look as neat upon her arrival at the station as she had on her departure from home, but repressed a small shudder when contemplating Caleb's probable state. He had many miles yet to acquire that patina of dirt that seemed to be particularly his.

Her family having passed under review, Susannah turned to the arrangements for the comfort of their new employees. Anything to keep the fear at bay, she resolved. Their house, cleaned and furnished with the essentials, passed muster. Each of the three bedrooms contained a bed, pallet, and shelves. The kitchen, in addition to a table and six chairs, had a good-sized work surface. The pantry was small, but provided adequate storage for dry goods.

Jackson's installation of a pump and closed stove, combined with Susannah's stocking of the kitchen with basics and a tin of cookies, assured the Browns of a warm welcome. Emily's loaf of bread occupied a place of prominence on the table, nestled beside the dish of butter she had made. Each offering sported a brand new tea towel covering to preserve its freshness and guard against flies. Susannah's pleasure at the thought of soon being able to present a wedge of her cheddar faded with the realization that her days with her little family were almost finished.

Caleb, at the cost of a bruised thumb, hung the match safe beside the kitchen stove, then filled it with Eddy matches. He also, perforce, filled the wood box. Jackson's contributions, in addition to the pump and stove, included kindling and a healthy start on a woodpile.

Her trepidation grew as they neared the town and the inevitable meeting. She straightened when she realized that her torso, pressed against Jackson's arm, caused her bonnet to brush against his shoulder.

"It will be all right, Susannah, you'll see." Only a fierce determination and iron control let her keep a façade of calm as she looked down to see one of his hands cradling hers. How would she bear leaving the love of her life, All the loves of her life, because the children were inextricably entrenched in her heart. Laughter, so long absent, burst forth from every member of her family every day: at the antics of the kittens, things the children said, or her and Jackson's teasing of each other. Even the unremitting labor of housekeeping, meals, laundry, gardening and the dairy seemed light because she loved and was loved in return.

Now her bright new world would shatter. Jagged shards of pain would wreak bloody havoc on heart and soul and mind. Because of her actions, her family in Yorkshire and her beloved husband and children would suffer. She made an excuse to adjust the folds of her skirt. Screened by their voluminous folds, her fists clenched so tightly that the nails caused crescent bruises in her palms.

Jackson realized that his grip on the reins tightened as the horses began to toss their heads and increase their speed. In spite of his constant reassurances, he really had no idea of what they would do when, inevitably, the truth of their bigamous marriage became common knowledge.

Social and financial ostracism would be the least of it. No matter where they went, their past was sure to haunt them. In spite of this, Jackson pledged to keep his wife and children. They were more important to him than his farm, his business or his reputation. His efforts in foiling Susannah's plans for leaving on several occasions had met with success. They did not guarantee that she still wouldn't disappear to save him and the children from disgrace.

Locked in their own thoughts, they paid little attention to the passing scenery, in spite of Susannah's vow to remember every minute of this last happy time in her life. Neither noticed the frequent brushing of shoulder against shoulder, a contact that provided comfort in their shared pain. Caleb and Emily's behavior was so exemplary that Susannah turned to make sure that all was as well as it seemed. They huddled together on one of the quilts spread over the hay, exchanging confidences of what they would do with their new friends. Emily had a handkerchief she proudly stitched to give to that girl from England (Uncle Ethan not being forthcoming with such minor details as the names or ages of the children), and Caleb had some special stones to show that boy. Both children hoped that their new playmates would be close to them in age. The steady clop, clop of hooves and soft jingle of harness formed a background to the busy minds of the wagon's occupants.

# # #

Jackson and Susannah, each clutching a child's small hand, stood on the train platform waiting for the Brown's arrival. In spite of her best efforts, Susannah had been unable to leave her little family. Jackson seemed to have an uncanny knack of knowing just when she had managed to screw her courage to the sticking point, and cleverly blocked her every move.

"When is the train coming, Uncle Jackson? We've been waiting an awfully long time." Caleb, unimpressed with the concepts of graciousness and punctuality, wanted to see the great steaming, puffing monster sweep into the station with its attendant roar and shrill whistle. Waiting time equaled wasted time in his mind.

"Caleb, quit bothering Uncle Jackson. We got here early to be polite and to greet the Browns. It's rude to be late, especially when we're the hosts." Emily, at her most pious, poked her nose in the air. Her voice dripped with scorn and condescension.

"A lot you know, Miss Emily. You're just repeating what Aunt Susannah told us earlier." Caleb remained unimpressed with his sister's air of superiority. His outthrust chin told of imminent physical retaliation. He knew his sister could out talk and out argue him, but his efforts to develop a good, solid punch showed great progress. One day it would be his turn to get even.

Susannah and Jackson deftly inserted themselves between the combatants. "Look, Caleb, way down the track. Can you see the smoke from the engine?" It was an excellent ploy. Held firmly by his uncle's hand, Caleb duly squinted, then began to jump up and down with excitement.

"Yes, yes, Uncle Jackson, I see it." His chest puffed out as he eyed his sister. "Hah! I saw the train before you did. So there," he taunted with a particularly unbearable smirk. Just as

Emily inhaled in preparation of annihilating her obnoxious brother, fists clenched at her sides, Susannah intervened.

"Come over here, Emily. I have a feeling that there will be a great deal of dust and dirt when that big engine comes through, and we don't want to spoil our good clothes." Willing to be distracted for the moment, Emily promised herself that later Caleb would pay dearly for being so insufferable.

Susannah whisked her reluctant charge into the station house. Even the false protection of a few more steps before meeting her fate was welcome. She realized, as she braced herself, that there was little chance of the Browns confronting her as their feet met the station platform. Logic had nothing to do with the panic that almost consumed her. Virtually her whole attention and will focused on presenting a composed appearance. A display of guilt or apprehension was simply not an option.

"If we look out this window, we'll see the train pull up to the platform. The men are welcome to all that soot and steam. We'll look like real ladies when we greet our guests." Susannah held her breath. Emily, usually amenable when appealed to partake in a ladylike activity, sometimes exhibited an odd kick in her gallop. Always willing to reinforce the vision of herself as a fine lady, she graciously consented to the scheme; but, given time, opportunity and privacy, retribution would be exacted from her pesky brother.

Confident that the incoming train commanded all of Emily's attention, Susannah let herself sink into despair. Her entire world was about to be destroyed, and the lives of those she loved so dearly, too. Only a very small part of her attention was directed to watching for the Browns. She turned away from the train to caress her menfolk with her eyes. They were so precious: stalwart Caleb who tried so hard to be a man, and Jackson, her dearest husband and protector. Her spouse was convinced that they could work out their problems and remain an integral part of the community, but she couldn't imagine how it would be possible. Her determination to focus on the moment was paramount. Nothing she could say or do at this time would make the slightest difference.

Puffing, steaming and shrieking, the train roared to a stop a hundred yards from the station platform.

"Why isn't it pulled right up here, Uncle Jackson? People will have to make a big step to get onto the ground, and then they could fall in the ditch. Wouldn't that be funny?" Caleb saw no reason to hold back mirth at the discomfort or embarrassment of others.

Jackson smiled. The question was so predictable. "See, Caleb, Mr. Henderson is riding his horse down there. He's expecting some cattle, and the engine has to stop there to line up the door of the stock car with the ramp."

"I see Rory Henderson, too, Uncle Jackson. He's one of the big boys at school. Is he going to help his pa drive the cattle home? Can I help?" Caleb's reach habitually exceeded his grasp.

Jackson tightened his grip, under no illusion that his charge would voluntarily remain at his side. "No. Remember, we're here to welcome the Browns. It would be very rude to ignore them just because you saw something that looked more interesting." While not the first time Caleb heard such a theory proposed, its value and relevance failed to increase with repetition. He looked with longing and determination at his young neighbor. Visions of cowboys and stampedes danced in his head.

Meanwhile, the stationmaster settled his cap, adjusted his vest, and stepped onto the platform as the train, livestock duties completed, pulled to a stop. He grinned in appreciation: the engineer made it a point of pride that the baggage car door should align perfectly with the cart. His assistant was on the way to handle the paperwork relevant to releasing the stock to the Hendersons. He prepared to assume his secondary duties as receiver of baggage and mail.

Susannah noticed that Caleb's attention alternated between inspecting the engine as closely as Jackson would permit, and offering his assistance in pushing the luggage cart. The train hissed in self-congratulatory satisfaction at the anticipated and perfect meeting of door and cart. The conductor swung down, placed a stool in front of the steps of the first passenger car and prepared to help with disembarkation. The senior Stansfields braced to meet their fate.

The first to alight were the Brighton sisters, complete with their obnoxious pug. Two strangers, both men, followed them, and then a thin man appeared. His weather-beaten face attested to work in the outdoors. His collar and tie contrived to give the impression that they more closely resembled a noose than articles of fashion. One raw-boned hand clutched the handle conveniently placed to help passengers descend to the platform. His head swung from side to side, obviously seeking someone.

Just as Jackson raised his hand to wave, he let go of the handle and transferred his grip only to the jacket of a young lad of about seven or eight years of age, who was attempting to rush past. With an expression of resignation and annoyance, he remonstrated with the boy and changed his grip from coat to wrist as he stepped onto the platform. The boy wriggled, but, after contemplating the expression on his captor's face, stood quietly.

Jackson again prepared to wave, only to have the man turn quickly and offer his hand to a woman whose bonnet hid her face. Her dress, while crumpled from being in a portmanteau, was obviously her best, and the white collar and cuffs glistened with starch. Her other hand clasped that of a young girl of about five, also dressed in Sunday finery. Susannah and Emily hurried across the platform.

"Wait here, Susannah, I think those are the Browns," Jackson threw over his shoulder, waving and striding toward the couple. Through habit, his hand remained firmly wrapped around Caleb's, who trotted willingly behind his uncle.

"Mr. and Mrs. Brown? I'm Jackson Stansfield." Receiving a nod from Brown, whose shoulders relaxed, he held out his hand. "Welcome to Marcher Mills. Did you have a good trip?" Brown's hand met his in a firm grip.

"That's right, sir, Harold Brown. This here's my wife, Martha, and our two children, Rudolph, Rudy, that is, and Anna." Brown was patently glad to have reached his destination unscathed. Jackson, having observed Rudy's attempted vault from the train, trembled at the thought of two intrepid and curious young boys on his acres.

"The young lad here, Caleb, is one of my wards." Catching a glimpse of Susannah and Emily hurrying to meet the Browns, he turned to introduce them.

"Susannah, here are the Browns, Martha and Harold, with their children, Rudy and Anna. This is Susannah, my wife. Emily is my other ward. She and Caleb are brother and sister." Susannah, pasting a smile on her face, extended her hand, first to Martha and then to Harold. "It's a pleasure to meet you at last. Did you have a good journey?" Anything, anything, she thought, to put off the dreaded moment just a little longer.

"Yes, it was very interesting," Martha replied. "Are these your children? Oh, no, I forgot, your cousin, Mr. Parridge explained that they are your wards, and Mr. Jackson just said so, too." Martha put her hand over her mouth, horrified at her gaffe.

"They are our children to all intents and purposes, Mrs. Brown. They have filled our lives with joy and interest." Susannah smiled more easily as the conversation drifted to safer shores.

"Thank you, Mrs. Stansfield. I hope I didn't say anything out of place," she quavered.

"Not at all. It's an easy mistake to make and a real compliment." Seeing Martha's confusion at her response, Susannah explained, "We think of ourselves as a family and have tried very hard to become one. You've just told us that we've succeeded."

As was inevitable, the men and boys had drifted off. Anna and Emily eyed each other with approval. Finally Emily summoned enough courage to speak. "I brought a present for you, Anna," she said, as she pulled a somewhat crumpled handkerchief from her little reticule and handed it to the girl she hoped would be her best friend.

Anna's eyes lit up as she accepted the gift. "Oh, thank you Emily, it's lovely." She continued, after a parental nudge and a whispered comment, "Did you do the embroidery?"

"Yes, Aunt Susannah has just started to teach me. This is the first hankie I've done. I'm practicing to be ready to start my sampler next." Susannah and Martha smiled at the girls.

"Why don't you show Anna where we put the wagon? I see that Uncle Jackson and Mr. Brown have gone to collect the baggage." The little girls scampered off hand in hand, giggling and exchanging confidences.

The two women made their first forays into friendship. Susannah proposed to wring what joy she could from the situation. "How was your crossing, Mrs. Brown?"

"Oh, please, call me Martha. It was a nightmare on the boat. If there was one bit of trouble that Rudy missed, I don't know what it might have been. Anna was sick for the first week." Susannah smiled in sympathy as they began comparing notes on their voyages while keeping the girls firmly under their gaze.

"Mr. Stansfield, Mr. Parridge sent you three more heifers. The bloodlines are completely different from the ones you have." Harold seemed relieved to have such a ready topic of conversation. "He said they'll pretty well set you up for a while with your breeding program. He wanted to know if he should keep his eye out for more, or for a different breed, if you wanted to try some crosses."

Jackson halted. "Are they on this train, Harold? I saw one of my neighbors picking up stock, today, but I don't recall seeing any Aryshires, or any young cattle at all." He was surprised and pleased at his cousin's thoughtfulness.

"No, sir. He directed me to arrange for them to come on the next train, as he said you'd have enough to do just getting us settled. And after seeing your young man and my Rudy, I'd have to say he's right." Harold smiled, but he was clearly nervous of his new employer.

"That's very thoughtful of Ethan, Harold, and I thank you for following his orders so well. Please let me know if you're out of pocket, and I'll reimburse you directly." Jackson reached for his pocket, but Harold jumped in.

"No, no. I've some left over funds to give you. I just thought I'd wait until we'd reached our journey's end." He was torn between delivering his messages and striving to keep both hand and eye on his son.

"Harold, before we go any further, please call me Jackson. I know it's not usual back home, but here we're much more casual. We'll be working together very closely, and it's foolish to stand on ceremony." Jackson, too, kept a weather eye on the two scamps as he tried to put his new employee at ease. He had released his hold on Caleb, but with an admonitory glare so potent that Caleb, at least for the present, behaved himself. His intense interest in his new friend, coupled with a vivid and inventive imagination for future pranks, occupied him fully.

"Oh, I don't know sir...Jackson...sir. I'll try, but it'll be mortal hard." Harold vacillated between gratification and nervousness.

"Well, Harold, whenever you're comfortable. We've plenty to be going on with as it is. Hie, Caleb, come away from there before you're hurt!" Jackson, with Harold on his heels, ran toward the two boys who circled back to investigate the engine more closely. Rudy and Caleb's skill in evading unwanted parental guidance was equal. The men shared a glance that acknowledged a shared challenge.

Susannah and Martha continued their exchange of the horrors of shipboard when traveling with curious and active youngsters. Although Susannah's journey, seemingly interminable, included boredom and fatigue, at least it escaped copious amounts of baggage and two lively youngsters. The memory of her exhaustion at end of such a long and arduous journey still caused her to shudder. At least she had only herself to manage. The excitement of train travel soon palled, and the culmination of a month's restricted physical activity had stretched Martha and Harold's patience to the limit.

Harold had spent considerable periods of time checking on the stock. His one attempt to relieve his wife of Rudy's presence had resulted in an emergency stoppage of the train. The boy tested the purpose of the cord that, he had been assured, would cause the train to grind to a halt if it were pulled. He pulled. It stopped. He was tender of sitting for the next few hours.

The four ladies stopped and looked around for the rest of their party. Two of them were unsurprised to see the men sprinting after boys standing much too close to the engine.

"I'll be very glad to have Rudy get rid of some of his energy. It's very trying for Harold and me, but I also realize that neither he nor Anna have been able to run and play for almost a month." While addressing her remarks to Susannah, Martha kept a monitoring eye on the action by the engine.

Susannah, similarly anxious about the two boys, checked on the girls. They were happily standing by the wagon, heads together. The words kitten, barn and sampler that drifted to her ears assured her that all was well in that quarter. Glancing back at the platform, she put her hand in front of her mouth to stifle a smile. Each man, boy in tow, assumed exactly the same expression and posture. There was no doubt that words of some gravity and exasperation fell about the miscreants' heads.

"Susannah, we've decided to have most of the baggage held for now. Harold and I will take the important pieces with us. Once we've got you settled at the house, we'll come back for the rest. I misjudged just how much luggage would be required for a family of four. Harold and I have to make arrangements for the cattle, too." A swift interchange of glances assured Susannah that nothing said or hinted at this point caused him anxiety. She nodded, her attention directed to settling Martha, Anna and Emily in the back of the wagon. She and Jackson, when discussing the seating arrangements for the homeward trip, agreed that placing two small boys between their fathers made the most sense. Wise in the ways of those same small boys, Martha and Harold heartily endorsed this program.

The wagon travelled at a walking pace. Conversation, thankfully, focused on the geography and flora of the surrounding fields. Jackson chose a route from the station that bypassed most of the town and its traffic. As they turned into their driveway, the horses picked up speed, sure that their stalls and a good rubdown awaited them. Jackson pulled up in front of the Brown's new home.

"Here you are, Harold and Martha. Welcome to your new home." He helped the boys down as Harold went to the back of the wagon to assist the ladies. The children immediately headed for the barn, only to be stopped by a chorus of adult voices. Emily and Caleb raced towards their home to change into play clothes, and the Browns followed the Stansfields into their new abode.

"Why don't you go ahead and look around, Martha. I'll just start the tea." Susannah pumped fresh water into the kettle before setting a match to the kindling laid ready in the firebox. So far, so good, she thought. No sign of knowing looks were forthcoming from either Harold or Martha. Indeed, they seemed to be very straightforward and obviously consumed with longing for the end of their journey.

Washing her hands in the basin, Susannah set the table for four, realizing that the children would be wild to explore their new surroundings. Sure enough, she had just put the tea to steep when two whirlwinds tore through the kitchen and out to the backyard where Caleb and Emily's voices could be heard greeting their new friends. Trusting that they would heed the stern admonitions from Jackson about just where they could go this first afternoon would be heeded, she put some cookies on a plate and turned to greet the three adults.

"Emily and Caleb have just returned, Martha. Did you want to have Rudy and Anna change their clothes before they charge off?"

"Thank you, Susannah. Harold, if you call them in, I'll find their play clothes and they can get rid of some of that energy." Martha bustled toward the bedrooms and the luggage the men had carried up the stairs.

"Anna! Rudy! Come back here!" Harold's stentorian tones stopped four children in full flight. They reversed their direction and reluctantly returned to the adults. "You two are in your best clothes! Inside with you. Your mother is getting out your play clothes. Put them on and then away you go." Never had two children moved so quickly.

"And Emily, Caleb, you remember what we talked about and just exactly what you may show your new friends." Jackson's stern mien convinced the children that there was no room for creative interpretation of his instructions.

"Yes, Uncle Jackson," they chorused.

Martha came back to the kitchen, children safely in play clothes. "Oh, Mrs. Stansfield, I mean Susannah, this is wonderful. It's so much more that we expected. A place of our own, at last. Back home we lived with Harold's family, and sometimes it was, I mean, this is just beautiful! Thank you so much!" Martha's face glowed, her pleasure banishing the harsh lines of fatigue.

"Yes, uh, Jackson, sir, it's absolutely wonderful! But perhaps we shouldn't take time for tea if we have to go back for the luggage." Harold, clearly pining for a cup, would forego tea and show himself willing.

"Oh, I think we have time for a quick cup, Harold. You must be glad of the opportunity to sit on something that isn't moving." Harold grinned his agreement as the four sat down to become better acquainted.

CHAPTER TWENTY-ONE

"Yep, them are good cattle, if I say so myself, sir," asserted Harold. "Mr. Parridge asked my opinion when he chose the beasts." Harold was proving to be talkative, as well as willing and knowledgeable, Jackson thought. He, too, was very sensitive to any indication from his new worker about knowledge of Susannah's past. He was especially cognizant of the fact that he and Harold would often be working together out of sight and sound of the women. Surely, if Harold had any concerns, he would take advantage of their privacy to broach the subject. Jackson was also aware that the Browns might be biding their time. As immigrants, they would surely want a chance to establish themselves and discover enough about their new country and community to ensure a safe harbor in the case of abandoning the Stanfield ship.

The two men stood beside the railroad's holding pen, waiting for the paperwork to be completed. Having carefully chosen a position upwind from the stock, they enjoyed the breeze that swept across the yard, free of unpleasant odors. Jackson contemplated the irony of idyllic weather, new stock to keep the bloodlines healthy and to provide well for his family. He shuddered at the prospect of losing everything. He

257

felt as if he were holding his breath, just waiting for the revelation of his and Susannah's supposed perfidy.

There was something very wrong in a world that condoned the beating and degradation of one human being by another. There was something very wrong with a system that gave one person life-and-death control over another. Perhaps the greatest irony of all existed in the fact that if he and Susannah had lived together without the sanctity of marriage, they would be judged and reviled by a great many in the community, but in no danger going of jail.

"Them'll be fine milkers." Harold shifted a stalk of grass to the opposite side of his mouth. "Want me to go and see if the papers are ready, sir...I mean...um...uh...." Torn between a strong desire to please and the conditioning of a lifetime, he floundered, stopped, cleared his throat, and then continued. "Won't take but a minute." The grass retraced its journey.

Jackson lifted his hat, smoothed his hair, and resolved to keep his mind on the present, and not on what the future might hold.

"Yes, yes, Harold, I'd appreciate that. You go and check with the station master." He used the ensuing quiet to review the excellent lines of the latest additions to the herd. He'd breed the heifers to calve in the spring. Preparations for their accommodations and subsequent integration into his existing herd occupied his mind until Harold reappeared, paperwork in hand.

"Here are the documents, um, uh, all proper and accounted for. We can take them home now. I'll get the wagon, so it won't take a minute." True to his word, Harold trotted off to bring the vehicle alongside the holding pen. Tying the animals to the back of the wagon by means of ropes attached to their halters took little time. Wrestling the beasts and having them remain still while they did so challenged the men's patience. Jackson welcomed the concentration required to overcome the extreme reluctance of two of the beasts to be restrained. It took both persuasion and swearing to coax them to follow and not set off in a new direction or plant all four feet and refuse to budge. Coping with balky animals provided an excellent anchor for his thoughts. When he knew that they were safe from escape, he headed home, knowing that there would be no lack of conversation, although monologue might come closer to the truth. The fact that Harold had to keep his eyes on the cattle in no way affected his garrulousness.

# # #

Susannah's hands kneaded bread with all the vigor of her trepidation. Neither hints nor innuendos suggested that Harold or Martha recognized the bigamous wife of a Yorkshire farmer.

Martha and she worked together throughout the morning. She waited, braced, shoulders hunched, for Martha to refer to such a wife, or even to question her outright. Martha, she discovered, let the words escape and then clapped her hand over her mouth, too late to hold them back. She appeared unaware of Susannah's tension. Her exploration and subsequent praise of the dairy was rewarding and genuine. She proved to be a cheerful and competent worker, moving smoothly from milking to straining, churning, and cleaning. She claimed that she had never seen a dairy so well appointed, and offered a recipe for what she called a quick cheese, should Susannah care to try it. She suggested that Martha make some for sampling before the next market day. Martha's work habits were exemplary.

Susannah gritted her teeth, ready to scream with the unrelenting anxiety. She knew her pregnancy made her more emotional. The greater portion of her sorrow and fear resulted from the possible loss of their home. Surpassing even that was her fear of Jackson, Emily and Caleb's shame and persecution when her crime became common knowledge.

Placing the dough in a large bowl, she covered it with a towel before setting it in the warming oven for its first rising. She changed into her garden shoes and vented her fear and frustration on weeding and bringing in the vegetables for supper. One of her mother's favorite axioms was that it was better to be busy and do something than to waste energy on worrying. She found herself sobbing as she ruthlessly yanked weeds. Her movements slowed to give her time to control her tears.

An hour later she straightened, placed her hands on her hips and bent backwards to counteract the ache. She admired that portion of garden that now boasted a weed-free status and began collecting the vegetables to be added to the stew. The carrots, onions and potatoes came easily from the soil, and the cabbage offered little resistance as she tugged its roots free. Sage and parsley were gathered on her way to the pump. She fetched the knife and basket she had forgotten from the house and settled on the back porch for the initial preparation. The aroma of cooking chicken wafted through the screen door as she began to trim, scrape and peel.

At the crunch of wheels and the sound of bawling cattle she raised her head in time to see Jackson and Harold heading toward the pasture. Once again she began to compose a letter to be left for Jackson.

My dearest Husband. Only my promise to you that I would not run away keeps me here. But it's hard, so hard. Surely if I removed myself from your life and that of the children, it would be easier for everyone. You could say that I had to return to England because of a family emergency. Little would they know that my journey would be in quite another direction, and that my absence would be permanent.

She remembered so clearly her joy when she learned of the children. Dreams mitigated her exasperation with the five rambunctious boys supervised on the voyage to give her an opportunity to add to her store of coins. Dreams of small children at her knee to say their prayers. Dreams of shiny faces at the table. Dreams of rocking them to sleep or holding them when they were hurt. Dreams that she might have been given a chance to begin a new life. Those very dreams banished thoughts of what might happen should her secret be discovered. Now her world teetered on an abyss; the shining dreams made of fool's gold.

Living on a knife edge of terror demanded its toll of her, Jackson and their relationship. It affected the children, too. They were sensitive to the strain between the adults, and showed it in their actions—less amenable to direction, clinging, refusing to go to sleep, whining, and, "forgetting" to do their chores. Even the distraction of having Rudy and Anna to play with did not entirely free them from the fear that held the entire family in its thrall. Lost in thought, she failed to notice that Martha stood in front of her, holding a covered plate.

"Hello, Susannah. My, you were a thousand miles away." Martha, much less hidebound by tradition than her husband, adapted easily to addressing Susannah and Jackson by their first names.

More than three thousand miles; across an ocean and most of a country, as well, she mused. Raising her head, she tried to smile.

"I'm sorry, Martha, I was just thinking."

"Well, they didn't look like happy thoughts, to be sure. Why don't I put the kettle on and we can sample these jam tarts I just baked. I made sure to get them here right away. Those children of mine can smell tarts from anywhere on the farm, and I wanted to share some with you." She bustled into the house and Susannah heard the whoosh of the pump, the splash of water, and the clang as the kettle met the surface of the stove. The rattle of dishes followed as preparations were made for a good chat.

"Now, you just finish up those vegetables, Susannah. I'll get out the cups and saucers. I can see that you're almost done. We can cut them up together and pop them into the stewpot in no time at all! It surely smells fine. I hope you'll give me the recipe."

Grateful for time to compose herself, Susannah quickly finished off the last potato, dumped the peelings on the compost heap, and took the cleaned vegetables into the house. True to her word, Martha had the table set for their tea and a board and knife ready to help chop the vegetables. By the time the kettle had boiled and the tea finished steeping, the stew was complete. They prepared to savor their treat.

"Susannah, here's the recipe for that one meal cheese I told you about. It's real easy and quick—a lovely rich cheese that should sell well. I could make some tomorrow for you to try. If you like it, we can take it to the market on Saturday."

"Thanks, Martha. I've heard of that kind of cheese, but this recipe explains it so clearly. Please do make some and we'll dazzle them." She smiled dutifully.

Harold and Jackson gratefully turned the new stock into the temporary pen knocked together last night. It adjoined the cow's night pen to give the animals a period of adjustment before putting them all together. The last two miles of their journey tried the patience of both men. Neither horses nor cattle conceded leadership to the other in the matter of forward, or backward, motion. Leaving Harold to put away the wagon and take care of the horses, Jackson headed for the dairy and Susannah. He found her stripping the udder of the last cow. He was shocked at the defeat evinced by her slumping shoulders.

"Susannah, whatever is the matter! Are you ill?" He rushed forward to take the pail from her hand, sliding his arm around her waist. "Is it the baby?" Placing the pail on the counter, he led her to the stool she used when she churned. "Where's Martha? I thought she was helping in the dairy."

"Well, she is, but she just left to check on her supper preparations. I'm fine. Just worried and upset. The baby's in no danger, nor am I. And speaking of the baby, how did you know? I've only been sure for the past week."

"Susannah, I'm a farmer and quite familiar with the facts of life. I didn't say anything because I waited for you to tell me." Jackson regarded her gravely. "Don't you want our child? I thought you'd be happy."

"Oh, Jackson, I am happy. I didn't tell you because, well because, that is…"

"Come on, Susannah, spit it out. You were still planning on leaving." He braced himself. She could see the pain in his eyes.

"I don't want to leave, Jackson, but it's not fair that you and the children should suffer for my actions." She reached out to touch his hand. He recoiled.

"I've told you and told you, Susannah; we're a family, and families stay together. Now, enough of this nonsense! I want your word that you won't try to leave, that you love us enough to stay." His eyes were suspiciously bright.

"It's not knowing if, or when, we'll be found out. I'm not sure how much longer I can go on." Running her fingers over his hand, she turned her head into his shoulder and slid her arm around his neck. Such strength, she thought, as she let him support her. It's there for the children, and for me, and for Harold and Martha and their children, too.

"I love you, Jackson. No matter what happens, please remember that I love you." With a mighty sniff and a swipe of each eye, and she straightened her back. "Now, my love, let's have supper. The stew is ready. If you call the children, I'll set the table as soon as I strain the milk. By the time you're washed up, we can eat." She kissed his cheek and gave him a wavering smile.

He didn't move as he dropped his arms from around her waist. "I'm still waiting, Susannah, for your promise. I know if you give me your word you'll keep it."

"I promise, Jackson."

Somewhat reassured, Jackson regarded his wife with love and pride. Most women would have succumbed to terror and despair, but not his Susannah. She had her moments, but generally she faced life on its own terms, asking no quarter. Not for the first time he wished for just fifteen minutes alone with Mr. Albert Ashton. He patted her buttocks, grinned to hear the gasp he knew would be his reward, and set off to fetch the children.

"Come on now, Emily and Caleb, your aunt is just finishing in the dairy. By the time we get washed up she'll have supper on the table." They grumbled, but only for form's sake.

"Anna and Rudy, your mother will have your meal ready, too. I know she's checking her pots right now. Scoot!"

Susannah gazed at her little family, overflowing with love. *No matter what happens in the future, nothing can take these last months away from me. I've discovered the love and support of a good man and these two precious children who have filled my heart. The babe who rests in my body has a good chance of survival. I have been truly blessed.* But no amount of blessing counting could eradicate the ever-present fear of discovery. The terror and pain of possible exposure overwhelmed her.

# # #

By the next week Susannah's body was beginning to show her pregnancy. She still cared for her family and managed the dairy, but the unrelenting tension showed itself in dragging feet and dull hair. On the rare occasions that her laughter was heard, it had a hollow sound.

Jackson's appearance remained unchanged, but his temper grew shorter. His nightly checking of animals and property took longer and longer as he braced himself to bolster his wife's spirits.

# # #

The Browns and Stansfields, plus numerous articles of food, filled the wagon. Harold and Martha's excitement knew no bounds. The first community social event since their arrival, the Browns anticipated meeting neighbors and experiencing one of the bees they had heard about. The children were ecstatic at the prospect of playing various games and making new friends. Susannah and Jackson wondered how many more of these occasions they would enjoy together.

Harold and Jackson's team placed a respectable second in the race to see which team would get their side of the barn up first. Martha discovered someone who knew one of her distant cousins. They immediately began to reminisce and exchange news of their respective villages. Susannah, included in the group, but not part of it, let her mind wander. Suddenly she was jerked back into the present by what she heard.

"...and they say he killed his wife. Ashton was his name, Albert Ashton. He took a spill off his horse, dead drunk as usual, of course, and he broke his neck. When they went to the farm to tell his wife, she wasn't there. Never did find her, they didn't. He was a wife beater. And I think they were right. He probably did kill her." Martha obviously relished telling the story.

"How do you know he beat his wife?" clamored an avid listener.

"It wasn't hard to figure out. My cousin, Alice, used to go the same market. She told me that his wife wore long sleeves and high necklines. Sometimes she limped, and more than once she had a cut or a bruise on her face. Some men is just animals. Thank God my Harold's gentle. Manly, mind you, but gentle. He'd no more lay a hand to me than fly to the moon." Martha waxed indignant on the plight of the poor wife.

Her heart beating wildly, Susannah cautioned herself to be very, very careful. She found it almost impossible to control her breathing, but managed to rasp, "Excuse me, did you say his name was Ashton? Anthony Ashton?" Desperately fighting to keep her complexion from flushing, she waited.

"No, no, it was Albert Ashton, from a small village near Upper Worthing. A nasty piece of work he was, too. His poor wife. Too bad she didn't survive. She certainly deserved to be well rid of him! Did you know him?" Martha looked at Susannah askance.

"No, no. I thought you said Anthony Ashton. I once knew a Tony Ashton, and wondered if it could be him." She prayed her words sounded plausible. The edges of her world blurred as a black curtain began to close in on her.

"When did it happen? I think you mentioned that they never found his wife?" Holding her breath and fighting to keep the encroaching blackness at bay, she waited for the response.

"That's right. They never did find her. Such a commotion it caused. I'll never forget the date. It was early in May. Now, just let me think here a moment. Yes, that's right, it was Cousin Alexander's birthday, May 7. Of course, it might have been May 8, as we don't rightly know just what time it occurred. But it was definitely the night of May 7 or real early on May 8."

"And you say they never found his wife? Not even her bones?" Susannah hung onto consciousness by sheer willpower alone.

"No. I heard that they dragged the pond on the farm and looked for graves in the woods, but she just disappeared. It was real uncanny like. I wonder what happened to the poor soul. Oh, well, at least she's out of her misery. I'd have run away long since." Martha continued to wax indignant on behalf of the missing wife.

"Were there any children?" Susannah fought the nausea and joy that battled for supremacy in her heart. Although she was desperate to escape the scrutiny of others, she played the part of someone hearing the shocking news for the first time.

"No, thank the Lord. At least there weren't any orphans. I heard that a distant relation of that brute's got the farm, and I wish him well of it."

Questions shot at Martha from all sides.

"How old was he?"

"Her?"

"Do you think she ran away?"

Susannah was oblivious to both questions and answers. She staggered back, frantically trying to take deep breaths and not faint. It was impossible! Unbelievable! Albert was dead! Her heart pounded and a ringing began in her ears. *Don't faint, don't faint*, she instructed herself. *Get away and sit down.*

"I'll just see how they're coming along with the punch," she murmured her excuse. "Perhaps I could be of some assistance." As she turned away, her knees buckled, and she succumbed at last.

"Susannah, Susannah, wake up. Are you all right? What happened? Is it the baby? Is the baby all right?" Jackson's frantic voice penetrated the fog that surrounded her.

"Take me home, take me home. It's all right! Everything is all right. Everything will be fine." Susannah knew she was babbling but was unable to stop. "Take me home now, please."

"Yes, yes, darling. I'll get the wagon." He looked around frantically, torn between getting the wagon and leaving Susannah.

"Mr. Stansfield, please bring your wife to the house. She's in no condition to be jostled and jolted about in a wagon. I'll make her a nice cup of tea and she'll soon feel better." His hostess stood at his elbow, concern and determination on her face.

"No, yes, thank you. I'll just...." Susannah's voice interrupted him. Aware that she was the center of attention, she was desperate to escape and give Jackson the wonderful news.

"Please, Jackson, that's a much better idea. There's no need to spoil everyone's afternoon. Help me to the house, but don't leave me." Prying her hands from his coat sleeves, Jackson swung her up into his arms and headed for the house, his hostess leading the way.

As they waited for the promised tea, Susannah told Jackson what she had overheard. "Do you understand, Jackson? Do you understand? Isn't it wonderful? We have no more worries. We've committed no crime. Not only is Albert dead, but he died before I left the farm and well before we were married. We're legally married." Her smile lit up the room.

Jackson's arms tightened around his wife as he buried his head in the cove of her shoulder and neck. His eyes burned and his throat stung. He gulped several times in an effort to gain control. Giving her a damp glance, he whispered in her ear,

"Thank God! I can hardly take it in. No more plans for hasty escapes, no more worries about the effect it will have on the children, no more wondering where we'll be when your time comes. Susannah, I can hardly wait to go home. I feel as if I could embrace the entire world." She relished the joy in his voice and on his face.

"Yes, my darling, we can make plans for the farm, for the children and for each other and know that they'll have a reasonable chance of coming true. Our grandchildren will know their grandparents' farm and all of the family history that it contains. Now I can write to Michael and Miranda, those dear friends who made this possible! Oh, Jackson, my heart overflows with joy." Her face glowed with happiness. "Let's go back to the party."

"Now hold on a minute, there, Sweetheart. You just fainted and scared the bejabbers out of a lot of us. I hardly think you're in any condition to attend a party." He smiled at her enthusiasm and rapid recovery, not entirely convinced that rejoining the others was a sound idea.

"Absolutely no one is keeping me from a party on the happiest and most wonderful day in my life! I'm going to dance every dance. If you're such an old man you can't keep up with me, I'm sure I'll find many who can!" As Mrs. Stevens bustled in with the tea tray, she was astounded to see her guest not only sitting up, but smiling and laughing. Her face was flushed with a healthy color.

"Well, this is a turnaround, to be sure, Mrs. Stansfield. You look so much better, and will be even more so after a cup of tea." She placed the tray on a small table Jackson hastened to draw up beside the couch. "I'll just pass the word to your friend, Martha, that all is well and that you'll be out shortly."

"Thank you, Mrs. Stevens. My wife is feeling so much better that she's threatening to dance every dance. I think I might have to sit on her to keep her from doing such a foolish thing." He smiled and patted Susannah's hand.

"You just try and you'll see how strong I really am. Thank you, Mrs. Stevens, a cup of tea is just the thing to set me right. You can see that I'm increasing, and that's probably what caused me to faint. I really do feel much better now." Sipping her tea, she sent a demure glance at her husband.

"I'll have a cup of that excellent tea too, Mrs. Stevens, and then I, too, really do think Susannah will be able to enjoy herself. We are greatly in your debt for your care." Jackson's joy and relief matched Susannah's. He relished the long years of happiness that awaited them and their little family.

"Oh, pshaw, Mr. Stansfield. After all the work you and the neighbors are doing to help us put up our new barn? A cup of tea is a small thank you, indeed." Mrs. Stevens preened herself. Mr. Stansfield's reputation as a community leader was growing. It never hurt to have good relations with people in a position to put in a timely word—or to be able to drop their names in casual conversation. She would further consolidate her position by paying a visit to Mrs. Stansfield in a few days.

# # #

Susannah and Jackson listened to the murmurs of Harold and Martha as they relived the barn raising. The Browns insisted on staying in the back of the wagon for the trip home. The children succumbed to sleep, lulled by the clop-clop of the horses' hooves and the soft jingle of their harnesses.

"We're going home, Jackson." Susannah could not keep the exultation from her voice. "Our home. A home that we'll never have to leave." She glanced back at the other couple. Seeing that they were engrossed in their reminiscences, she gave Jackson a quick peck on the cheek.

Jackson, not nearly so reticent, snaked his arm around her shoulders and hugged her tenderly. "We are, indeed, my dear, home to heart and hearth."

***

Made in the USA
Lexington, KY
12 December 2012